WITHDRAWN

No longer the property of the
Boston Public Library.
Sale of this material benefits the Library.

ALSO BY VIVI BARNES

OLIVIA TWISTED
PAPER OR PLASTIC

OLIVIA DECODED

vivi barnes

LOVE BYTES.

This book is a work of fiction. Names, characters, places, and incidents are the product of the author's imagination or are used fictitiously. Any resemblance to actual events, locales, or persons, living or dead, is coincidental.

Copyright © 2016 by Vivi Barnes. All rights reserved, including the right to reproduce, distribute, or transmit in any form or by any means. For information regarding subsidiary rights, please contact the Publisher.

Entangled Publishing, LLC
2614 South Timberline Road
Suite 109
Fort Collins, CO 80525

Entangled Teen is an imprint of Entangled Publishing, LLC.

Visit our website at www.entangledpublishing.com.

Edited by Stacy Abrams and Tara Whitaker
Cover design by Louisa Maggio
Interior design by Toni Kerr

ISBN: 9781633754904
Ebook ISBN: 9781633754911

Manufactured in the United States of America

First Edition September 2016

10 9 8 7 6 5 4 3 2 1

For Marlana—your unwavering support has meant the world to me. Thank you for seeing me through this story.

CHAPTER ONE

LIV

The white rose just a few inches from my nose is the first thing I see when I awaken on Valentine's Day—my first Valentine's Day in this huge mansion and the seventeenth without a boyfriend. Which leaves my grandfather as the rose culprit. Surprising, considering he rarely steps foot in my room.

It's fine with me. I have exactly zero interest in a boyfriend, considering the last—and only—love in my life was a hacker who refused to leave that life for me. My therapist told me I should try to make more friends, maybe even go out with one of the guys at school who'd shown interest. Why would I want to talk to some immature guy? The only person I'd ever told my secrets to was a secret himself. Nobody can know about the boy who was Z to everyone else, but Jack to me.

The boy who saved me, then broke my heart.

Twirling the rose in my fingers, I walk out on my

balcony. The sun has barely crept over the horizon, slivers of pastel hues breaking the sky. It used to be my favorite time of day, when the world around me is silent and I can actually think. But even after eight months, the painful memories of Jack are what fill my mind these days. His face is burned in my brain—kaleidoscope eyes that looked straight into my soul, blond hair hanging long over his forehead, even the warm smell of his jacket—an intoxicating mix of leather and spice that hinted at danger.

I haven't heard from him since that night on this very balcony. The night when he gave me his heart, then left me to go back to his "family," the home of foster-kids-turned-cyber-criminals. The rumble of his Ducati as he pulled away became the background music of my nightmares.

Not that my life isn't great. I love my grandfather. It was because of Jack that I was reunited with him in the first place, so I should be grateful for that. I am. I just wish—

Stop, Liv. Face the fact that he's moved on.

The longer I'm away from Jack, the more I wonder if what we had was even real to begin with.

A knock sounds before I hear my bedroom door open. I don't need to turn around to know it's Mrs. Bedwin with a cup of oolong tea, a morning ritual since I first came to live here. A year ago, I'd have laughed if someone said I'd be living in a mansion, waited on hand and foot. Funny how quickly a person can get used to being rich.

Mrs. Bedwin brings the tea out to the balcony where I'm still standing, staring over the wall past the huge oak that partially blocks my view of the street.

"It's chilly out here," she says, handing me the cup and rubbing her hands together.

"At least it's not snowing," I tell her. I run a hand over

the fluffy pink robe she gave me for Christmas.

She smiles. "I don't mind the snow. A good hard freeze rids us of summer's bugs. Where'd you get that?" she asks, nodding at the white rose in my hand.

I lift it to inhale the faint scent. "It was on my pillow this morning. I guess Grandfather snuck in before heading to work."

"Really?" Her eyebrows rise. "Odd thing for him to do."

"That's what I thought. Has he already left for work?"

"He left an hour ago. He said your dinner reservation is at six thirty this evening."

I smile and turn my gaze back to the street.

"What are you looking for out here each morning?" Mrs. Bedwin asks curiously.

"Nothing, why?"

"Well, you stand on this balcony almost every morning and stare at the street, or maybe the tree. Either you're wanting to become an arborist or you're searching for someone."

I don't answer. It wouldn't help to lie to her. She always seems to know what's going on in my head. Not everything, exactly, but my feelings in general. It's strangely comforting from this sweet, caring woman who once loved my dead mother, too. I can tell her almost anything, though I don't tell her about Jack. I'm sure she's heard about him from my grandfather, whose questions early on made me realize he'd come to his own conclusion that Jack was no good for me. Sometimes I get the feeling my grandfather's asking her to fish for information on him.

Mrs. Bedwin touches my cheek gently. "You look tired. Still having a hard time sleeping?" She sighs. "Sweetheart, I really think we should talk to your grandfather about restarting your therapy sessions—"

"No," I interrupt a little too quickly. "I'm fine." They had me see a counselor after I'd been kidnapped by Jack's hacking ringleader, Bill Sykes. Though it did help to get me over some of the horrible things that happened in my past—things I wouldn't have shared except that the therapist already knew them from my foster-care records—there was no way I was going to tell her *everything.* "I just had a bad night."

"Do you want to talk about it?"

I shake my head. I don't share with anyone the thoughts that keep me up at night, sometimes causing my heart to race so fast it might as well thump its way out of my chest. Some are based in memories, like visions of my last foster father Derrick trying to force himself on me; some are based in fear—Julia at Child Welfare knocking on our door and telling my grandfather that this has been a big mistake and that I'm ready to be shipped off to the next disturbing home, or Jack begging me to return to his life of hacking.

Mrs. Bedwin squeezes my hand. "You're safe here, remember? We're not going anywhere and neither are you." She winks at me. "Well, that's not exactly true. You'd better get downstairs—Juliette is making ham and eggs and will be awfully upset if you skip breakfast before school again."

only have a couple minutes to shovel down breakfast before slipping on my coat and gloves and running out the door to my car. I slide into the driver's seat and start the engine, then crank up the heat. A square white envelope on the passenger seat catches my eye, my name printed on the front in plain block letters. Behind it is a pink and white striped bag with pink tissue paper. Good thing I left the car unlocked last night. Smiling, I slide the card out of its envelope. First the rose, now this. Grandfather is obviously trying to overcompensate for years of missed Valentine's Days. Much like Christmas morning, when I swear there were more gifts under the tree for me than I'd received in my entire life.

The picture on the front of the card is a white rose with a simple message:

Thinking of you on Valentine's Day.

There's nothing inside—it's completely blank. Grandfather didn't even sign it. I know he probably hasn't gone out with anyone since my grandmother died before I was born, and he doesn't have any other family except me, but seriously, he's got to know how to write in a card.

I set the card down and pick up the bag, pulling out the tissue paper and a rectangular white box. Inside lays a delicate gold link bracelet, accented with emeralds and diamonds that twinkle in the stream of sunlight. In the eight months that I've been here, Grandfather's supplied me with almost enough jewelry to open a store—pearl earrings and necklace, a diamond necklace that belonged to my grandmother, a gold infinity bracelet. How much jewelry can a person wear?

I start to slip the bracelet around my left wrist but stop, my eyes on the bracelet Jack gave me that I never remove. My fingers trace the slender gold chain lightly. It's the simplest of jewelry, something that belonged to his mother, but aside from the locket that once belonged to *my* mother, I've always treasured it most. I wrap the new bracelet around my other wrist and shoot Grandfather a quick text: Thank you for the gift. It's beautiful.

Emerson is just behind me when I drive up to Dalton Academy for the Obscenely Wealthy. It's not a bad school, just filled with the richest, most entitled kids in the world. And not a single one with a past like mine—not that they'll know about that. Grandfather was quick to change my name to Brownlow, his last name and also my mother's before she ran away with the guy who got her pregnant. Something he never talks about.

"Happy Valentine's Day," Emerson sings through her window as she pulls her Audi into the parking spot next to mine. She gets out of her car with a big heart-shaped box of candy and presents it to me with a flourish.

"This is for me?" I ask, taking the box.

"Of course, silly!"

"But I didn't get you anything." I had no idea friends got each other gifts. I thought Valentine's Day was a relationship kind of thing.

She laughs at that and wraps an arm around my shoulders. "You didn't have to. I just felt like getting it. But if you want, you can give me a truffle from the box. I won't mind."

I let her browse through the box until she finds one and pops it into her mouth, grinning. Emerson, my best—and really only—friend here at Dalton, was the first person to even say three words to me my first day of school. Those three words happened to be, "Need a friend?" And I did—very much. Having someone as well-liked and genuine as Emerson made my first months at Dalton more tolerable.

"Check out my present from Kade." She holds up her

hand to show me a ring with a small emerald in the middle. "Sneaky guy, he gave it to my mom last night so I'd have something first thing this morning."

"It's pretty. Is it like a promise ring or something?"

Her mouth drops open, then she closes it. "No. At least, I hope not. Oh my God, do you think he's thinking like engagement or something?"

I bite back a grin, surprised that she didn't come to that conclusion herself. Emerson's a total romantic. "No, he probably just thought it'd look great on you."

"Oh. Good." She frowns, stretching her hand out to stare at the ring. "I guess."

"It matches my bracelet," I tell her, holding up my wrist.

"Wow, who gave you *that*?"

"My grandfather. He left it on my car seat this morning."

"Oh, boo. I thought maybe you had a secret admirer or something." I try not to smile at her obvious disappointment. Emerson's been on me to date for months now. She knows I had someone back in Richmond who was special, but only that we broke it off before I moved here. She doesn't know anything else about Jack. No one does, because what would I say? *The last guy I dated is a criminal, and the last time I saw him was right after we got kidnapped by his horrible boss and almost died trying to escape.* That'd go over really well.

"I don't know, what do you think?" Emerson breaks into my thoughts as we walk down the hallway to our lockers.

"About what?"

She sighs. "Where Kade's taking me tonight. Girl, you are not with it today, are you? Are you doing anything tonight?"

"My grandfather's taking me to dinner."

"Sweet. Not so romantic, but sweet."

I smile. "Yes, he's sweet. But a little over the top on gifts sometimes." Even after eight months of living the wealthy life, I'd be happier if he gave me a gift card to a bookstore instead of extravagant jewelry I rarely wear.

My phone starts buzzing, and I pull it from my pocket. Grandfather's text reads: **What gift?**

I frown, typing, **The bracelet you left in my car.** I snap a quick picture of the bracelet on my wrist and send it to him. Maybe his text was a hint to send a picture, though I doubt it. He's usually pretty direct about things.

"What's up?" Emerson asks.

"Looks like Grandfather forgot he left me the bracelet." But even as I say it, it doesn't sound right. He's one of the sharpest people I've ever known, *and* he runs a financial institution.

"Maybe he gave it to one of his *staff* to put in your car." Her voice has the usual bitter tone whenever she's thinking of her parents. They're hardly ever around, and when they are, they don't pay much attention to her.

"Yeah, you're probably right." I don't believe that, though. Even though it's possible Mrs. Bedwin did put it there, I doubt it. Grandfather is the type to handle things himself when it comes to me. But Emerson's parents travel so much for their business that they often let their staff handle things like birthdays and other events they think aren't important. So as grateful as I am that Grandfather's always there for me, I don't like to rub that in Emerson's face.

"Maybe you really do have a secret admirer," she says hopefully.

I roll my eyes. "I doubt that."

"Oh, really?" She stops in her tracks, her eyes fixed straight ahead. I follow her gaze, a sharp sense of dread creeping down my spine. A white rose is dangling from the vent in my locker.

A rose I know wasn't placed there by my grandfather.

CHAPTER TWO

JACK

I ride the Ducati through the main entrance of Briarcreek House, my eyes on the three-story home at the end of the long drive. The house is beautiful from the street. Sometimes I stop halfway down the drive and look at it through narrowed eyes, trying not to see the rust overtaking the archway sign or the weeds growing onto the drive. It looks especially bleak in the winter—everything brown and worn. The glory days of Monroe Street have passed, and all we have left is this shell of a life, barely eking out enough money to hold on to this property.

I had no idea how much we relied on Bill.

As I walk into the house, the noise of Xbox and laughter sounds normal enough to make me relax a bit. We're still a family, even if we don't have all the money we had before.

"Z!" Dutch comes out of the kitchen to slap my hand. By the slightly acidic smell of tomatoes mixed with smoky garlic, I'm guessing we're having spaghetti tonight. It's the cheapest thing Nancy can make for so many kids, so it's on the menu every week, and sometimes twice. I have to hand it to Nancy—she's pretty good at stretching the ol' dime.

"Been out on a killing spree?" I ask Dutch, pointing at the spatters of red sauce all over his shirt.

"Yeah, pretty much. I won," he says, his voice warbling slightly. Only in eighth grade, Dutch is the youngest kid in the house. His hacking skills are pretty impressive for his age. Or they were, before Nancy pulled the plug on our business.

"You're kitchen duty tonight, huh?" I ask him.

He nods. "Better than cleanup. That's Jen." His grin is slightly evil, which makes me laugh. Jen hates having any kind of kitchen duty, but since we took in some of the girls from Bill's prostitution ring that most of us tried to forget existed, Nancy's had to reassign duties to accommodate everyone. Not only that, by playing "mom" to all these extra kids, she suddenly decided that we all needed to stop hacking. Live a good example and all that crap, just because Bill's crazy idea to kidnap Liv for her grandfather's money almost got us caught. Never mind that we'd gone years without any incident. I wouldn't be surprised if she carts us all off to church soon.

The frustration of knowing we *can* do something about our situation but *won't* is almost more than I can take. We need the money. Her work-at-home job as a remote computer tech isn't cutting it. She'd be upset if she found out I saw a pretty hefty credit card bill on her desk, but it's stuck in my head now. We, the Monroe Street family, who not long ago had so much money that we never had to even think twice about buying a new car or computer, are now ringing up debt on credit cards and struggling to pay bills. And it's for that reason I'm shocked she doesn't allow us to continue hacking for profit. It's also one reason that I haven't stopped.

I'm not going to let my family do without if I can help it.

Nancy calls to me from the office as I start toward the stairs. "Close the door behind you," she says. Her eyes are fixed on the monitor in front of her, her hand pressed to her lips.

"Something wrong?" I ask, shutting the door and sitting across from her.

"I don't know. Did you buy some jewelry lately?"

I start laughing until I realize she's not even smiling. "Um, no, why?"

She turns the monitor toward me. "Well, someone has. Two thousand dollars' worth from our emergency account. You know you and I are the only ones who have access to it. Did your debit card get stolen?"

I peer at the monitor to see the line she's pointing at. The transaction is with Abbott & Peterson Jewelers, a jewelry store about a mile from our house.

What the…

I reach for my wallet and find the debit card tucked inside its normal slot. I show it to Nancy, who cross-references it against the information on the monitor. "Are you sure no one else here has access?"

"Of course not."

I believe it. Nancy's protective of that account. It's supposed to be a last resort in case the regular house account runs dry—something I think is pretty close to happening. Nancy's been involving me for the past year just in case something were to happen to her so I'd be able to take it over for her. But I've never actually used the card.

"Well, if you didn't and I didn't, then someone decided to help themselves," she says.

"Did you ask anyone else in the house? One of the girls?"

"No. And don't just assume it's a girl. Guys can purchase jewelry, too."

I roll my eyes at the *You're a sexist, Z* insinuation. I'm not—at least, I like to think I'm not—but it's not worth arguing over.

"Obviously I disputed the charge, canceled the cards, and requested new ones sent to us. Why would someone steal money from this account just to buy jewelry, of all things?" she mutters at the monitor as I stand to leave.

"Maybe someone's got a problem with the fact that we can't make our own money from hacking," I tell her. She looks over the monitor at me, her eyes speculating. I get it—I'm the one who's most vocal about the fact that we shouldn't have stopped hacking. I wonder if she suspects I haven't really stopped, either. Most of my hacking has involved small deals—little transactions here and there, just to keep from getting rusty. Nothing major.

"It's not me, so don't get that idea in your head," I tell her quickly. "But I could see someone else getting desperate enough to steal."

"Desperate? This isn't a loaf of bread, Z. It's jewelry. Go ahead and cut up that card. It's no good anymore."

I head upstairs, hesitating as I pass by Maggie's door. The music inside is cranked up, and I know she hates loud music. Of all the girls who moved in recently, Maggie seems to be having the hardest time. Everyone's all over my back to help her acclimate here. I've tried to get Nancy to reassign that particular duty to someone else, but unfortunately, I'm the only one Maggie trusts. Me, the ex-boyfriend she can't seem to get over. It's one of the most uncomfortable situations I've been in, and that's saying a lot.

I grit my teeth and knock on her door. The door is yanked open by a spiky blue-haired girl with tattoos creeping up over her tank and piercings invading her face. "Yeah?" Sunny says, her hand moving to her hip. "What the hell do you want?"

I've never known a bigger contradiction in terms than Sunny's name and personality. "Is Maggie in here?"

She slams the door on me. So much for that.

I thought Jen was bad, but Sunny is like having a lightning storm living in the house. It makes me wonder what kind of escort she was, considering Bill's preference for higher-class women like Maggie and Nancy. Although I don't think I want to know.

I head to my room and sit in front of my laptop, the picture of Liv and me I once took with my phone now the screensaver image that tortures me. She's laughing—her eyes lit up like she just heard the funniest thing. I miss those eyes. I miss *her*. The only one besides Nancy who knows my real name...my real story. The only one who ever loved me for the person I really am.

I can't even say that for myself.

I really need to change my screensaver.

A light tap at the door sounds, then Maggie opens it. "You were looking for me?" she asks meekly. If it were anyone else, I'd go apeshit on them for opening my door. With Maggie, one angry word will freak her out, so I just say, "Come in."

Withered—that's the only word I can use to describe

Maggie. This once happy girl who loved life now shrinks into the corners of Briarcreek. The dark rims under her eyes and limp, dull hair that once bounced over her shoulders only emphasize how much of a shadow she is now. It hurts every time I see her. I brought her to Monroe Street a long time ago, when it was too easy to convince a lone girl without home or family that she needed us. Maggie was a pretty girl with a knack for hacking—though she never got to be as good at it as the rest of us. And she loved me too much. Really, she loved the bad boy image of me, same as Jen. When I broke it off with Maggie, it took no time at all for her to join Bill Sykes's escort service. A sad life of prostitution in another house.

And I let it happen.

Maggie is a constant reminder that the damage I did by bringing her into this life in the first place can't be undone. It's always going to be a knife stabbing me in the gut. Which is probably why I don't have the balls to tell her to back off.

Maggie perches on the edge of my bed, her thin legs poking out from her dress like skin-covered bones. I sit next to her.

"Happy Valentine's Day," she says, handing me a small envelope.

Uh-oh.

There's no card inside, just a photograph. It's a selfie of Maggie and me. I'm looking off camera and she's smiling into the lens, happier than I've ever seen her. "Um… thanks." I glance at her and she smiles, her eyes on the picture.

"When I was moving stuff from the other place to here, I found this. I'm giving it to you because I want you to know I'm okay with us being like this. I mean, like, just friends. I know you don't look at me the same as you used to. But I don't want you to forget me."

Forget her? My gut clenches. "You okay?" I ask. Stupid question—of course she's not.

"Yes. But I need a favor," she says, her voice as thin as she is.

"Of course," I tell her quickly. "Anything you want."

She smiles at that. "I want my own room."

This again. "Did you talk to Nancy?"

She laughs, and it comes out slow and soft like punctuated sighs. "Yes. She said it's better to have Sunny with me. She thinks I'm suicidal. I'm not, you know," she says, her voice pitched an octave higher. "I…I just need some space. Sunny's so intense, and she never leaves me alone."

"I don't know." As much as I can't stand Sunny, I have to admit that keeping her around Maggie is probably smart. No matter how much she'll try to convince me she's fine, I can't be sure that she's not going to take a razor to her wrist at any moment. We're all worried about it, and now she's giving me a picture of us and asking me not to forget her? Nancy explained to us when Maggie moved in that it's not that Maggie misses being a prostitute or that she misses Bill. She misses what had become her family at the other house. The girls she was closest to ended up moving out and getting other jobs. I don't know why she didn't join them. Maggie never did feel like she belonged with us. And as bad as it sounds, I never felt like she did, either.

"Z, please. Please," she says, sliding her cold fingers through mine. "You can talk to Nancy. She'll listen to you. Please."

"I doubt she'll listen, but I don't think it's a good idea

anyway. You hardly ever eat anything, and you spend all your time in your room."

"I'll eat more, if that'll make you happy. Please." Her eyes move to the picture of Liv on my computer's screensaver, and she frowns.

"Okay," I tell her quickly, knowing she's wondering why I keep a picture of Liv on my computer when I never kept hers. "I'll think about it."

Her face softens. "You still care about me, don't you?"

"I care." I put my arm around her. Of course it's at that moment that Jen walks by the open doorway, glaring at us. She's hardly ever around anymore, and when she *is* here, she acts pissed because Maggie's back in the house. Which I don't get because it's been a long time since I was with either of them.

"Do you ever miss home?" she asks.

"Monroe Street? Sometimes."

"Me, too." Maggie rests her head on my shoulder. I'm actually surprised to hear her call Monroe Street home, considering she ultimately ran away from there to join Bill's escort service. Then again, there was something about the Monroe Street mansion that was home to all of us. A shared sense of purpose, maybe.

"This place is so crowded," she adds. "Do you think… Would you mind if I come here and hang out with you sometimes when I need to get away from Sunny? At least until I get my own room?"

"Sure," I tell her, removing the hand that's wandering along my thigh. How can I continue living under the same roof as two of my ex-girlfriends? One hates me, the other still wants me.

And the one *I* want is far from my reach.

"Thank you," Maggie whispers, and I can't remember what she's thanking me for. "I still want my own room, though."

"We'll see."

If I talk to Nancy about it, seriously put up an argument for how Maggie needs her own room, she'll listen. Nancy won't deny me, and I can't deny Maggie. Everyone in this house owes someone something. Give and take—it's how this house has run from the beginning.

I stare at the picture of Liv. I was happy then. I was Z, hacker who had it all. Corporations, banks—hitting them was easy. The chances of us getting caught are slim, no matter what Nancy thinks. The little transactions I do here and there in my own account are nothing compared to what I did before.

If only we could hack again, maybe life could go back to the way it was. We can only live off our reserve funds and investments for so long. Maybe I wouldn't feel stifled like I do now. It's an itch that won't go away, and I have a feeling I'm going to scratch it. No matter what promises I made to Nancy about trying to stop.

CHAPTER THREE

LIV

I can't take my eyes off the single white rose hanging from my locker door.

Emerson grabs my arm. "You really *do* have a secret admirer!" She sounds a whole lot more excited than I feel.

"No, I don't." I yank the rose free from the door, dropping it as one of the thorns bites my skin. "Ouch." A tiny drop of blood forms on my finger. Figures.

"You okay?" Emerson asks, picking up the rose from the floor.

"Yeah, it's just—"

"What?" she asks as I gingerly take the stem.

"It's sort of like the one my grandfather left on my pillow this morning." What is the chance I'd end up with two white roses today? It's not like white roses are rare, but who would do this?

"Maybe Theo?" Emerson asks.

My inner self gags. Theo Blakely, star basketball player

and self-proclaimed "great guy," has been asking me out for months, mostly by telling me it'd help my social status. I almost laughed in his face at that. If he knew my history, he'd run away from me, screaming.

On second thought, maybe I *should* tell him.

"Open your locker to see if there's anything else," Emerson suggests.

I turn the combination lock until it clicks. I cringe a little as I pull open the door, almost expecting something to jump out at me. It's not like anyone at this school has been cruel to me. No mean girls picking on the foster kid who was too afraid to stand up for herself. At this school, where I'm just another girl from a wealthy family, nobody bugs me. And I'm not the awkward, insecure girl I once was. Well, at least not completely.

There's nothing weird inside the locker. I exhale heavily. "Someone just put this on the wrong locker," I tell her, grabbing my history book and slamming the door.

"What are you going to do with it?"

"With what?" Emerson's boyfriend, Kade, walks up and grabs her around the waist, lifting her up to plant a kiss on her lips. "Happy Valentine's Day, babe."

"Liv has a secret admirer," she tells Kade, nodding at the rose in my hand.

"Really?" Kade's face lights up. "Awesome. I told Theo he should get you some flowers or something."

"Kade, please don't do that." I don't care if Theo is his friend—there is no way I'd go out with him.

"What? He's not a bad guy."

"Tell that to Becca," Emerson says, shoving him lightly. "Texting a girl that she's too boring to date is not cool. Some guys deserve to be alone."

I reach out and deliberately drop the rose in the nearest trashcan. Hopefully Kade will give Theo the message. "I'll see you guys later," I offer over my shoulder as I head toward my first class. I'm sure Emerson is expressing her concern about my sad state of mind to Kade, who will try to think of which of his other friends he can set me up with.

The sucky thing about being single is that no one believes you really want to be alone. They think you're either playing hard to get or hoping for a "special someone" to ask you out. Even Emerson doesn't get it, though she always tells everyone else to leave me alone. At least she respects my feelings on that one.

My classes drag by all morning. But as soon as I walk into fourth period, my phone finally buzzes with a text from Grandfather.

That bracelet is not from me.

I stare at the text. Not from him? It has to be. Who else would send me a fancy gift like this *and* put it in my car that was sitting in my driveway? That doesn't seem like a move Theo would make.

My eyes move from the new bracelet on my right wrist to my left arm, where the simple chain Jack gave me rests. The blood whooshes faster through my veins at the thought of him. Could this new one be from Jack? Is he telling me he's finally leaving Monroe Street?

Whoa. Jack coming back after eight months? Highly doubtful. I'd made it pretty clear last time I saw him that the only chance we had was if he stopped hacking. For a hot minute, I thought that was going to happen. Eight months later…yeah, no. I shouldn't even be wearing his bracelet anymore, but it didn't feel right to mail it back to him.

Besides, Jack wouldn't leave jewelry in my car. He would come directly to me. Maybe even climb up to the balcony like he did the last time, like I've imagined a million times since the night he left me to continue his life of crime.

He's climbed up before.

My stomach clenches in on itself, and the room is suddenly twenty degrees hotter. I take a shaky breath. As romantic as I once pictured that scenario, thinking he'd actually climb up in the middle of the night to leave a rose while I'm sleeping is more stalker-like than romantic. But he's not like that. Not the Jack I know.

But you don't know him anymore. Eight months apart—

I text my grandfather: **The rose?**

A couple minutes later, I get a response: **What rose? Is there something going on? Can you call me?**

I'm suddenly very aware of the weight of the emerald bracelet, as if every single link is searing my skin. I unclasp it and shove it into the side pocket of my backpack. The other chain rests as comfortably on my wrist as it ever has. I leave it alone. I text my grandfather that everything's fine and that I'm in class.

During the rest of science, I rest my forehead on my fingertips, staring at the book in front of me that's become a jumble of symbols and formulas. Did Jack really put that rose on my pillow? Was I even covered by a blanket?

Stop getting ahead of yourself, Liv. This doesn't sound like Jack at all.

I have Jack's number programmed in my phone, though I haven't used it once in the eight months we've been apart. Maybe I should text him. But now that I think about it, do I really want to call him back into my life when I'm finally starting to feel like a normal teenager?

And if he didn't do it—who did?

Emerson catches up to me as I walk toward the parking lot after school. "Hey, you okay?"

No. "Sure."

"Sorry about this morning. Kade doesn't mean anything by it," she says.

This morning seems so far away, and I have no idea what she's talking about. "By what?"

"Trying to set you up with Theo. I keep telling him that Theo's an idiot."

"I think it'll be easier to teach a monkey to talk than to get it through Theo's head that I'm not interested."

She wrinkles her nose. "Well, monkey would definitely describe him."

"Describe who?" Theo comes up behind us and rests his arm on my head. I pull away from him.

"Not now, Theo," Emerson says to him. "We're in a hurry."

"Whatever. Plans tonight?" he asks me, turning to jog backward in front of me.

"Yes. I'm having dinner with someone."

He stops suddenly, tilting his head. "Really?" The way he says it is like he's shocked anyone else would ask me out. It shouldn't bother me, but it does. Too much of a throwback to my foster-care years when no one wanted anything to do with the weird new kid.

I open my mouth to snap back, but Emerson beats me to it. "Yeah, and the guy's scorching hot, too. Plus, he doesn't have to resort to shoving a rose with thorns in a girl's locker."

I wink at Emerson as Theo's smirk drops into a scowl.

"Well, good luck with that," he says with the air of someone who's offended but pretending not to be. He turns to jog toward the parking lot.

I breathe a sigh of relief. "Obviously Theo put the rose in my locker." Theo putting a rose in my locker is a normal thing. Jack riding his Ducati two hours to do that is not.

Emerson glances at me. "Why, did you think it wasn't him?"

"Yeah. I— With the bracelet and, well, stuff, I just wasn't sure."

"You said your grandfather gave you the bracelet."

"He said he didn't. I don't know—I'm so confused. I should've asked Theo if he gave me the bracelet, too." *And the rose on my pillow.*

"He'd probably be dumb enough to give you an expensive bracelet," Emerson says, huffing. "Dude doesn't know you at all."

Hopefully I can get through the rest of Valentine's Day without any more "gifts," but I have a feeling that's wishful thinking. As I get closer to my car, I can see that I'm right. Four thick flower stems without their flowers attached lay like dolls without a head on the hood of my Infiniti. *What the actual hell?* I look over at Theo, but he's already driving away. Seems like if it were him, he'd be standing there, waiting to see my reaction.

Maybe I shouldn't have refused the mace my grandfather tried to get me to carry.

"Who did *that*?" Emerson says, clutching at my arm.

"Someone who thinks he's being funny, I guess." Which rules out Jack—he's too serious to play practical jokes. I know he wouldn't do something like this. I gingerly pick each stem from the hood and toss it to the ground.

"Funny? If this is Theo, I'm going to kill him," she says.

I yank open the door to the car, inhaling so sharply I'm sure I just froze my lungs. "I found the rest of the roses." Emerson rushes to my side.

"Liv, this is the creepiest thing I've ever seen," she says, her voice shaky as she stares at the white rose petals on my seat.

I almost tell her it's not the creepiest thing *I've* ever seen, but I'm not going there. This is bad enough without bringing up my past. I take a deep breath. *It's just someone pulling a prank. Like stupid Theo.*

"Should we call the police?" she asks.

"To say what? Someone put roses in my car on Valentine's Day?"

"Well, at least you should lock your car door from now on."

I stare at her. "But I did lock it." Except for when I'm at home parked behind Grandfather's gates, I always lock my car, even if I'm just running into the gas station for a soda. It's become a habit to press the lock button, even more than once to make sure. I run my hand along the window frame, but it doesn't look like someone tried to force it open.

Someone unlocked my car.

Which would leave the only person who has a key—my grandfather, which is about a zillion to one chance—or someone else who might know how to break into cars without leaving a mark. I look quickly around the parking lot, but there are only students climbing into their BMWs and Maseratis to head home. No Ducati. And I can't even tell if the trembling inside my body is from fear or disappointment.

"Are you okay?" Emerson reaches out to grasp my arm. "You look like you're going to pass out or something."

"I'm fine," I tell her, my voice anything but fine. "I'd better go."

"Maybe you should let me drive you home."

I smile at her, trying to look sincerely unaffected. "It's okay. I'm just a little freaked out. Maybe you can call Kade and ask him to tell Theo to back off?"

"Hell yeah I will. This is ridiculous." She glances at my car. "Let me at least help get that crap off your seat." She sets her bag down, walking around the door to scoop the petals out to the ground. She steps on them, turning her boot heel to grind them into the pavement. "Dumbass Theo," she mutters. She looks up at me. "Text me later, okay?"

I nod as she hesitates, her gaze moving back to the ground, to the petals lying on their bare stems. "Actually, can you call me when you get home? I just want to make sure you're safe."

Safe is never a word I'd have used to describe my situation until I came to live with my grandfather. Now apparently that's not even a sure thing. "Yeah, I will."

As soon as I slide into the car, I pull out my cell phone. Should I text Jack? Maybe he's gone off the deep end or something. I need to rule him out and move on. But if it wasn't him, texting him would be a really bad idea.

Instead, I scroll down to the one other Monroe Street connection programmed in my phone. My fingers fly over the keys, and I press send before I can think twice about the text.

Then I start the car and head home, rolling down the windows to let the cold air blast away the heavy stench of roses.

CHAPTER FOUR

JACK

Nancy tells everyone at dinner about the money stolen from our emergency account. Tells us we need to cut back on our spending. I know she's disputed the charge and will get the money back. This is just an excuse she's using to tell everyone to stop living off our reserves and get real jobs. But we don't need to flip burgers to make money—we had the perfect job before. We can do it again.

I follow her to her office after the meeting. "So I was thinking, maybe we could start the business again. Small scale, I mean. Just a few hits," I add as she shakes her head firmly.

"I told you. With Bill gone we have a chance to start fresh. Everyone else is willing to try, so why aren't you?"

"*Everyone* is willing to try? Yeah, did you see their faces tonight? Have you seen anyone go out and get a real job?"

"Z—"

"And I certainly don't see Maggie getting a job, do you? Or Jen either, as lazy as she is," I add.

"That's enough," she says firmly. "Maggie has her issues. I'm working with her on those. You and Jen have been at each other's throats for a year now, and that's a year too long for me."

"Her problem, not mine." Ever since I broke up with her a year ago, Jen jumps at any chance she can get to take me down. The only time it'll get resolved is when one of us moves out.

Nancy keeps her sympathetic but firm gaze on me. I try a different approach. "Nancy, I know we need the money—"

Maybe it's the way I emphasized "know" that makes her eyes narrow. She holds a hand up, her palm flat. "Keep your eyes on your own bank account, Z. The house is my business, and you're only on the accounts as a precaution. You have enough to worry about with graduation right around the corner." Her expression softens. "I know you worry about us. Don't. An honest job may not make as much money, but it won't get you arrested or killed."

There's nothing I can say to change her mind. I get it— knowing how much she loves us. In her mind, hacking will ultimately land one of us in jail. In her mind, she is saving us.

But we never asked to be saved.

I head out of the office, but right before I reach the stairs someone grabs the collar of my shirt and yanks me backward. I swing around, ready to clock the idiot, when I come face-to-face with Sam.

"What is your problem?" I ask, glaring at her.

"Why don't you tell me?" she asks. Sam takes any chance she can to poke at me these days. The happy-go-lucky, sometimes irritatingly optimistic partner in crime I knew before is gone. These days she's annoyed at everything. She blames me for our situation, I know. She's pretty clear about that. She doesn't care that Liv drove us off that bridge because Bill was going to kill us or how evil he was. All she thinks about is our life *before* he died. Our money, the luxury of Monroe Street, the time when we didn't have as many kids in the house.

Obviously, I can relate to that.

Sam wags her phone in front of my face. "You cut off all ties with her, huh?"

I grab the phone from her and stare at the text from a 757 area code. There's only one person I know in that Norfolk area code.

Hey Sam it's Liv. I got some roses and jewelry—did Z send me anything for Valentine's Day?

"Sending her roses, huh, Romeo? I thought you were going to leave her alone."

The first text I see from her in eight months, and it's about someone sending her shit. Someone who's not me. What, is she trying to show me she's got a rich boyfriend now? Is this her way of telling me she's moved on? I'd expected that after eight months, but I didn't expect her to throw it in my face. I clench my jaw and hand the phone back to Sam.

I turn around and head toward the front door, stopping to grab my leather jacket and keys. "Where are you going?" Sam calls out, but I don't turn around. All I know is I need to get out of here. Now.

By the time I get back to the house, it's been at least two hours and all I've managed to accomplish is near-hypothermia. Still, I feel better. That's the best thing about having a bike. The faster I go, the harder the wind beats away my stress.

A black truck sits in the driveway where I usually park, and a man in a fedora is climbing into it—Frank, a man I only knew as Bill Sykes's driver. He came around a couple of times to talk to Nancy after Bill died, but I haven't seen him lately. I assumed he'd split. His eyes catch mine as I wait for him to move his truck, and for a second his expressionless gaze stays on me. I wonder if he thinks about Bill when he sees me, about the fact that his employer died because of us. Though he drove the car when Bill kidnapped Liv and forced her to try to hack her grandfather's account, he wasn't with us when Liv drove Bill's car into the river. I'm not even sure if he knows what happened. As far as I'm concerned, Bill's life was fair game as soon as he kidnapped Liv.

Nancy is at the window when I walk in. "Are you okay?" she turns and asks.

"Yeah," I say, trying to keep my teeth from chattering. "Why was Frank here?"

She shakes her head, her gaze returning to the window. "Just had a few questions about things."

"Things?"

"Bill's death left everyone in the dark. I think a lot of us were floundering there for a while. Do you want me to make you something hot?"

"No, thanks."

"Z," Nancy says as I walk away.

"Yeah?"

"Are we okay?"

"Sure." I flash her a smile. I never can stay mad at Nancy.

I head upstairs and take a long, hot shower, grateful to have one of the few rooms in the house with a private bath. And a private room, for that matter. It's a big house, but nowhere near what we had before. And when there are this many kids in the house, it's good to have a room to escape to.

Wrapping a towel around myself, I walk back into my room. *Jesus.* Maggie is sitting on my bed, her eyes wide at the sight of my half-naked body. So much for the private room. I move to my closet quickly and grab a T-shirt and jeans. "I'm tired, Maggie. This isn't a good time." Not that it's ever a good time for what she wants from me. The line between me showing kindness and something more is too fine for Maggie.

Her eyes are fixed to my body, the heat in them too apparent. Great. She isn't going anywhere soon.

"Fine, you can stay here. I'll go somewhere else." I step into the bathroom to quickly slip on my clothes and then leave before she can say anything. It's my room, and I can't even crash if I want to. I head down to the office instead and lie back on the soft leather couch, closing my eyes.

It's Valentine's Day, and I didn't send anything to Liv. Someone did, though. But isn't that the reason I left her on that balcony? So she could have a real life with real family and friends and non-criminal guys to send her flowers? She deserves nothing less.

I choke on the thought. The idea of her with another guy is a knife to the heart. It's been eight months—has she really moved on? Forgotten what we had? I need to know for sure, and the longer I wait, the higher the probability that I'll chicken out. I pull up the weather on my phone. It's going to be frigid tomorrow. So much for taking the Ducati for a long ride. I text Sam: **Can I borrow your car tomorrow?**

To which the immediate response is a bunch of swearing.

I go back upstairs and stop at her room, rapping on the door several times before she finally yanks it open.

"May I come in?" I ask politely.

She opens the door wider and steps back. "I am *not* giving you my car. Go ask Nancy or bother someone else."

"There isn't anyone else, and I don't want to ask Nancy. I just want to keep this between us."

That grabs her attention. She leans back on her desk and stares at me hard. "What? That you want to drive up to see your girlfriend?"

"Listen, I just want to see if she's okay. I—I need to know if there's—"

I can't even say it. Me, the guy who's not affected by anything, is scared shitless of seeing Liv. I can say this is what I want for her all day long, but it doesn't change the fact that I don't want to know that she's found someone else, some normal, decent guy who gives her the attention she deserves.

"If you care about her that much, why haven't you called her before now? Face it, she's moved on. You should, too, and stop sending her stuff."

She's right, of course. Staying here, I thought I could help my family with the fallout from the post-Bill days, and that I'd join Liv soon after. I didn't. I'm sure that'll be the first thing she thinks of when she sees me. A jerk of a guy who chose his life of crime over her.

I take a deep breath. "I didn't send her anything. I need to see if she's okay, that's all. And then we can both move on. Please."

I think it's the fact that I actually said "please" that makes her face soften. It's not a word I say much. She nods. "Okay. But only if I can come with you." I start to tell her no, but she holds up a hand. "Otherwise you can go to Nancy and beg her for her car."

"Why do you want to come?"

She shrugs. "I want to see what Liv's up to these days."

"This isn't research on a new target."

"Shut up. I want to see that she's okay, too. I liked her, remember?"

I have suspicions about her true motivation, but it's not like I can argue with her. Now that Sam is officially with Cameron, another hacker in the house who's loved her since he first joined our team, she's on this mission to hook up everyone else. "Fine," I tell her.

"Don't worry, I'll turn around when you guys start making out."

Ignoring that, I turn to walk out. "Be ready at ten," I tell her over my shoulder. When I get to my room, I'm glad to see Maggie isn't there anymore. I lock my door and lie down on my bed. Tomorrow I'll see Liv and know for sure. This may be it, and she may blow me off, but at least I'll know. Regardless of what Sam thinks, there will be no making out. I'd be surprised if Liv doesn't throw something at me, like a fist.

And I wouldn't blame her, either.

CHAPTER FIVE

LIV

The whole way home from school, I can't get the roses and bracelet out of my head. Was Theo responsible? Or was Jack? Sam never texted me back, so I don't know. Was he trying to be romantic for Valentine's Day? But if so, why would he cut off the petals and put the stems on the hood of my car? The questions circle around and around in my brain until they're one big muddled mess, leaving me no closer than I was to solving this creepy mystery.

As soon as I get home, I head up to my room to do my homework. But it's hard to memorize Shakespeare when Jack's face won't stay out of my mind. I almost even hear him saying the lines. Strangely, the persona of Hamlet fits Jack, which is more than a little disturbing.

Mrs. Bedwin taps on my door to remind me of my dinner date with my grandfather. "He got caught up in a work crisis, so he said he'll have to meet you at the restaurant. James will be ready to leave in an hour."

I nod and set aside my homework so I can get dressed. I usually prefer to eat at home, but tonight I'm glad to have something to distract me.

Picking up my brush, I glance at the photo of my mother sitting on my dresser, her dark hair pulled up in her usual French twist. When I first came to live here, I'd stop and stare for the longest time at the pictures of her that lined the hallway, fascinated. The only picture I'd had of her before was the tiny one in my locket. But here, there are pictures taken at the beach, in front of a Broadway theater with her parents, in her school play, even at a professional studio. I'd take a mirror and compare my reflection with her image, wondering what features we share. Some are easy—we have the same wavy hair, the same color and shape of eyes. But there are quite a few differences—my mouth is wider, my lips fuller, and I have this tiny dimple in my chin that shows up when I grin. My skin is paler than hers, and my ears stick out a little farther. I'm not quite as slender as she was, either. And in the photos as well as from everything I've heard, it's clear my mother was the life of the party, always with a big grin or mouth open in a laugh, and everyone staring at her like she's the most amazing person. Whereas I'd rather fade into a crowd than shine.

So many unanswered questions when I look at my reflection in the mirror now. More than I ever considered before moving here. How much like my father do I appear? Is there anything Grandfather sees when he looks at me that reminds him of the guy who took his only child away from him? Even though I know I shouldn't worry about him sending me back to foster care, there's still a part of me that worries I won't live up to his expectations, or that he'll just write me off as being just like my father.

I sweep my hair into a French twist, apply a little makeup, and slip into the long, flowing mint-green dress that I'd bought just for this occasion. My grandfather is the type of person who appreciates a more classic look, so when we go to restaurants or shows, my clothes are always as impeccable as his.

Mrs. Bedwin breaks into the biggest grin as I walk down the staircase.

"Oh, sweetie, you look absolutely beautiful." An exaggeration, in my opinion, but her sincerity touches me. She lifts a hand to my hair when I reach her. "You look lovely with your hair up."

"I look like my mother, right?" I ask, unfortunately sounding more eager than I intended.

"Yes, you do." Mrs. Bedwin tilts her head, frowning slightly. "You know, you are your own person, Olivia. Be yourself. That's all anyone wants from you."

She pulls me into an embrace. Mrs. Bedwin isn't blood-related to me—she's part of Grandfather's staff—but in so many ways I feel a bond with her that I've never had with anyone. She makes me think of what it would be like to have an aunt—supportive, kind, one who offers advice but doesn't nag you constantly to take it.

"You know I love you, don't you?" I whisper, the words easy when I say them to her, and her arms tighten around me.

"I love you, too, honey," she says. She releases me and dabs at her eyes. "Now go have a wonderful time."

• • •

The restaurant is in downtown Norfolk at the top of an elegant, historic hotel. Grandfather is already seated next to a window overlooking the city. His eyes light up and he stands as I walk toward the table with the hostess. As always, I'm impressed by how "put together" Grandfather always appears—perfectly pressed gray suit, clean-shaven, silver hair only slightly receding, sharp gray eyes that always soften for me. The only time I've ever seen him even slightly out of sorts was when he came to the hospital after I nearly drowned trying to escape the clutches of Bill Sykes. I'll never forget the fear that tightened his eyes when he saw me in the hospital bed, or the rumpled, untucked shirt that told me he'd probably been pacing around the hallways until I woke up. Funny the tiny details I noticed, but with someone like Grandfather, they mattered. Looking back, that moment was when I truly started to feel like I was part of a real family.

"You look lovely, Olivia," he says, his voice thick with emotion. He pulls out my chair for me to sit down. "Happy Valentine's Day."

"Thanks. To you, too."

The server shows up to take our drink order, so Grandfather orders a merlot for himself and a glass of sparkling water for me. He steeples his hands under his chin when she walks away. "Now about this bracelet—"

I paste on a bright smile. Grandfather doesn't waste time. "Oh, the bracelet. Yeah, apparently I have a secret admirer. One of Kade's friends."

"Secret admirer?" He sighs. "Look, Olivia, I know the children who go to your school are rather affluent, but if someone's spending that much money on you—"

"Don't worry, I'm going to give it back to him. He stuck a rose in my locker, too." I wrinkle my nose. Thinking on it, it probably was Theo, after all, who gave me the bracelet. And maybe I didn't lock the car door like I thought I did. Now I feel like an idiot texting Sam.

Although there was the rose on my pillow. But Theo could've paid a member of the staff to put it there. He'd be proud of himself for that one.

"Speaking of bracelets, and one of the reasons I was rather confused about this bracelet you received today, I have something for you," Grandfather says after the server comes back to deliver our drinks. "It's something I've held on to for a while." He slides a blue Tiffany box over to me. More jewelry. This box is slightly faded, though. "It belonged to your mother. Well, it was your great-grandmother's, then your grandmother's, then she gave it to your mother. Much like the locket you wear."

My fingers automatically move to touch the locket at my throat that I never remove. The pictures of my grandparents and my mother inside the little heart are the reason Jack found out my grandfather was alive—the same day he was supposed to hack into my grandfather's business account. Well, the day *I* was supposed to hack into it—my very first target. The memory still haunts me. I was *this close* to stealing money from my own family.

I pull the white ribbon and open the box. Inside is not what I was expecting—instead of expensive jewelry, it's a small antique gold heart charm, connected by a chain to a key that appears to fit in the tiny carved keyhole. "Oh, wow." The fact that it belonged to the women in the family means more to me than anything. "Thank you."

"The bracelet your mother wore with it was broken, so I was going to get you a new one until I remembered you already have one that you wear all the time." He points at Jack's slender chain around my wrist. "It's nice—where did you get it?"

I yank my arm back, my face burning. Hopefully it's dim enough in here that he won't notice my blush.

"A…a friend gave it to me. I thought it was pretty so I've kept it."

His eyebrows pinch slightly as he stares at me, and I have a strong feeling he's remembering Jack. I unclasp the bracelet nervously and smile at him. "Thanks for the charm. I love it."

He doesn't say anything for a moment as he watches me slide the heart on the chain. The server comes back to take our appetizer orders, and when she walks away, he says, "You know, Olivia, I worry—"

"Oh, there's Natalie." I wave at a girl I barely know who's in a couple classes with me, sitting across from her boyfriend. She looks at me and waves slightly, then goes back to eating. I feel stupid, considering I've hardly ever spoken to her, but for the moment, I'm grateful she's provided a distraction.

"Didn't look like she recognized you," Grandfather says. "Do you want to go say hi?"

"No, it's okay."

He takes a sip of wine, studying me. "Not really a friend of yours, huh?"

"Well, she's in a couple classes with me."

"Ah." He sips his wine, his eyes still on me. I know I'm about to get the "why don't you make more friends" speech. Ever since I moved in, he's worried that I'm not having enough of a regular teen life, even going so far as to set up dinners at his country club with some of his friends and their daughters.

"I do have friends, Grandfather," I tell him before he can start. "You've met Emerson."

"Yes, and I like her very much," he says. "But she's the *only* friend I've met since you've been here. There are other nice girls, you know."

I take a deep breath. I want to snap back that I know this, that I have absolutely nothing in common with most of the girls who go to Dalton Academy for the Ridiculously Loaded, not to mention the fact that I really don't have the bright personality that Emerson does to attract friendships anyway, even if I did want them. My natural avoidance of people who could ask me about my past means I'll probably always be somewhat of a loner.

But I keep the thoughts to myself. Considering Grandfather is one of the very few adults who's ever cared about what's going on in my life, I know I should appreciate his concern.

He sighs. "Okay. I know you're tired of hearing it, but you don't ever go out or anything. I just want to make sure you are enjoying your life here. I don't want you to feel like you should be attached to your previous life."

I recognize the slight jab at Jack but choose to ignore it. "I am enjoying it. Seriously. You've given me everything I could possibly want. I don't need anything else."

He smiles. "Okay, so back to the fancy bracelet you got today—"

By the end of the meal, I have him pretty much convinced that Theo's behind the bracelet and that I'm going to return it to him. I keep my hand under the table as often as possible throughout dinner the rest of the night, my fingers playing with my mother's tiny heart charm on Jack's bracelet. *Jack, why couldn't you have been just a normal boyfriend?*

Not that I expect to get an answer to that. Ever.

CHAPTER SIX

JACK

Nancy is in the kitchen when I go downstairs in the morning. It's already ten. Sleeping in today felt good.

"No school for you, either, huh?" she asks, eyeing the clock.

I shake my head and glance at Sam, who's already sitting at the table, calmly eating a bagel and scrolling through her phone. She doesn't seem as agitated as usual, which is to say she's not glaring at me.

"This is your senior year—you should be in class," Nancy says.

"It's fine." Besides, I can always adjust my grade if I need to, something Nancy knows well enough, though she doesn't approve. Stealing from banks is okay, but changing your grades is not, as far as her weird morals are concerned. Well, stealing from banks *was* okay before she got on this no-hacking kick.

"So where are you headed today?" she asks.

"Nowhere," I say. Normally I wouldn't hesitate to tell Nancy, but this feels way too private.

"Ah," she says, frowning in a disappointed way, and by the slightly guilty expression on Sam's face, I'm guessing she told her.

"I'll go warm up the car," Sam says, draining her coffee.

"Did anyone come forward about the stolen money?" I ask Nancy after Sam leaves.

She frowns at me. "No. Nobody knows anything about it. I talked to my friend at the bank this morning. She's going to get a receipt." She hesitates, her eyes staying on me. "Z, this drive—"

I raise a hand to interrupt what I know she's going to say. "Don't start. I'm just checking things out, that's all."

"You've both moved on. You said so yourself."

I don't say anything. Funny, because I know Nancy would like nothing more than for me to be with Liv and stop hacking. Maybe this is her way of trying out reverse psychology. Why she thinks that would actually work on me is the bigger question.

Her lips twist slightly as she stares at me. "Okay, fine. See you at dinner?"

I nod. "I'll be here."

Sam grins when I show up at her car. "About time. Ready?" she asks, the excitement in her voice unmistakable. It makes me nervous. Maybe I should've taken a chance on freezing on my Ducati rather than involve her.

In a couple hours we'll see Liv. For better or for worse, I'll finally be able to move on with my life. And I'll learn to live with this empty pit of a feeling in my heart when she says she's ready to move on with hers.

"Are we going to stop by her school?" Sam asks.

"I figured we'd just head to her house."

"What if she doesn't go home right after school? And her grandfather could be there. You said you want to avoid him, right?"

"Yeah. Okay, so I guess we go to her school, if we knew where she went to school."

She looks over at me, her eyebrow raised. "I'm shocked you didn't search for that yourself."

"I told you, I cut ties with her." Truthfully, I do know where she goes to school. But I don't want Sam to know I looked her up, either.

"Well, lucky for you that I already found out. She goes to some rich private school called Dalton Academy. Snootiest school in the state. We can stop for lunch to kill time before it lets out. And I already have it programmed in my GPS."

"Of course you do," I mutter, though she's right—it's the only choice. I definitely don't want to run into her grandfather at the house. That'd be a little hard to explain, although just explaining to Liv herself why I'm there will be hard enough.

Once we get to Norfolk, we stop for lunch, then head to the school. Sam shows her driver's license to the guard at the gate and charms him into believing she's picking up a friend. Probably because her Camaro fits right in here. And because he's a guy. Sam's smile has that effect on most of the male population.

"Fancy," Sam says, whistling at the various luxury sports cars parked in the lot. Everything from Mercedes to Jags and even a Viper are situated in the spaces like they're doing the pavement a favor. As the students trickle through the parking lot, the nerves take over. What if she freaks out when she sees me? Maybe Sam should've texted her to warn her we're coming.

Sam pulls around to take a spot midway up as soon as a car leaves. About three minutes later, I see Liv walking alongside another girl.

And a guy.

Two guys, actually. One is clearly paying attention to Liv's blond friend, wrapping his arms around her and making her laugh. My jaw clenches as I watch the other one—a tall, skinny kid wearing red basketball shorts—move in on Liv, his arm wrapping around her possessively. He leans down to either kiss her cheek or say something in her ear. Liv pulls away from him. She's not laughing, but she didn't shove him away, either.

The guy calls out something else, then turns to walk toward his car. For no apparent reason, I make a note of his vehicle—a red late-model BMW convertible.

"Breathe, Z," Sam says to me, tugging at the fist I'm driving into the leather seat. I'd forgotten she was even next to me. "You knew this when you came up here."

I nod shortly. Of course I did. Someone sent her roses and gifts—am I really that surprised that she'd have a boyfriend? It shouldn't bug me. It shouldn't make me want to get out of this car and kick out his headlights. She's moved on...just like I should've. The barriers around my heart strengthen, and I allow my anger to melt away into indifference. "Let's get out of here," I tell Sam.

"Too late," Sam says quietly, nodding toward Liv, who's walking in our direction. We'd have to drive past her to leave, and she'd see us. As much as I wanted to talk to her before, it's the last thing I want to do now.

CHAPTER SEVEN

LIV

I walk toward my car, leaving Emerson and Kade to make out at Kade's car. My tired brain still can't shake whatever is going on. Theo said he didn't know anything about the roses in the car and on my pillow, just the one in my locker that he seemed to think was such a sly move. And nothing at all about the bracelet. At lunch, I even stole his phone and spent my next class period hacking into it in the media center. There was nothing about roses in his emails or his texts. No phone calls to a jewelry store. The only thing I found that creeped me out was a chat with Kade about throwing a fake party so he could get me to his house. Thankfully, Kade shut that one down fast. I turned his phone in to Lost and Found, not feeling the least bit guilty about it.

Besides, as arrogant as he is, if Theo bought me the bracelet, I'm sure he'd own up to it right away. He seemed pretty irritated that I might have a secret admirer who's not him. As glad as I am that I couldn't find evidence pointing at Theo, I'm back to square one.

"Hey, wait up." Emerson joins me, looping her arm through mine. "I wish you'd tell me what's going on. You haven't been yourself. Does this have something to do with those beheaded roses yesterday?"

I shrug, my eyes following a group of girls walking past us, laughing and talking over one another about stuff that I wish mattered to me more. Life should be that easy for me, too, instead of having to worry about someone creeping on me.

Emerson sighs when I don't say anything, her breath white in the chilly air. "Okay. Just let me know if you want to talk."

"I will. I'm sorry. If I could tell anyone anything, it'd be you."

"But you just need some more time. It's okay," Emerson says. "I'm still your friend, no matter what."

"Thank you," I tell her. "I really appreciate that."

She nods, her lips twisting slightly in disappointment, then she smiles. "I was thinking about throwing a party for graduation. My parents won't care, you know, since they'll be in Costa Rica. Want to help me plan it?"

"Sure." Sometimes I'm not sure who has it harder—me, who has no parents, or Emerson, whose mom and dad are never around. The only time I ever hear a bitter tone in her voice is when she talks about them. Though she appears on the outside not to care, I know she does.

"I'm going to make it an all-out event with tons of half-naked guys and kegs and all kinds of stuff my dad would disapprove of." She lifts her chin, then chuckles ruefully. "Of course, this is me, so it'll probably just be me, you, and

Kade playing dominoes or something."

"This is you, so you'll have a bazillion people show up."
I laugh. "And I'll help as long as you help keep Theo from
trying to get me into the hot tub."

"Deal." She gives me a quick hug and slides into her
car, promising to call me later. The totally normal moment
between us lightens my steps as I continue toward my
car. I have to remember that this is not a foster home.
It's *my* home. My school. My family and friends. And it's
permanent and normal. I can be normal, too. First, I need
to stop looking like I have more secrets than the CIA.
Emerson will stop worrying about me if I act like every
other person around here. My entire past can be just that—
past.

My light steps grow heavier as I get to the other side
of the parking lot and notice a familiar red Camaro parked
a few spaces away from my car. I almost trip over my feet.
Only one person I know drives a Camaro like that.

Oh, no.

So much for leaving the past in the past. I only sent her
the text because I figured she'd just respond and let it go,
not show up here. Or maybe she came to tell me to stay out
of their lives.

Times spent with Sam crop up in my mind—the moment
she convinced me to steal a shirt at that store, the hacking
competitions at Monroe Street—memories from a life I've
tried so hard to bury. We were friends, but she used that
friendship to try to recruit me into their crime ring. I don't
know that I've forgiven her for that yet.

Of course, I forgave Jack for pretty much the same
thing, so…

I look over my shoulder to see Emerson driving away. I

consider flagging her down and hitching a ride, pretending I don't notice the Camaro. But Sam might've already seen me, and what's to keep her from following me to my grandfather's house?

Taking a deep breath, I walk to my car and open the door to place my bag on my seat. The thick whomp of a car door shutting tells me there's no use pretending I didn't see her. I turn to face Sam, who's now leaning against her car, grinning at me, but she's not alone.

Jack is next to her.

My.

Heart.

Stops.

Then it starts zigzagging around my chest like it's trying to bang its way out. Jack's here, right in front of me, just like I've thought about too many times. He looks exactly like he did the last night I saw him eight months ago on my balcony—thumbs tucked in his jean pockets, leather jacket, blond hair hanging longer in front—but no, there's a hardness in his stance that I don't remember. He isn't smiling at me, either. His eyes tighten as I step forward. I do see something I recognize in him, now, and it makes me go cold.

This isn't my Jack, who once looked at me like I was his world. The guy who tracked down my grandfather so I could have a chance at a safe, new life. The guy who's occupied the better part of my mind for eight months.

This is Z, criminal hacker with a twisted agenda and an arsenal full of anger.

"Hey, Liv," Sam says brightly, stepping forward. I keep my eyes focused on the scowling guy in front of me as I let her wrap her arms around me lightly. Her clean ocean-like perfume filling my nostrils is the only indication that I've started breathing again.

Releasing me, Sam looks at Jack, then me. "So, um, your text had me—us—worried."

"Yeah, sorry about that, but I'm fine," I tell her. "Really. Turned out it was a guy here at school." The heat rises to my cheeks and I'm not sure why. Maybe because I know I said it just to jab at Jack. His eyes narrow at my blush.

"Oh. Okay, well, that's great!" Sam gestures at Jack, but he doesn't say anything. What the hell is his problem, anyway? Sam obviously feels the same. She throws up her hands. "Oh for God's sake, Z. Did you drag me all the way up here just to stare at her?"

Drag Sam here? It certainly doesn't look like Jack has any interest in being here. Sam, as I recall, is a manipulator, though I don't know what she gets out of this. I cross my arms in front of me and decide to address my question to her. "Why did you come all the way here?"

"You know, I have no idea now. He wanted to see you." She looks back at Jack. "So now you've seen her. Is that all?"

He shrugs, as indifferent as if Sam was asking him about his color preference. Seriously? The emotions roll over me like a wave—regret, sadness, and most of all, anger. *How did I ever think a guy who clearly doesn't even like me anymore was sending me roses?*

"Okay, so, thanks for coming," I tell Sam, trying to sound as bored as he looks. "It was great to see you." I look over at Z with my most polite eat-shit grin. "I've got things to see and people to do—"

Sam snickers at my word slip, but Z glares at her. "Anyway, I need to go," I tell them. "You can head back to

Monroe Street so you can, you know, plan your next big heist."

The last few words crack as my throat tightens, the tears pressing against the backs of my eyelids. I whip around to walk toward my car. *Jerk.*

This is the point where he should call to me, to tell me he misses me. But there's nothing. I finally turn around, hoping I'm far enough away that he can't see my totally fake don't-care attitude crumbling. For the space between two heartbeats, I catch a flicker of pain in his eyes. It's gone so fast, I wonder if I imagined it.

"You know, I have something to return to you," I tell him in a voice that's as cold as the air. "If you'll wait right here, I'll get it, then you can leave for good."

I open the door to my car and reach into the pocket of my bag to pull out the small box containing the bracelet, my fingers trembling. Whether he gave it to me or not, I don't care anymore. I want this thing gone.

I want Jack gone.

Sam is talking in a low voice and gesturing angrily at him. He doesn't answer, his eyes fixed on something in the opposite direction. His jawline is tensed, the muscles twitching. It's satisfying to know he's not as dismissive as he's pretending. With him not looking at me, my heart softens for a moment. This is the guy I love. Loved. Whatever.

He just didn't love me back. Not enough.

They both look surprised as I step up and hand the box to Jack. He opens it and removes the bracelet, his eyebrows pinched in confusion. "Why are you giving me this?"

"I don't want it."

"I don't want it, either. Shouldn't you give it back to

your boyfriend?" He practically spits out the last word.

I draw myself up taller. "Is that why you're really here?" I ask him, unable to keep the sharp irritation out of my voice. "To see if I have a boyfriend? I'm surprised you even care."

"Maybe I don't."

"Okay, okay," Sam says, waving her hand between us. Her worried eyes flick from him to me—what did she expect, that we'd run to each other with open arms? "Um... so, I thought you said your, um, boyfriend gave this to you. Why are you giving it to Z?" She takes the bracelet to examine it, whistling softly as she holds it up to let the emeralds sparkle in the light.

"He gave me roses, not the bracelet."

"You think *I* sent it?" Jack asks. "Why would I send you something like this?"

"Good question," I say. His face is confused and more than a little irritated. He didn't do it, and a mix of annoyance, relief, and fear wells up in me. I hate to ask him the next question, but I have to know. "What about the rose on my pillow?"

"Someone left a rose on your pillow?" Sam and Jack ask together, their eyes widening.

"Yeah. I think someone paid one of my grandfather's staff a tip to do it." My attempt at an excuse doesn't work on Jack. I recognize the anger boiling underneath by the way his chin juts out slightly.

"A secret admirer, maybe?" Sam prompts. "This is a pretty rich school, right? If it's not your, um, boyfriend, couldn't it be someone else?"

I stare at the ground without responding. If it's not Theo, and it's not Jack, I really do have a secret admirer.

Or a stalker.

"Apparently so," Jack says drily when I don't answer.

I ignore him. "Theo could afford it. But he told me he didn't do it, and I couldn't find any evidence that he did."

"We could go find this Theo and ask him ourselves," Sam says to Jack, but I grab the bracelet and its box.

"No. I appreciate you coming here because you were worried. Really, I do. But this is my problem, not yours. I'll handle it. Just—" I close my eyes for a second, and an image crops up of Jack pounding on Theo. Just like he did Tyson, a guy in Richmond he once believed drugged me at a club. He thought he was protecting me then, but I don't need his protection anymore. I open my eyes and focus only on Jack. "Just leave me alone." The words are too final, and as soon as they're out, I wish I could pull them back.

Z's eyes tighten at the corners, and he nods. "We won't bother you again." He gestures at Sam. "Let's go."

"But—" Sam starts, but Z's already walking back toward Sam's car without another word or look. He'll soon be in her car and gone, and that will be the end of us. The final good-bye. The pang in my heart burns—and it's too familiar.

"So that's it?" I say loudly. "After eight freaking months, after you came all the way here, that's all you have to say?"

He turns around, and I envy and hate his emotionless expression. "What do you want me to say?" he asks calmly.

I step closer to him. "When I saw you here, I thought—I thought— You know what? Never mind. At least now I know where we stand."

"Go back to your life, Liv. It's obviously a good one." His eyes flick to my car before he turns and gets into the passenger side of Sam's car. I can feel the door slam like it's attached to my heart.

Sam touches my shoulder. "I'm so sorry, Liv. I thought— He's been messed up since you left. I figured he'd get closure this way. You really did a number on the guy's heart." She sighs. "Probably best thing for both of you to cut ties anyway. There's too much going on at home with Maggie and the others moving in for him to be so distracted."

"Maggie is back at Monroe Street?" This surprises me. Z had once said Maggie made it clear that she wanted nothing more to do with the hacking side of the business. Or, more than likely, just him.

"Briarcreek House," Sam corrects. "It's definitely not the same as Monroe Street, unfortunately. And yeah, Maggie's living with us, and boy is it fun to watch Z try to avoid her while she's being all sappy over him. Sorry, but it's true. Anyway, now you can both go on with your own lives, right? This is a good thing."

She gives me a hug. "It was good to see you again," she says softly as she releases me. Her hand touches my hair, straightened and styled since she's last seen me. "You look amazing. Very rich." She winks at me, then turns to leave.

"Sam?"

She turns around.

"Take care of yourself." *And him.*

"You, too." She smiles, then like a blink, she's in her Camaro. An invisible string still connects me to them, tugging angrily at my heart as they drive away.

I lean against my car and breathe deeply. Definitely not the fairy-tale reunion I'd once dreamed of. I've moved on and so has he. The end of Jack and Liv, a romance that was over almost as soon as it had begun. Could I really even call it love, considering I'd known so precious little of it before I met him? Maybe it was my infatuation with the excitement of Z that I thought was love. Maybe he only cared about me because I was a sad, lonely foster kid. I'm not that anymore, so he's moved on.

This is for the best.

You're such a liar.

You still love him.

Admit it.

I slip into my car and press my forehead against the steering wheel. Then I straighten up and start the engine. Forget Jack. Work on figuring out who's stalking me—that's what I need to do.

Forget him.

CHAPTER EIGHT

JACK

Liv and I are over. She's going to move on with her life with her grandfather and have her rich boyfriend and go to college. And I'm going to move on with mine. Return to being Z, a glove that fits a hell of a lot better than *Jack* ever did.

It's a good thing. Really. It's what I wanted. Giving her a better life was the whole purpose of finding her grandfather and reuniting them.

I didn't know it would actually hurt.

The whole way back, I say nothing, and Sam doesn't press me except for a comment at one point about how she knows I'm full of crap and that she knows I'm not giving up on Liv. I ignore her.

We get back to Briarcreek House late in the afternoon, which surprises Nancy. Obviously, she thought I'd be running away with Liv or something ridiculous.

"You okay?" Nancy asks as I pass her on my way to the stairs.

"Yeah."

"Want to talk about it?"

"No."

I get to my room, glad that Maggie isn't camping out in here, and lock the door behind me. I crank up my stereo as loud as I can handle and sit at my computer, noticing that instead of the screensaver image of Liv, the screen is dark. It's almost like the monitor knows we're done. I'm grateful not to be smacked with the image of what I'll never have again. I type my password, then go into the files and delete the few pictures I have of her. Liv's face is not going to torture me anymore.

I stop at the last one. Liv's head is tilted back slightly, her mouth opened in a laugh. Long, wavy dark hair flying wildly over her shoulder. This is how I remember her. Not the girl I saw today, with her perfectly lined eyes and styled hair. That girl is meant for the good life. Now she's just another ex-girlfriend to me.

But as soon as I close my eyes, I see her ridiculously beautiful face, large brown eyes that see right through my bullshit, her soft smile that breaks down all the barriers I've worked so hard to build up. Her touch that unravels me. The memories rip my soul apart. I'm one of Freddy Krueger's victims who can't escape the nightmares. They'll probably end up killing me, too.

Someone bangs on my door. I get up and jerk it open to see Sam. "What?"

"You might want to escape after dinner. Nancy says she's taking an online class about choosing the perfect career that she's going to share with us." She motions gagging on a finger. "You need to talk to her. She's becoming *boring*."

"Thanks for the warning." I close the door again.

Choosing the perfect career? I chose it a long time ago. I miss the Monroe Street house. Miss the easiness of the life, the puzzle-solving challenges that hacking presented. Mostly, I miss not having to think about anything past today. Now I feel like I have to worry about everything, and the fact that money tops the list really sucks.

It's not that I personally need money right now—I have plenty saved in my bank account from so many years of cracking banks. Nancy won't let me give any of it to her for the house account. She wants me to save it. If I moved out right now, I'd have plenty to live on for a while. So would Sam, Micah, and many of the others. But Nancy, who uses everything she has for the house and the other kids—she's the one I worry about most. Our situation right now reminds me too much of being poor when my mother was alive and knowing that she had to scrape and save every stupid penny while my father had billions of dollars. He didn't give my mother any of it. Just went back to his perfect family while we suffered.

My father really gave me my first lesson in taking what you want. He's the main reason I refuse to work for some bullshit corporation, no matter how hard Nancy tries to convince me otherwise. Those guys are no better than us, except they somehow manage to convince people they're doing well.

I pull up news on ICL Investments, the main financial support behind my father's campaign for senator in the upcoming New York election I've been following. So many articles about his talent with money, his family values, and— my personal favorite—his work with local foster homes in his community. My lips press tightly together. What would people think if they knew the so-called generous, compassionate, wealthy John Dawkins Winslow III had an illegitimate son by a woman he got pregnant and then dumped without so much as a penny? A woman who then committed suicide and left their son in, surprise, foster care? The media loves a story like mine, especially when they can use it to take down a mogul like him.

I stare at the picture of my father in the midst of a bunch of kids, standing in front of a brand-new group home his money helped build. Building homes left and right while mine falls apart.

The ICL icon flashes in the corner of the screen. It's been a few months since I touched his accounts. I once was a frequent customer, filching here and there from it anytime I thought about my mother. It was my own personal act of revenge, I guess. The hacking stopped after I realized it wasn't helping me feel better.

No, I correct myself. I stopped stealing from my father after I met Liv. My feelings for her gave me the ability to look past all the shit he put me through.

But now she's gone.

Gritting my teeth together, I do the usual precursory check of my computer's settings, then log into the back door of one of ICL Investment's accounts through Tor. The access hasn't changed—idiot security. It doesn't take me long to transfer money to my dummy account, then send it to my overseas account. So ridiculously easy. It's not a large amount—not by ICL's standards. They won't even notice it's missing. But it's enough to satisfy me. For now, at least.

I ignore the stab of guilt at what Nancy would say if she found out I did this. But she started up our group home intending us to be hackers. She can't just tell us to stop now—not when it's a part of who we are.

My fingers tap at the keys idly. Nancy's always behind her computer these days, sorting out bills. She deserves better. So does everyone in this house. Considering his political platform, I'm sure my father would agree.

I open our house account and redirect the money into it. Hopefully she'll just think I'm pulling from the reserves in my own account. She won't be happy I'm transferring my money, but she'll be much less angry than if she found out it was stolen funds.

I relax back in my chair, linking my hands behind my head. Sam and I can't be the only ones having a hard time with Nancy's new look on things. Maybe if enough of us speak up, she'll listen.

I head to Cameron's room, but stop when I hear Sam inside. Bad choice anyway—Cameron's happy enough with the way things are now. Especially since Sam finally got with it and realized that he's a good guy. I turn and head instead to Micah's room. He's sitting on the bed, talking on the phone and waving me away. I sit on his desk chair to wait. He rolls his eyes.

"Hey, my brother just walked in so I gotta go. I'll call you back." Micah laughs at whatever the other person is saying to him before hanging up.

"How are things going?" I ask, nodding at the phone.

Micah grins. "Great, especially since Alec finally came out to his parents."

"Have you told him about us?"

Micah throws his hand over his mouth in fake shock. "Us? Are you finally coming over to the dark side, love?"

"Shut up. I mean the house. Does he know what we do?"

Micah's grin falters.

"I didn't think so. When are you going to tell him you're an expert cracker?"

He fiddles with the edge of his comforter. "I don't need to tell him that. We're not doing that anymore, remember?"

His voice is just soft and unsure enough. I shove the door closed with the back of my foot. "Don't you miss it, though?" I ask. "You're the best. You can get through almost any firewall. You made more money in a month than a lot of people make in a year. You can't tell me you don't regret Nancy's decision."

"Yeah, her decision that was made because *you* screwed up," he says, his voice stronger. He stands up, the happy-go-lucky attitude clouding over into something more like anger. *Perfect.* "You screwed us all over when you brought Liv here and were stupid enough to fall in love with her."

"I didn't screw up—Bill did, by keeping information about us on his computer. Except we don't know that he did for sure, do we? Everything is based on *maybe*. Aren't you tired of being held back by *maybe*? We could be doing so much better right now, instead of going out and getting a boring dead-end job. Unless you'd like working at some help desk with a corporation that cares more about its bottom line than its people."

I choose my words intentionally, since I overheard Micah telling Nancy that no way was he going to be stuck at some corporate IT help desk. Micah stares at me for a long moment—by the way the muscles around his eyes twitch, he's thinking hard about this.

"Think about why we came here," I add. "No one should be able to decide our fate except us, remember? That's what Nancy told us from the very beginning. Don't you still believe that?"

Micah's eyes drop to the floor and he sinks back down on his bed. "I do. I just…I don't know. Maybe we could talk to her."

"I already have."

He looks up at me, his eyebrows pinched. "So what do you suggest? And don't tell me to do it behind her back," he adds. Micah's always been good at reading my mind. "I'm not going to go against Nancy."

"I wasn't going to," I lie. "But maybe you can help her see reason. Talk to her yourself. Maybe she could relax her ban a little bit. Like once a week or Saturdays only or even set a limit as to how much each month. Something. Think about it, okay? You could even make enough to get an apartment with Alec instead of some crappy dorm at UVa."

Micah barely nods, lost in thought. I leave him and head back to my room. Micah's a pretty easy sell. He's the one who loves hacking the most—besides me, of course. Being in a relationship could change that, but it also might make Micah realize he needs more money to be on his own. And if Nancy says no, I'm sure it wouldn't take too long to convince him to work with me in secret.

I put all thoughts of Liv out of my mind for the next couple days. School, home, repeat. My life.

Nancy calls me to her office when I get home from school. She hands me a piece of paper—a scan of a receipt. "The jewelry store faxed over a copy of the receipt to my friend at the bank."

My jaw literally drops open. My name, or at least the name I use as Z, is written on the signature line, though the handwriting isn't mine. "Nancy, I didn't—"

"I know," she says, holding up her hand. "For one thing, you're not stupid. Someone must've used a skimmer to get the data."

I'm familiar with the technology used to capture people's credit card information so they can open their own card on your account, though we never used them ourselves. The fact that someone stole credit card information isn't what unnerves me. "Why would they use my name?" I ask. "Thieves who steal card data don't need the real cardholder name."

She shrugs. "Maybe they found your name on a receipt somewhere and thought it'd look legit. I don't know."

I can't help but laugh at the irony.

Nancy raises an eyebrow. "I fail to see the humor in this."

"Poetic, don't you think? We stop stealing and then someone steals from us."

"Maybe we're getting our just desserts for stealing money all those years."

"Or maybe it's a sign that we never should've stopped." I make no effort to hide my irritation. "I know we need that money, Nancy."

"I know you know that." She cocks her head, her eyes probing. "Interesting how a rather large sum of money miraculously showed up in our bank account the other day from an offshore account."

She taps her finger on the desk and stares at me, trying to intimidate me. It won't work. I noticed how the pantry was full yesterday. Regardless of where she thinks the money came from, she used it, and I'm glad.

Nancy sighs when I don't say anything. "Are you aware of how lucky we were that we were never caught? We could've so easily been found out. It's for our own good that Bill died. Now we can actually live like people are supposed to. Normal, honest lives."

"Yeah, normal, honest lives like all the other suckers out there who work seventy hours a week and have nothing to show for it."

Her smile is the worst kind of sympathetic. "I know this is hardest for you. But I think it's not so much the money as the thrill of hacking you miss. You have this image in your head of the glory days of Monroe Street and how cool you were then. But it wasn't cool. It was wrong. We were wrong."

She reaches across to take my hand but I jerk it away. "You are the one who pulled us into this life, talked us into hacking, and now you want us to just walk away? Forget it. I'm not going out and getting a job scooping ice cream or flipping burgers. Or turning into a corporate drone at some help desk."

"You say that like those are the only options. There are so many more opportunities for someone as smart—"

"Are we done here?" I stand up to leave. It's not that I like being rude to Nancy, but I'm not going to sit there and listen to how we need to start living productive lives. She makes hardly anything at the job she's working at now, barely enough to live on herself, let alone with so many kids. That's supposed to be my goal now? I'd even consider it if she'd at least let me help with the house expenses, but no, she wants us to save money for college. Which is in itself a complete waste of time.

"Jack."

"Don't call me that."

"Okay, then Z," she says firmly. "You've got to stop blaming everyone else. You need to start being responsible, and being a thief isn't going to land you anywhere except jail. You and whoever thought it was okay to steal money from us for a bracelet, of all things."

My hand freezes on the doorknob. "Bracelet?" I walk back over to look at the description that I somehow missed.

"Yes. Two, actually, costing almost a thousand dollars each. I would understand more if it were something necessary, like food. Not jewelry. You okay?"

I look up from the receipt and force the muscles in my face to relax. "Sure. Just surprised."

"Don't worry, we've disputed the charge," she says, thinking I'm concerned about the money taken when that's not even on my mind anymore. "They see this kind of thing all the time."

I look back down at the swirling script letters *A* and *P* that begin the Abbott & Peterson's name at the top of the receipt. I know I've seen those letters before. "Can I borrow this receipt?" I ask. "I'll help you figure it out."

She hands me the receipt. "Let me know if you come up with anything."

As soon I get back to my room, I look up the jewelry company online. They don't have any stock available online at all, but that A&P—I'm pretty sure it was on the jewelry box of the bracelet Liv tried to give me. The only way I can know for sure is to ask her for a picture of the inside of the box, but that'd be the ultimate dick move considering how we parted a couple days ago. Instead, I grab my helmet and keys and head over to Abbott & Peterson's.

Abbott & Peterson's is a small jewelry store in a plaza,

along with a grocery store, dry cleaners, and Chinese restaurant. The receipt had the name of "Robert" as the salesman, and since there seems to be only one person working the front area—a woman who's already helping someone else—finding Robert might not happen today.

I look around the long glass cases to find the bracelets, and even though there are plenty of styles, I don't see one that has emeralds. I take a cautious breath of relief. Maybe it is a coincidence after all.

The woman walks over to me. "Can I help you find something?"

"I'm looking for one of the salespeople, Robert."

"He's off today. Can I assist you?"

"I was wondering if you carry a gold bracelet with diamonds and emeralds all around." I make a circular gesture around my wrist. "I have the item number, if that helps." I hand her a slip of paper with the item number and description written on it. I don't want to show her the actual copy of the receipt in case she knows it's being checked for fraud.

She peers at the paper. "Hmm...yes, I believe I know which ones those were, but I don't think we have any in stock at the moment."

"Do you have pictures of them?"

She shakes her head. "We've been trying to get our inventory posted on our website, but Mr. Abbott says it invites thieves. He's a little paranoid." Then she looks up at a black orb in the ceiling, embarrassed. "I'm sorry. I shouldn't have said that." She leans over slightly. "Mr. Abbott's on vacation but he likes to keep an eye on us anyway." She rolls her eyes. The door's bell jingles with another customer, so I thank her and leave. But not before

I note the Avatar Security sign on the door.

I call Micah once I'm back on my bike. "Hey bro, can you hack into a wireless camera system?"

"Probably. Can't you?"

"Yeah, but you'll be faster. I need surveillance off a camera from a jewelry store called Abbott & Peterson's. From about a week ago." I read the date and time stamp from the receipt. "Looks like it's a remote access system with Avatar Security."

"No prob. What am I looking for?" I can picture Micah cracking his knuckles, his expression going from bored to all business. He lives for this shit. Same as me.

"Someone who bought two emerald bracelets, and the salesperson was a guy named Robert. That's all I know. If you can just get in, I'll sort through it. Need every angle they've got on the store."

"No worries. I was getting bored anyway. It's kind of like the old days, huh?"

I smile at the excitement in his voice. "Yeah. Just like them."

I hang up, then stare at the receipt. If these are connected, and anyone in the house finds out about Liv's bracelet—considering it was my name on the signature line on that receipt—they might think it was me who skimmed our account. I'd be screwed.

Royally. Screwed.

CHAPTER NINE

LIV

Mrs. Bedwin tells me I'm out of sorts. In other words, I haven't talked much to her or my grandfather in the last few days. This card she handed me when I got home from school today didn't help.

The red envelope in my hand has no return address, only a postmark from Richmond and a small heart drawn on the back. The card inside should make me happy, but it doesn't. It doesn't sound like Jack at all—not the cutesy picture of the boy kissing the girl under an umbrella nor the verse inside:

No matter how much time passes
You are always on my mind
And this Valentine's Day
I want you to know
My love is yours
(Forever.)

The word *Forever* has a heart around it, hand-drawn with a red pen. Nothing else, not even a signature, is included in the card. Not to mention that it's days past Valentine's Day.

Nobody in Richmond sends me cards—except for the one I received at Christmas from Bernadette and Marc, the foster parents I lived with before I moved to live with the Carters. That one had been forwarded to me from the Child Welfare agency in Richmond.

And Jack...he'd never send me a card out of the blue. Especially after we left things the way we did.

I video chat with Emerson to tell her about the creepy-ass card. "I think you should tell your grandfather you have a stalker," she says seriously when I hold it up to the camera.

"I don't know."

"Why not? I don't get how you're so calm about all this. I'd be freaking out, big time."

I stare at the card, biting my lip. "My grandfather would probably overreact and never let me out of the house."

"It takes a lot to get you out of the house on a normal day. That's not it, is it?" She waits, but I don't say anything. What can I say? One weird thing on top of another, and I still don't know who sent me the bracelet.

She frowns, sitting back in her chair. "Just one more thing you don't want to tell me, huh?"

I must look like such a jerk to her. I've had friends before, but only the shallow kind, where you eat lunch at school together and talk about homework and boys and that's pretty much it. Not the real deal.

Why she's friends with me, I have no idea.

I know she's frustrated, and for the hundredth time I wish I could confide in her. She knows nothing about my life before coming to live here. In the beginning, I was too skeptical. And even now, knowing Emerson has such a huge, kind heart, I can't tell her. What would she say about my being abused? About being abandoned by a mother on drugs? Would she feel sorry for me? Be disgusted? Think I'm some hapless kid from the foster-care system?

Not to mention the secret I still have to keep about the Monroe Street gang of criminals and the fact that I was naïve enough to get caught up in their scheme.

And fall in love with one of them.

"I suck at friendship, I guess," I finally say.

She sighs. "No, you don't, and I'm sorry I made you think that. I think you've just been burned a lot, am I right?"

"No, I—I've just never had a friend where we tell each other things. I don't know how to do that stuff."

She tilts her head. "Ever?"

"Ever." I did with Jack, though it was different with him. We were two lost souls with little in common except a shitty past.

She sits up straight and clasps her hands together, all business. "Okay, so here's how it works. You don't have to tell me anything if you don't want. You only should tell me what you want to tell me. Things that are burning a hole in you and you feel like you're going to explode if you don't tell somebody."

"What does that do?" I ask, my voice sounding stupidly small.

"It shares the problem so it's not just yours. Helps relieve some of the pressure. Well, it does for me, anyway.

Try it. Tell me something that's been bugging you that you haven't told anyone. Even something small."

Something small that bugs me, except there's nothing that fits that description. It's more like huge things I'm terrified of. The list is way too long, and most of them I can't tell her at all. "Okay. So that guy I liked back in Richmond—he was here a couple days ago."

Her eyes widen. "Your Richmond boyfriend was *here*? Liv, how could you keep that a secret? I'd be freaking out!"

I half laugh. "Yeah, I sorta did, but it wasn't that kind of visit. I mean, he was here with a friend and came by to see me because I had texted his friend about the roses I'd gotten and so he was worried about it and came here and it turned out it wasn't from him but we aren't, like, seeing each other anymore so it doesn't matter and, you know…"

We're both silent for a moment, then both of us break into laughter. "Wow, when you spill, you *spill*," Emerson says.

"I'm sorry. I told you I wasn't good at this."

"No, you're perfect at it. Let's go back a bit." She pulls her blond hair over her shoulder and purses her lips in thought. "Okay. So your ex-boyfriend was here and you guys broke up—wait, I thought you were already broken up. Did you break up again?"

"Well, we kind of were. Long story."

"And he lives in Richmond, so he probably sent the card."

"I don't think so."

"There's only one way to find out," she says. "Call him."

"But that'd look weird. Since we're not together anymore and all." I pick up the envelope to shove the card back inside, but it catches on something. I fish around and pull out a small square picture.

Emerson is saying something, but the words don't go through to my brain. This picture—this was taken at the restaurant on Valentine's Day. I'm smiling across the table at my grandfather. It's close enough where it looks like whoever took it is either sitting at the next table over or farther back with a high-power zoom lens.

What the—

I flip it over, but there's nothing on the back.

"Liv!" Em says. I look up quickly.

"Huh?"

"Are you okay? You look freaked out."

I shake my head. "I have to go," I whisper. "I—I'm not feeling too good."

"Oh. Okay," she says. "But call him. And then let me know."

We hang up, and I stare at the picture. It could be Natalie, the girl I awkwardly waved to, but then no…this is a different angle. And the envelope was postmarked Richmond.

Screw this. I pick up my phone to call Jack. It goes straight to voicemail, his recording short and to the point. When it beeps, I start babbling: "It's Liv. I'm wondering if you know anything about this, um, card and picture that someone took of me that I got in the mail. The postmark is from Richmond. You and Sam are the only people I really know there. You don't have to call me back, just text me yes or no. Okay, thanks, bye."

Immediately, even before I hang up, I regret the call. I wish there was a way to delete the recording. Jack would never in a million years do this. What is he going to think?

Roses, jewelry, now a weird card and an extremely

creepy picture taken of me. I open my bag and take out the box with the bracelet, running my finger over the gold A&P initials imprinted on the interior white satin. I do an online search for an A&P jewelry store. Nothing comes up. I search for jewelry stores that start with *A* in Norfolk, but nothing shows up. Gritting my teeth and already knowing what I'll find, I do the same for Richmond and find an Abbott & Peterson's Jewelers. In the same swirling font. Of course.

I jump as my phone buzzes. Jack's name lights up the screen. At the same time, Mrs. Bedwin taps on the door and calls to me, so I flip up the automatic response window and send Jack a text saying I can't talk, then turn the phone over on my lap. I don't need Mrs. Bedwin to hear me talking to him.

"Dinner, sweetheart," Mrs. Bedwin says, opening up the door a bit.

"Okay, thanks," I tell her, trying to keep my voice calm.

"Your grandfather is already downstairs, waiting for you." She waves for me to hurry, then pulls the door closed behind her.

The last thing I want to do is go act normal and happy at dinner. But unless I want to pretend I'm sick and have Mrs. Bedwin ferret out the truth, I have to go. I quickly change from my sweatshirt and jeans into a simple blue dress and join Grandfather downstairs in the formal dining room. The room only gets used when we eat together; otherwise, I eat my dinners at the breakfast table in the kitchen or up in my room. Lately, he's been so busy at work that he ends up missing dinner at home. I wish this were one of those nights.

"You look lovely," he says, standing to pull out my chair.

He glances at my wrist. "And I see you're wearing your mother's charm."

I touch the charm dangling from Jack's bracelet. "Yes, I love it."

He beams. "Sometimes I wonder if you're just saying these things to make an old man happy. It's working, you know."

I smile, trying hard to focus on his words instead of Jack, the card, the picture, and the jewelry store in Richmond. I seriously doubt the store is so amazing that someone from Norfolk would order from there. It's possible it could be someone here who's trying to make it look like it's coming from Richmond, but that would make no sense. Regardless, whoever it is sent that picture to freak me out. But why?

"Olivia? Are you okay?" Grandfather asks.

Oh, crap, what was he saying? "Sorry. Just thinking of something else for a moment."

He moves his hands back as Juliette places a bowl of French onion soup in front of him. "I asked if you have big plans for the weekend."

"Not really. Studying for a test I have on Tuesday."

He raises an eyebrow. "Studying? That's all?"

I nod, sipping on a spoonful of soup. His face is expectant, and I feel the "why don't you have a life" speech coming on. "Well, I might go over to Emerson's for a while. We'll probably go hang out at the mall or see a movie. Maybe meet up with a couple other girls in her neighborhood." Which is a bunch of bull. Emerson always complains about her neighborhood having no other kids her age. But I know that's what he wants to hear. He'd probably be thrilled if I told him I was going to a big party at someone's house, just to show I had some kind of social life.

"What about this secret admirer of yours?"

I drop the spoon in my bowl a little too hard. "Oh. I told Theo I wasn't interested."

His lips twist as he considers that. "That's probably wise, considering the jewelry he thought appropriate to give you before even asking you out. Did you give it back to him?"

I hesitate.

"You haven't." He lifts his chin. "Is there something else going on? Is this young man getting aggressive with you?"

"No! It wasn't even from him." I bite at my lip. I didn't mean to tell him that.

His eyebrows pinch.

"I'm not sure who it's from. Another secret admirer," I tell him, trying to laugh casually. "I guess people here like me more than I thought they would."

"That doesn't mean they should be buying you expensive jewelry out of the blue."

"I know. I…I just have to let whoever it is down nicely. I don't want to hurt his feelings."

"Best to do it quickly. That way he knows immediately how you feel. Relationships are difficult to manage when you're so close to graduating and heading off to college, too." He tilts his head, his eyes softening. I know this look— and the question that usually follows. "Are you happy here, Olivia?"

"Yes, of course I am."

"You have everything you need? I know it's hard not having a parent around—someone younger who can give you advice about things like love and boys, um, things like that."

Love and boys and things like that. Surprisingly enough, I actually appreciate my grandfather's attempt at "the talk." Much better than Derrick's awful sex talk last year. Of course, Derrick had other things on his mind. I shiver slightly. "I've had plenty of foster parents in my life," I tell him. "Most of them knew less about these things than you. I haven't missed out on anything by being here. I'm grateful for all you've given me."

I should've left out that last part about being grateful. It doesn't sound *family* enough. Sure enough, Grandfather frowns, his fingers twirling his wineglass slowly. "I worry sometimes that you feel uncomfortable here. This is your home, Olivia. You own it as much as I do, and I'm proud to have such a wonderful, smart girl as my granddaughter."

This isn't the first time Grandfather's had this conversation with me. It warms my heart, but at the same time, the more he tries to tell me I'm part of this family, the more I worry he has this expectation of me that I'll never live up to. Half of me is my father, the person who stole Grandfather's precious daughter away. The one time I asked him about my father, he went stone-cold silent on me, later apologizing for his reaction and telling me he knows my mother's character is stronger in me than my father's, that I have the better half inside me, and that I'm better than "that lowlife" ever was. I can't help worrying that I'll say or do the wrong thing and he'll see that side of me and realize I'm not fit to be a part of this family. Knowing I feel this way would probably upset him, so I just put on my brightest smile and tell him what he wants to hear.

After dinner, Grandfather leans back in his chair. "Mrs. Bedwin informed me that you received a card in the mail."

I should've known she would've told Grandfather. He

probably told her to alert him to anything unusual that concerns me. "Yes. I'm not sure who it's from. It wasn't signed."

He tilts his head. "Mrs. Bedwin said there was a heart drawn on the back of the envelope."

"Maybe my secret admirer." *Maybe not.* The last thing I want to do, though, is worry Grandfather. If he saw the picture someone took of us in the restaurant, he'd freak out.

"With a postmark from Richmond?"

I sigh. "It's not who you think it is. I haven't seen that guy in a long time." As far as I'm concerned, Jack showing up at my school for a few minutes doesn't count. "Maybe the mail got misdirected."

His eyebrow rises in skepticism. I glance at the clock over the fireplace. "Oh, crud, it's already eight thirty. I told Emerson I'd watch *Boston Watchman* with her tonight."

"You're going to her house this late?"

"No, we're just talking on the phone while we're watching it. I'll be up in my room." I stand and he follows. "Thanks for dinner."

I cringe at his disappointed expression. I shouldn't have said that. He's probably worried again that I'm looking at everything as charity. Maybe I should give him a hug. I don't know. That's the weirdest thing about being in the foster-care system for so long—you learn all the school stuff and things like how to survive in a group home and how to handle changing schools every year, but nobody bothers to teach you about basic things like how to give casual hugs and be a good friend. Or a good granddaughter. Things I didn't realize I was missing until I came here.

"Olivia," he calls out as I walk away.

"Yes?"

"You'll return the bracelet as soon as you find out who gave it to you, right?"

"Of course I will. I don't want it." That's the truth. I smile, and he nods, satisfied. I have to admit, I love that he cares this much. I remember when I was in seventh grade, one of my friends at school kept talking about how her parents nagged her all the time about boys and school and stuff. I was really jealous of her—my foster mother at the time couldn't care less if I had clothes to wear, much less whom I was hanging out with.

As soon as I get up to my room, I check my phone. It shows a missed call and a text from Jack, asking if I'm okay. I run my thumb over his words, picturing him in his room, picking at his guitar or tapping away at his laptop. I miss him, I'll admit. It's not easy to pretend I feel nothing for him anymore.

Contact with Jack is doing nothing to help me get over him. I shouldn't have called him. I text that I'm fine, apologize for the call, and let it go at that. My eyes move to the picture that was in the envelope. Whoever sent me the bracelet I'm sure took that picture, too.

My phone rings and Jack's name lights up the screen. Shoot, I should've turned it off. At the same time, I'm the one who called him and freaked him out. Like the mature person I am, I throw the phone into my nightstand drawer and wait for it to stop ringing before I take it back out. Jack left me a voicemail.

"Hey. I know you're not fine, and I figure you aren't answering because you think I'll get the wrong idea about us. Don't worry, I know we've both moved on. But I wanted to apologize for showing up there randomly the other day. That wasn't cool. And this bracelet you got—well, there are some weird things going on here, too. I think someone's trying to link us. I don't know why. Just…be careful, please."

There's a pause, then the voicemail ends. I play it again. And again. What does he mean, someone's trying to link us? With the bracelet?

I sit at my computer and go back to the A&P jewelry store website. There's not much there—just a picture of the storefront, a map with the location, women who look like they're from the sixties displaying arms loaded with diamond bracelets and rings, and an "about us" page featuring how the store is one of the oldest in Richmond. Old is right—they don't even have any of their jewelry listed for sale online.

I start to navigate away from the site when I notice a small shield at the bottom corner of the screen. I click on it and it takes me to Avatar Security. Why would they need website security when they don't sell jewelry through their website?

The answer hits me as I look at Avatar Security's services. I go back to the website and zoom in to the storefront window. It's not a clear image, but there appears to be a sticker on the door that resembles the Avatar Security shield on the website. Surveillance cameras—it's got to be.

I call the store and tell the saleswoman who answers that I am looking for a particular date that someone bought a bracelet. She is nice enough to give me her work email address, so I send her a convenient link to a picture of the bracelet. She responds about a half hour later saying one of the salesmen in the store said he sold a couple bracelets like that a day or two before Valentine's Day but doesn't know anything else and apologizes for not being more helpful. I smile as I capture the IP address—she's helped plenty.

Hopefully, the storeowners haven't figured out that they need to change the factory settings on their security system. I do a quick search online to walk myself through the hack. Surprisingly simple. It takes all of five minutes to get in after only a couple attempts at username and password—"admin" and "1234." It's so weird to me—the more technology people have, the more careless they are about their security.

I start at the archived footage for February thirteenth. Mostly I fast-forward until someone appears, then I fast-forward again.

By midnight, I've sorted through all of February thirteenth without so much as seeing one bracelet sold and all I've accomplished is to give myself a massive headache. Yawning, I open up the February twelfth footage. Tomorrow is going to be hell, but I can't sleep until I know. Which sucks, because it might've been purchased a week before.

The clock reads 1:00 a.m., and I find myself nodding off while scanning through the video. I've had to rewind a couple of times. Of course, it's when I finally decide to shut it down that I see a salesperson holding out a bracelet to a man in a hood. I jerk up straight and rewind it. The man is completely hidden by the hoodie, which sucks because all I can see is his hand. Nothing like a tattoo or missing finger or anything, and the grainy footage on this cheap camera system isn't helping with any other details. The salesperson comes back with a receipt and places two identical-looking boxes in a bag. Two? I watch the man sign the receipt. The way his hand moves, it looks like he's signing an initial for the first letter. I rewind again and again, but I can't get a better view. It could be a 2, or an L...or a Z. But this guy seems taller than Jack.

The man walks away, and it looks like he's gesturing to someone off camera. I save the video to my computer and try to find other camera angles. There is only one other—pointed at the desk in the back office.

The guy obviously bought something else in addition to my bracelet, so maybe there's some mistake. Maybe the bracelet was actually intended for someone else. I shake my head. I'm not naïve enough to believe a coincidence that big. Jack said someone is trying to link us. What does that even mean?

Something about this nags at the back of my mind, but I'm too tired to sort it out. I'm sure tomorrow it'll make more sense.

Though, nothing so far has, so why would this be any different?

CHAPTER TEN

JACK

Liv leaves me a voicemail telling me she got a card from a mystery person in Richmond and then texts me she's fine? My guess is she looked up the jewelry store, too, and is freaking out because it's in Richmond. She's going to tell me she's okay because she either doesn't trust me or she doesn't want me to worry. Neither makes me feel better.

And what picture is she talking about? It sounds like someone sent her a picture that they took of her. Which is creepy as hell. My plan was to find this salesman Robert today and see if he had a description of the guy who bought the bracelets. But maybe it would trigger his memory if I brought in the actual bracelet.

Yeah, I know how that sounds, and I'm honest with myself enough to know I'm making an excuse to head to Norfolk again. I start to text Liv to let her know I'm on my way, but at the last minute I don't. Better if I just show up before she has a chance to conveniently not be home. I can't expect she'll be happy to see me. Not after the way I left her, and not with all stalker signs pointing to Richmond. She didn't even take my call last night, so why should I think showing up would make her any happier?

The weather is warm for February, and it's Saturday with little traffic on the road to Norfolk. It takes an hour and a half to get to the mansion. I pause outside the open wrought iron gates, wondering why Mr. Brownlow leaves them open during the day. I can get inside without a hassle, but so can anyone else. Obviously.

I ride in and park behind Liv's car, an Infiniti Q60. At least she's getting all the best things now. The bitter knot in my chest tightens as I stare at it. I should've just asked her to send a picture of the bracelet. The last thing I need to do is look like a stalker to Liv, especially after she told me to leave her alone. But if someone really is after her, I can't turn my back.

I switch off the engine and remove my helmet, placing it on my bike. I walk to the front door, take a deep breath, and ring the bell. A tall, lanky man in khakis and a polo shirt opens the door, his eyebrows pinching slightly as he looks me over, then over my shoulder at my bike. *Yeah, dude, I get that I look like a thug to you. Deal with it.*

"Is Liv here?" I ask politely. He doesn't say anything. "Olivia?" I press.

"Who is it, Terrence?" a woman's voice calls from behind him. The man opens the door wider as a round, older woman steps into view, wearing a black dress and carrying an iPad.

"Hi, I'm looking for Liv," I tell her, smiling.

She smiles back. "Are you a friend from school?" I

notice—and appreciate—that her eyes don't skim over and judge me like his did.

"I'm a friend of hers, yes."

She gestures me inside. I step onto the marble floor, glancing around at the bright chandeliers, mahogany walls, and enormous staircase. The kind of house I picture my father living in.

"I'll let Olivia know you're here, um—"

"Jack."

"Jack. Okay, just a moment."

She disappears up the staircase as Terrence closes the door. He doesn't leave, though. Keeping an eye on me. I wonder how often Liv has friends over. My guess is not too often, considering how surprised he and the other woman are to see someone at the door for her.

"What are you doing here?"

A gray-haired man steps into view from behind a large mahogany door off the foyer. Her grandfather hasn't changed since I last saw him, the day I turned his granddaughter over to him. He's not wearing a suit this time, but he still carries himself as if he's dressed for business. He was pretty nice then, from what I remember, and grateful to me for reuniting them. But as he approaches me, I can feel his gray eyes slicing through me. Carlton Brownlow is definitely *not* happy to see me again.

I straighten and nod at him. "Mr. Brownlow."

"Answer my question," he says sternly. "Why are you here?"

Calm. Stay calm. "I'm here to see Liv."

"For what purpose?"

"That's my business, sir," I say, keeping my voice even and polite. By the flash in Brownlow's eyes, I can tell he's not impressed with my attempt at composure.

"Olivia *is* my business now. You are not in her life anymore. I suggest you go back to where you came from."

"After I speak with Olivia."

He steps closer, his eyes narrowing, and for a moment I'm actually a little afraid of him. This honest man is nothing like Bill Sykes, but in a way he's even harder. If he could make me feel like this with a glance, I can imagine what he's like conducting business deals. Despite the situation, I can't help but respect that intensity.

He nods at Terrence, and the guy disappears. "Young man," Brownlow says quietly, "I imagine you're here because you wish to be with my granddaughter. I see it in your eyes, and I see that you're not a man who gives up easily."

He enunciates the word *man* carefully, and I get the feeling it's a threat. I swallow hard. Liv is still seventeen, and my being eighteen could cause a problem that I don't want to deal with.

"I just need to talk to her, that's all. I'm not stealing her or anything."

He glances toward the empty staircase, then back at me. "You think I find that funny? I know you had something to do with Olivia's kidnapping last year."

My composure finally crumbles. No wonder he's so cold to me. I can't blame him. "That wasn't me," I say, a little too fast.

"But you were involved somehow, weren't you?" He shakes his head when I don't answer, the corners of his lips tightening in disappointment. "Exactly. Why would you come back here now, after she's worked so hard to get past all that happened to her? Do you know how long it took for her to recover? All the sleepless nights and breakdowns she's had to overcome with therapy?"

No words come out of my mouth. What can I say? Liv has been in therapy? The thought of the only person I've ever come close to loving sobbing in a therapist's office, having to relive all the shit I was responsible for putting her through, stabs over and over at my heart. I was right—I should've stayed far away and let her live her life.

Brownlow's eyes relax, now that he sees I'm giving in. He puts his hand on my shoulder. "I'm sure you're not trying to cause trouble for her, Jack. But Olivia has only just started relaxing into her life and making new friends— normal kids who want the same things she does. She wants a normal life. She needs this. Surely you can understand if you really care about her, which I can only hope that you do. Leave her alone."

I nod. What else can I do? As I step out the door and it shuts tight behind me, I know Brownlow is right. I shouldn't have come here. It's not what is best for her or for me. Not for the first time, I wish I'd never met Liv. Everything about her wormed its way into my heart and soul and mind, and I'm worse off for it.

I climb onto my Ducati, staring at the Infiniti in front of me. I should go back to Briarcreek and leave her alone. But I know that I can't. The card Liv got from Richmond— it's not from me, but it is from someone. Same with the bracelet. A stalker. And if the bracelet is the same one that was purchased with our house money, it has something to do with me. I care about her too much to let Brownlow stop me.

My phone buzzes with a text. Thinking it's Sam or

Nancy asking if I went AWOL or something, I'm shocked to see it's from Liv. **Meet me at Latte Café on First in 30.**

Smiling slightly, I ask her to bring the bracelet, then start the engine and pull the helmet over my head.

Carlton Brownlow, you don't know Liv like you think you do.

CHAPTER ELEVEN

LIV

I stare out the window as Jack's Ducati pulls away. Emerson said it'd take her fifteen minutes to get here. I just need to stay put until then so my grandfather isn't suspicious. Thankfully, Mrs. Bedwin told me Jack was here before Grandfather could stop her. From my hidden vantage point upstairs, I was only able to hear part of the conversation, and my heart ached for the way my grandfather talked to him. It's my fault he's here, after that crazy call I made to him. I should've called him back last night instead of letting him drive all the way to Norfolk. But despite everything, the fact that he's here sends pinpricks of electricity pulsing through my bloodstream.

Minutes later, I see Emerson pull into the driveway and park. I head downstairs as she makes a point of loudly greeting Terrence and Mrs. Bedwin. Grandfather comes out of his study, full of smiles for Emerson where he had only glares for Jack.

"Hey," I call to her, my voice as bright as I can get it.

"What are you girls up to today?" my grandfather asks as I walk toward them. His eyes are tightened slightly—nervous, if I had to guess. I have to be very careful here. Not too cheerful-looking. Nothing that makes me look like I'm doing anything other than dreadful homework.

I hold up my backpack. "Studying, remember? We have a test on Tuesday, plus a ton of homework."

Emerson sighs. "I know, right? Mr. Lennox gives more homework than any other teacher. I thought in anatomy and physiology we'd just be dissecting animals and stuff. I should've signed up for something like macroeconomics instead."

Her face droops dramatically. *Overact much?* I glance at Grandfather to see if he's suspicious, but he's smiling.

"You never know when you might need any of these classes, so don't be too regretful," he says. "Plenty of time to learn macroeconomics."

She nods. "I just don't know how learning about a cat's intestines is going to make me a better lawyer, but whatever."

Grandfather nods approvingly. Clearly, Emerson going to law school ranks high on his list. I'm sure if Jack were headed to an Ivy League law school, Grandfather would be more accepting of him, too.

We chat all the way to Emerson's car about our homework assignments—which we don't have—until the car doors shut. Then she turns to me, her face mirroring her excitement.

"Spill."

"I need you to drop me off at the Latte Café on First Street."

"Why?"

"I'm meeting someone there."

"Who?" She folds her arms when I don't answer, one eyebrow raised. "This is where you confide in your friend, Liv. What is going on?"

She's not going to relent, and I'm actually glad about that. "The guy from Richmond. He came here, but my grandfather chased him away before I could talk to him." Her jaw drops. "It's not a big deal," I add quickly. "I just want to see what he wants, that's all."

"That's all?" she squeals, lightly punching my shoulder. "Wait, did you find out if the card is from him?"

I shake my head. "But I know it's not. He wouldn't do that. I left him a message about it, and he's here to talk. Nothing more."

"Nothing more," she repeats, rolling her eyes. "Okay. I'll take you there, but I'm getting a good look at him before I leave you, okay? Want to make sure I'm not dropping you off with some criminal."

My answering laugh is weak. If only she knew she was going to do exactly that.

Ten minutes later, we pull into the parking lot in front of Latte Café, right next to a very familiar-looking black Ducati.

"Nice bike," Emerson murmurs as she steps out of the car, holding her door carefully so as not to hit it.

"It's his."

She whistles through her teeth. "Well, what are we waiting for?" She gestures toward the door.

I take a breath and step stiffly toward the entrance. *This is Jack,* I tell myself. *You know him better than anyone.*

The café isn't large—just a few tables and a long counter near the window. As soon as we step inside, my eyes immediately land on him. He's sitting on a stool at the counter, watching me, his helmet propped on one leg. His blond hair is a bit shorter than before, still curling up slightly at the bottom. It's the only gentle thing about him. Everything else—the leather jacket and black boots, the hard look that seems permanently etched on his face—makes him look kind of dangerous. No wonder my grandfather freaked out.

No wonder my pounding heart won't let me breathe.

"Holy crap," Emerson whispers next to me.

My plan for when I saw him was to tell him thanks for coming but that he didn't really need to and that I could handle this.

It was a good plan, in theory.

I make my way to him, numb to everything around me. I'm completely lost in the swirls of green and hazel in his eyes, which soften as I get closer to him. As before, when he came to see me with Sam and all the horrors of my life flashed in my mind, memories rise to the surface. This time they're different. Memories of kissing at the waterfall, clutching his waist as we fly down the road on his bike, the trust in his eyes as he told me his real name. The moment he said he loved me. I reach out at the same time he does, the tips of our fingers barely touching.

But out of the corner of my eye, I see movement—a gray-haired man leaning forward to look at what I'm doing with interest. It's Mr. Tate, one of my grandfather's associates. I jerk my hand away and turn around, bumping into Emerson. "Go to the counter and order," I whisper to her. She nods and I follow her to the register. She orders lattes for both of us. I wonder now if my acting all weird is going to cause Mr. Tate to ask more questions, which he'll undoubtedly pose to my grandfather. If I had casually hugged Jack, he probably would've just assumed I had seen a friend and not thought anything of it. *Stupid, stupid.*

"Are you okay?" Emerson asks me quietly as we wait for our drinks. She takes my hand. "You're trembling."

"That man over there behind Jack is someone who works with my grandfather. If he says anything to him, I'm screwed."

"I could pretend to go kiss Jack or something," she suggests. "Make it like he's *my* boyfriend. I mean, I know it'd be a stretch, but I'd suffer through it."

"The way I acted when I saw him, I'm sure Mr. Tate's already figured it out."

Emerson glances over my shoulder. "That is one seriously hot guy, Liv. But I don't know about leaving you with him. He looks kind of intense. Like he's going to seduce you and then steal all your money."

She chuckles, but her laughter fades as she looks at me. "Are you okay? You look sick."

I nod, my throat tight.

She looks from me to Jack and back again, frowning. "Maybe I shouldn't leave you with him."

"No, I'm okay. Really." I take the latte from the barista and sip on it, noticing with relief that Mr. Tate is stepping out of the café. I watch as he gets into his Mercedes, only breathing again when he drives away. "Thanks for bringing me here, Em."

"Uh-huh." She follows me as I walk toward the door, letting my gaze catch Jack's briefly before I walk out into the cool air. When the door closes behind me, Emerson takes hold of my shoulders. "Listen—I know I don't know what's going on here, but if you don't text me twice in the next hour, I'm sending the police after you, okay?"

"Em!"

"I mean it," she says fiercely. "You're my best friend, and I can't let anything happen to you."

"I'll be okay. I promise." I smile at her, grateful for her concern. "But thanks."

She nods shortly and gets in her car, glaring at Jack as he steps out of the coffee shop. She holds up two fingers, then pulls away. As silly as the idea is of me sending her two texts while I'm with Jack, the thought that she cares that much makes me grateful.

"What was that about?" Jack asks as I toss my cup in the trash and zip up my jacket.

"She wants me to text her twice in the next hour to prove you're not a serial killer. She suspects something's up with you."

"Criminals all look the same, I guess."

I decide to ignore that. I follow him to his bike and climb behind him as he starts the engine, wrapping my arms around his waist and leaning against him. The familiar leather and spice fills my lungs and every empty space in my body. He hands me his helmet—always more concerned for my safety than for his. The familiar thrill of being on his bike pulses through me as he turns out of the parking lot, speeding up when he gets onto the highway.

Jack and Liv and the open road—and it feels like coming home.

CHAPTER TWELVE

JACK

I used to believe there was nothing in this world that was worth living for more than money, until I met Liv. When I left her on her balcony eight months ago, I thought for sure that I'd be able to move on, but she's haunted every thought and filled my dreams at night. I can't let go of those memories any more than I can stop my heart. But now, with her arms wrapped around me as we fly down the road, it's like I'm alive again. I know it's short-lived, but I almost don't care.

Once we get several miles from the café, I pull over at a quiet Mexican restaurant and we find a booth in the back. She sits across from me, and for a while neither of us speak. I want to take her hands, but it's important that I make as little contact as I can—for her sake as well as mine.

"It's warm in here," she says, shrugging off her coat after the server takes our order. "So how've you been?"

"Good. You?"

"Pretty good. School, homework, fun stuff like that." Her eyes move around the restaurant. Nervous. "So you're still at Monroe Street?" she asks quietly, and I have a feeling she's asking about more than just the location.

"We're at a different house now."

Her eyes flicker slightly, maybe disappointed in my response. "Oh, yeah, Sam mentioned it." She purses her lips for a moment, then adds, "Sam also said Maggie is living there now?"

I nod. "Her house closed down after Bill died, so a few of them are living with us. I'm not back together with her or anything," I tell her when her forehead puckers.

"Oh, I know," she says, waving her hand and blushing. "It's fine. Just weird, I guess. Are you still doing—you know—?"

"Nancy made us stop."

"But have you really?"

She sighs when I don't answer. Regardless of the guilt that occasionally pricks at my gut, I don't really plan on stopping. Not yet.

"I'm not here so you can judge me," I tell her, a little sharper than I intend.

"I'm not judging you," she says quietly. "I just...I can't go back into that world again."

"Nobody's asking you to." I flick at a sugar packet lying on the table. Just because I'm here, she assumes I'm trying to pull her back into the business. She doesn't trust me. Although, I have to admit, the kick-ass way Liv could hack into pretty much anything was what drew me to her in the first place.

Maybe hacking was all we had in common. A love for the game. Not to mention the fact that we both had royally screwed-up childhoods. Maybe it was never really love at all. I mean, if I really loved her, I would've given it all up for her, right?

The server brings some chips and salsa. Neither of us touches them.

"Jack," Liv says softly. I wonder if she's aware how it feels to me when she says my name like that, a velvet hammer striking at the bitter wall around my heart. Her fingers touch the top of my hand, and I automatically flip it over to hold them. "What are we doing here?" she asks. "I mean, really. Why did you come back?"

My eyes stay fixed to the chip basket. I know what she wants me to say, but I can't. Releasing her hand, I mentally distance myself from *Jack* and become cool, professional *Z*. "Show me the card," I tell her.

She draws her hands back, frowning. "Sure." She opens her backpack to pull out a red envelope. The card inside has a cheesy picture of a boy kissing a girl under an umbrella and a poem with a hand-drawn heart around the last word: *Forever.*

"This was sent with it." She pushes a picture of her sitting across from her grandfather in a restaurant. She tells me all the other things that have happened since Valentine's Day, including rose petals in her locked car and a rose on her pillow. Some jerkoff actually broke into her room.

"You need to call the cops," I tell her, my eyes still focused on the photo. It's all I can do to keep my anger under control when I really just want to track the guy down myself and beat the shit out of him.

"I was thinking it might be someone playing a prank."

"You don't believe that, though, do you?" I look up at

her. She shrugs, pretending to be okay when I know she's not. Either she really is scared of calling the cops—which isn't unusual for someone who's been in the foster care system—or she's afraid of what her grandfather would say.

She flicks a sugar packet at me. "I don't want to overreact and call the police for nothing."

For nothing? "If it happens again, you should. Do you have the bracelet with you?"

She pulls it out of her bag, handing it to me in its box. "I looked up the initials from the box. It's from Abbott & Peterson's Jewelers in Richmond," she says, her eyes on mine.

"I know. Someone hijacked the debit card for our emergency house account and used it to buy a couple bracelets at that store. Micah's working on hacking into the security cameras, so hopefully soon we'll—"

"Already done," she says.

"What?"

Her lips twitch at the corners. "I hacked in last night and found the video footage. It was a man wearing a hoodie." She reaches over to press my gaping jaw up with a finger, her eyes dancing. "Don't look so shocked. I know how to hack, too, if you remember."

I do remember, and it's all I can do to not climb across this table and kiss the hell out of her. It reminds me of the first time she visited Monroe Street with me and won the hacking challenge against Jose. And the time she bested me—

I tighten my fists and release them a couple of times to regain some control over myself. "So could you see his face?"

"No. It was hard to see because the quality was so bad

and the guy was wearing a hood. He looked like he was waving at someone right before he went off camera, so I think there might've been someone else with him. I tried to find other camera angles but there weren't any that showed them." She tilts her head. "Why would someone send the bracelet to me if they stole the money from you to buy it? That's too weird to be coincidence."

"Agreed. It's got to be someone connected to both of us."

She frowns, the little line between her eyes creasing as she thinks about that. I remember kissing that crease.

Focus, Jack.

"One of Bill's people?" she asks. She bites at her lip as she waits for me to answer that one. I'm sure it freaks her out just as much as me to think someone in Bill's organization could be stalking her.

"Nancy said they disbanded after Bill died. But there's this guy Frank who's come by the house a couple of times. Just to talk to Nancy, though. He doesn't stick around. He was Bill's driver."

Her face is frozen as she stares at me. "The guy who was driving Bill's car that time—" She doesn't finish the rest of the sentence.

"I'm sure it's not him doing this," I tell her in a calm voice, though I'm not sure myself. It makes too much sense.

"But if it is, he knows where my grandfather lives, remember? He drove us there after Bill kidnapped me so I could break into my grandfather's account. What if he thinks it'd be easy money to come after me again?"

Her voice is higher now, scared. I want so badly to move over to her and hold her. I drive my fists into the vinyl seat, trying to stay firmly on this side of the line.

"Think about it," I tell her. "If it was Frank, why would he go through the trouble of skimming our account when he could do the same from someone who'd be less likely to track him? It doesn't make sense."

She nods, her eyes clinging to mine almost desperately. Her expression tortures me. *If it wasn't for you, she wouldn't be worrying about Bill's gang in the first place.*

I slip the bracelet into my jacket pocket. "Let me take this by the store and see if I can track down more details on who bought it. In the meantime, if you get anything else in the mail or see anything suspicious, you should tell your grandfather."

She smiles a little. "If I did that, he'd think it was you. Considering all the evidence, I should think that myself."

"Why don't you?" I know I would.

"I did. I mean, just for like five minutes until I realized that it didn't make any sense. I know you, Jack."

We stare at each other for a long moment, neither of us saying anything. I'm glad I can't read minds. If there were any part of her that still wanted me, even a little, I'd never be able to let her go. But I couldn't do that to her. She deserves better than a criminal like me.

My phone buzzes, and I glance down to see a text from Sam. Have you checked your bank account lately?

My bank account? I stare at the text, the words sinking into my brain like quicksand.

"What's wrong?" Liv asks as my fingers fly over my phone.

"Huh. Nothing, I guess." The balance is the same as it was yesterday, minus the gas I put in my bike last night. I text Sam that it's fine, but she doesn't respond. Did Sam misunderstand the whole stolen debit card thing and think *my* bank account got hacked? "I probably should get back, though. Sounds like there's something else going on at home."

Neither of us are hungry, so I leave a tip for the chips and salsa and Liv and I head back to her grandfather's. I go as slowly as I can. Having her behind me, even for a short time, is like stealing back a piece of the happiness I've missed being away from her. The anger that's been my constant companion since forever fizzles when I'm around her, replaced by a pressure in my heart that's suffocating. I'm not sure which is worse.

Regardless, saying good-bye this time—maybe for the last time—is going to be a bitch.

She asks me to stop outside the gate, out of sight from the windows of her house. I cut the engine, and for a moment, she doesn't get off the bike. I keep my grip on the handles, my face forward. I hate good-byes. It's too easy to let things slip that you want to keep silent.

She slides off the bike, shaking out her long dark, windblown hair. It reminds me of the way it used to fall wildly over her shoulders.

Stay focused.

"Thanks for bringing me home," she says, handing me the helmet. I start to pull it down over my head but she touches my arm with her hand, frowning. "Jack, wait—"

"Thanks for coming with me today," I say quickly. "You sure you're going to be okay?"

She nods. "Trust me, I've been keeping my balcony door closed."

"And locked."

"Definitely."

"If anything else happens, tell your grandfather or call the police. Please."

She strokes her bottom lip with a finger. I stare at it, fighting the urge to pull her to me and kiss her. There is no scenario in my head where that'd be okay.

Her gaze moves to my bike, her eyebrows pinching slightly like she recognizes how I'm sitting, frozen in place. Ready to flee. "Will I see you again?" she asks.

"I think it's better if I stay in Richmond and figure things out from that end. I'll let you know if I learn anything. Just be sure to go to the police if anything else happens. And let me know, too."

A long pause. She's staring at me and I'm staring directly ahead at the quiet street, focusing on the white line in the middle. I rev the engine slightly, trying to hint that I'm leaving. I need her to back away and let me go.

"Jack."

She takes a step forward. I lock eyes with her.

And as fast as that, she's in my arms. I drop the helmet, pulling her to my lap. Her lips still taste like strawberries, her body so warm. My senses reel as I hold her, kiss her.

"Jack, I…I can't," she says, pulling back slightly, though she doesn't slide off my lap. "I know you're going to disappear again, and it'll be another eight months before I see you. I can't go through that again."

I rest my head against hers, wishing more than anything that I could tell her it won't happen. But nothing in my life is sure anymore, if it ever was.

"I have to go," she murmurs, kissing my cheek softly. Then she's gone.

Weirdly, the scenario is too much like the time I left her, that last night on her balcony. But this time it's Liv running as fast as she can away from me. And just like that, the aching void in my heart returns with a vengeance.

"Deal with it," I mutter to myself, pulling the helmet over my head. I pull out of her neighborhood and away from Norfolk as fast as I can.

The ride back to Richmond is long and chilly, giving me a chance to cool down. By the time I'm walking up the steps and opening the door to the Briarcreek house, I almost feel normal again.

As soon as I step inside the house, Sam finds me, trailed by Jen, Cameron, and a few others. "Where have you been?" she asks.

"What's up?" I ask.

Jen puts her hands on her hips. "He's a little too unconcerned, don't you think?"

"So what's the problem?" I ask Sam, ignoring Jen. "Does this have to do with the text you sent me earlier?"

She nods. "A lot of us are missing money from our bank accounts. You said yours is the same?"

"Yeah. Are you telling me—"

"We've been hacked," Nancy says, stepping out from the office. "All of us. Except, apparently, you."

CHAPTER THIRTEEN

LIV

Grandfather's in the study when I walk into the house. He's on the phone, smiling slightly and lifting a hand to wave as I move past the doorway. No indication at all that he thinks something might be up. I take a deep breath when I get to my room, then fall back on my bed, my fingers trailing over my lips.

What the hell was that?

A mistake, that's what. I shouldn't have kissed him. It sends all the wrong signals. Just when my life started to make sense, when I finally stopped trying to decode my past and move forward, Jack has to show up and send my common sense whirling into another dimension. The look on his face when I told him I hacked into the security camera—

I press my hand against my chest, breathing slowly to keep my heart from pounding its way out. I can't let my emotions get the best of me. Not this time.

I sit up then. This guy Frank who worked with Bill Sykes—I know him only from the eyes in the rearview mirror of Bill's car. He did get out at Bill's apartment and handed him the keys, but I can't remember anything other than him wearing a black uniform and black hat.

I sit at my computer and look up a variety of word combinations.

Frank + Bill Sykes + Richmond

Frank + hacking + Richmond

Frank + theft + Richmond

Frank + crime ring + Richmond

Nothing comes up. I do find articles on Bill Sykes, though. They're mostly focused on his death, though a couple do hint at his questionable past. Nothing really links him to any crimes. Nothing about the prostitution and hacking rings. He was a man who locked himself down pretty well. I'm glad to see nothing about Monroe Street or kids included in the articles.

In one article about his death, though, I see a chilling black-and-white image I've never seen. The picture is of his car being raised from the James River with a crane. From this view, I can zoom in on the picture to see what looks like a crack in the back window on the passenger side. It's the side where Bill was sitting—the one he busted his head on when he died. I remember seeing blood smeared on the glass as the car sank into the river water. And I caused it all by driving over the bridge railing. The memory always lingers at the edges of my mind, waiting to catch me unaware, reminding me that I've actually killed someone. Long hours with the therapist helped me come to grips with what I already knew—I had no choice. It was do that or die at Bill's hands. I could've just as easily killed myself or Jack by doing it. I try not to think too hard about that.

I move the mouse to close out of that window, then obliterate my computer history. I don't want that search to show up in my browser again. Ever.

Put your past behind you. Move on.

Easier said than done.

CHAPTER FOURTEEN

JACK

"**W**ho'd hack *our* accounts?" I ask. We're standing in the office, staring over Sam's shoulder at her laptop as she shows us the wire transfer to a person named Donald Smith. The others confirmed the same name on their accounts. Sam's missing a thousand, the others more or less the same amount. In all, a few grand was stolen.

And nobody touched mine, an observation I can't sweep under the carpet.

"What do you mean, *our accounts*? You didn't lose any money," Jen snaps. She looks at Nancy, her hands on her hips. "Pretty suspicious, don't you think?"

"My account's normal, too," Micah speaks up. "Why are you all assuming it was Z who did it?"

"Good point," Sunny tells him. "So it was you, then."

"Really?" He rolls his eyes.

"Did you shut them all down?" I ask Nancy.

"Of course. And Patty at the bank is working with the

wireless rep on it. Apparently, that Donald Smith account was closed yesterday, the money already wired to an account in the Cayman Islands." She pinches the bridge of her nose. "I doubt we'll find him."

"Was the emergency house account touched?"

She shakes her head. "I know what you're thinking, but I doubt the two instances would be linked. One any fool could do. This one—I don't know."

"Isn't anyone listening to me?" Jen whines.

"No," Sam tells her. She looks at me. "You might want to close your account, too, just in case."

"Good idea."

"Have any of you interacted with someone who might've stolen a checkbook from you, your debit card, or anything?" Nancy asks. We all shake our heads. "Check your past transactions, anything that could give us a clue."

"I still say it's an inside job," Jen says, staring pointedly at me. I ignore her, though I don't blame her. It is weird that nobody hacked my account. I'd doubt me, too.

"Have you looked into the guys who used to work with Bill?" I ask Nancy.

I watch her carefully as she thinks about that. Her eyebrows twitch just slightly, and I wonder if she's thinking of Frank, too. But she shakes her head. "I haven't the faintest idea how to find those guys. Bill dealt with them, not me, and they completely disappeared when he died."

"What about that Frank guy?" Sam asks. So I'm not the only one who's been paying attention. Interesting. "I've seen him here before."

"Oh, no. He wasn't one of Bill's—I mean, not like that. Just a driver. Besides, I managed our bank accounts—Bill didn't have access to your personal accounts. Now," she says briskly, "if any of you need cash until we get this cleared up, I do have some in our safe here." She's acting a little too stern. And too quick to tell us Frank's not involved. I try to catch her eye but she avoids looking at me.

"Try to keep it to things you absolutely need, not new cell phones," Nancy says, looking pointedly at Jen.

After the meeting, Nancy takes Dutch and a couple others to the kitchen, in deep discussion about dinner. Obviously, she doesn't want to be left alone where I can ask her my questions. Nancy should be worried about this Frank guy as much as me. She's too quick to blow him off. And as much as I would never admit it to Jen, she's right. Why would my account not be hacked as well? I probably have more money than most, if not all, of the kids in the house.

I reach into my jacket pocket and feel the box with the bracelet. The best thing I can do now is head to Abbott & Peterson's and try to find out who really bought this. It'll probably take some schmoozing, and I'm going to need someone who's a skilled schmoozer.

Which leaves the obvious choice: Sam.

It takes me all of two seconds to convince her to help me. I swear, the girl loves a mystery. I won't be surprised if she ends up being a detective one day.

"You know," she says as she turns in to the jewelry store parking lot the next morning, "if Nancy finds out you've got this thing, you're going to have a hard time convincing her it wasn't you who bought it in the first place."

"Trust me, I know. But like I said, it's probably a coincidence." I hand her the box with the bracelet. "Find out as much as you can, and try to get a description of the man who bought them. And see if you can get a scoop on whoever might've been with him."

"Yeah, yeah, I know. You've told me a hundred times." She opens the box, whistling through her teeth. "I could look at this all day and not get bored. Hey, do you think Liv would give it to me, since she doesn't want it?"

I level a look at her. She rolls her eyes and gets out of the car, assuming her brightest smile. "Be back in a jiffy, sweets."

Ten minutes later, Sam comes back to the car, a grin on her face. She tosses the box on my lap.

"That was way too easy," she says. "I pretended I wanted to find out who my secret admirer was so I could give back the bracelet. You wouldn't believe how fast he gave me the information."

"Just for telling him you wanted to return the bracelet?"

"Well, for that and the fact that I said I wanted to keep my options open for dating rather than getting serious with one guy. Then I did this…" She leans forward slightly and pouts her lips, batting her eyes. "He caved pretty quickly then. Guys are so one-dimensional."

I decide to ignore that. "What did he tell you?"

Her smile falters. "Well…the bracelets did come from this store, but he said it was a couple who came in to buy them."

"A couple?"

She nods. "A blond guy wearing a hoodie and a woman. Said they were all lovey-dovey with each other. Said he remembers because the lady was over at the other counter shopping for earrings, and she was all happy when he walked over to wrap one of the bracelets around her wrist." She shrugs. "He couldn't remember anything else. Oh, except that the guy had a weird name that was an initial." She *tsks*, shaking her head at me. "Really, why didn't you go with a name like Zack instead of Z?"

I stare at the box with the bracelet, my stomach churning. Someone wearing a hoodie came into the store with a woman but knew enough about the store security to keep the woman pretty much out of the picture. Then intentionally signed my name to set me up. And what about the second bracelet that was on the receipt? Liv said there were no other camera angles that caught them. What jewelry store doesn't have a lot of cameras? I stare at it, then the store next door.

"Hang on, I'll be right back," I tell Sam, getting out of her car. I walk toward the shop next to A&P. A pawn shop has bars on the window—surely it'll have an outdoor camera. Trying to look casual, I peer up at the overhang and find a camera pointing at an angle that not only captures people leaving its store, but possibly Abbott & Peterson's, too. I open the door and walk inside the shop.

"Excuse me," I say to the burly man at the counter. "I'm with Littleton Security. We're new here and would love the opportunity to give you a demonstration of our security cameras." Littleton Security is the name of the company that covers Briarcreek House.

The guy grunts. "We've already got a system with ABC."

"That's perfectly fine. We're running a special this month, and I bet I can undercut your current system by thirty percent. And get you out of your existing contract with absolutely no fees."

The guy's eyebrows lift at that. He hands me a business card and tells me to send him the information via email. Which I will—via a link to my "amazing sale," which will allow Micah to hack in through his system.

I head back to the car with his card in hand. Sam grins when I tell her what I did.

"Maybe you can get a look at the chick he's with," she says as I text Micah the information. "Do you think this guy's the same person who stole from our accounts?"

"No idea. Maybe."

"What about that Frank guy?" Sam asks. "He looks kind of shady and shows up at the house a lot."

"He's already at the top of my list. He's the one who drove us around when Bill kidnapped Liv. Drove her straight to her grandfather's house, so he knows where she lives. Problem is, all we have is his first name, and Nancy won't give me anything on him."

She nods. "Then we need to get the information from her when she's not looking."

Sam and I decide to wait until everyone's asleep. Around three a.m., she opens her door, yawning, after I tap on it. She sneaks into Nancy's bedroom to get her phone, pressing the button with Nancy's thumb while she's asleep to unlock it. Sam definitely likes to live on the edge. She brings it out to me and we search the phone contacts. I'm actually surprised to see Frank listed in her contacts. So she *is* keeping up with the guy—or maybe she's screening his calls. I capture the number in my phone. There are no texts between the two. There is a phone call, though, two days ago. I go into location services to check out the list of most recent places she's visited. I'm surprised that she left that function running. It was the first thing I turned off when I got my phone.

Nancy doesn't go out much, so the only items listed were the grocery store and home. Except for a visit two days ago to State Avenue.

"Who do we know on State Avenue?" I mumble. Sam shrugs. I hand her the phone and she returns it to Nancy's room.

We don't speak until we're in the office downstairs. I sit at Nancy's PC and boot it up in safe mode while Sam searches on the second computer for the phone number, owned by a Frank Jones. She finds an age—47—and several addresses as well as an associated name: Elizabeth Jones, age 38. Wife, maybe. Or sister. Maybe she's the woman who went to the jewelry store.

"Check it out," Sam says, pointing at the last address listed on State Avenue. "Why is Nancy visiting Frank at his house?"

"No idea."

"I wish there was a stupid metal filing cabinet," Sam says grumpily. "Pry it open, pull out a file labeled 'Frank Jones,' and we'd be good to go. Or look under the carpet for a key."

"I am looking for a key," I tell her, typing in the code that will get me in. "Just a different kind."

I hesitate, though, staring at the black screen in front of me. It's not like looking at her phone or listening in to conversations. This is a lot more personal. It'll be the first time I've ever attempted to hack Nancy's computer. I have no doubt that I can do it, and it might give me all the facts I need on this Frank guy. But if I do this, I'll lose the trust of the one person who's always believed in me. Would I even be able to look her in the eye?

"What's wrong?" Sam asks.

"I can't do it. Not to Nancy."

She stares at me for a moment, then her lips lift in a slight approving smile. If she says "good boy," I'm out of here.

"Besides, we have enough information to start with." I lean back in my chair. "So obviously this Frank guy is someone Nancy knows well enough to allow him into the house, to keep him in her phone, and to have a conversation with two days ago. She also was inclined to go to his house herself. And he knows where Liv is and that her grandfather's loaded, so it would make sense if he was going to blackmail her."

"But stalk her?" Sam asks in the middle of a yawn. "Send her roses? What would he get outta that? And why would he steal your debit card and use it to send her jewelry?" She laughs.

"What's so funny?"

"Nothing. I'm sorry," she says, wiping her hands over her eyes. "I'm getting loopy. I've got to go to bed. If you come up with anything else, let me know."

"Will do."

I browse around on the computer Sam was on, looking for more details on Frank or Elizabeth Jones but come up with nothing useful, other than the fact that they're both from Pittsburgh.

Sam has a point, though. What would Frank get out of sending roses to Liv? Unless he was related to Bill and is pissed off about his death or something. I didn't think Bill had any family. Not that any of us know about one another's families (or lack of them). No one except Nancy knows I have any family, either.

I look up my father on the web, and a different story pops up. This one's about his son Jeremy, who's a few years older than me and interning at a hospital right here in Virginia. I wonder how John Dawkins Winslow III would feel about both his sons—his precious legitimate son as well as the one he swept under the carpet—living in the same city. Not that he would've looked me up anyway to know shit about me. Maybe I should pay a visit to Jeremy and share our relationship, which I am sure he knows nothing about.

I stare at a photograph of my half brother, taken at his college graduation. Two fingers are pointed skyward; the other arm is around his father, who's smiling proudly at his Johns Hopkins graduate. His mother is on his other side, laughing at something off-camera, her hand clasped around a grinning little boy. Such a happy family. Bitterness surges inside my heart, but also a weird kind of ache. I zoom in to my father's face, imagining that look of pride, those shining eyes of approval, directed at me.

This is stupid. I don't need my father's approval. Anger at him is what kept me pushing forward to be an expert cracker. The antithesis to his perfect son. Wrecking every corporate life that I could. Make them hurt to take away some of my pain. Problem is that it doesn't work as well as it did when I was younger. The anger still boils under my skin, but it feels old, an ache that I can't cure.

I hack into his website and replace the word "honest" with "scumbag" in a sentence in his "about me" section. It probably won't even be noticed by his team for a while.

Then I close the browser and erase any trace I was there.

0 0 1 0 0 1 0 0 0 1 0 1 1 0 1 0 1 0 1 0 0 0 0 0 0 0 0 0 00
0 1 1 1 1 1 1 1 1 1 1 0 0 0 0 0 0 0 0 0 0 1 1
1 1 0 1 0 0 0 1 0 1 0 0 1 1 1 1 1 0 1 1 0
1 0 1 0 0 0 0 1 1 1 1 0 1 0 0 1 1 0 1 0 0 1
0 0 1 1 1 0 0 0 0 1 0 1 0 1 0 1 1 1
0 1 0 0 1 0 1 1 1 1 0 1 1 1 1 00 1 1 1 0 1 0 1
1 0 0 1 0 0 1 0 0 0 1 0 0 0 01 0 0 0 0 1 0
1 1 1 0 1 1 1 0 0 1 1 0 1 0 0
0 0 1 0 0 1 1 1 0 0 1 0 0 1 0 01 1 1 1 0
1 0 1 0 0 1 1 0 0 0 1 0 01 0 1 1 1 0
0 0 0 0 0 0 0 0 0 1 0 1 1 1 1 0 0 1 0 1
0 1 0 1 1 1 0 1 1 1 1 0 0 1 0 0 1
0 0 0 1 1 1 0 0 0 0 0 0 1 0 1 1 1 0

CHAPTER FIFTEEN

LIV

On Sunday, I sleep in, exhausted after staying up all night to get my homework done. The visit—and kiss—from Jack threw me a curveball, and I'm having a hard time concentrating on anything else.

I've replayed that kiss on his bike a hundred times in my head and come up with no conclusions other than the fact that I need to stay on my guard. Otherwise I'm going to end up falling hard again, just to have my heart broken. Again.

I go to the bathroom and brush my teeth, then come back to my room, put on my robe, and open the doors to the balcony. It's so weird how warm it is out—more like spring than February. The concrete feels soft to my feet. Soft concrete? I glance down, a chill creeping over my body until I'm numb.

Roses are cut up and strewn all over my balcony, red petals mixed with white. Hundreds of rose petals and stems, looking like blood leaking out of veins. It looks like someone took a hacksaw to them. *What the hell?* There's nobody in sight. Nobody running from the house.

Someone did this while I was *sleeping*.

I back away, only able to take shallow, whimpering breaths. *Keep it together, Liv. It's just rose petals. Someone trying to freak you out.*

I grab my phone off the desk and take a picture of the roses and text it to Jack without even thinking. I just swore to stay away from him, and here I am sending him a picture of...

I peer closer at the picture, at what looks like a glint of steel, then look up at the same spot on the balcony. A knife is lying on the petals. Not the kitchen kind—the kind you see on CSI shows that look like daggers. I step back, my entire body trembling. "I'm not afraid of you," I try to shout, but I can't find my voice.

I am afraid, though. Very. I edge back into my room, lock the balcony door again with my shaking fingers, and run to get my grandfather.

Less than an hour later, two policemen are on my balcony and in my room, taking pictures of the chaos of roses and making notes on their pads. I tell them about the rose petals on my car seat at school. I leave out the part about the flower on my pillow, not because I'm trying to keep it from them, but from my grandfather. He'd freak if he knew I'd kept that a secret this whole time.

The younger of the two police officers walks over to me, tapping his notepad against his pant leg and looking around the room as if there were clues they might've missed. "Any old boyfriends who might be trying to reconnect with you?"

I shake my head, doing my best to keep my face even. "No."

"May I see your phone?" the older officer asks.

My throat tightens. Of course, they'll want to check the call record. I should've thought of that before texting Jack. Stupid.

Grandfather nods at me. "Sure," I say, trying to act casual though the word comes out high-pitched.

The officer raises an eyebrow. "Well, where is it?"

"Oh, it's in the bathroom. I'll go get it."

"You keep a phone in the bathroom?" The officer looks at my grandfather, who shrugs.

"Yes, sir." I head into my bathroom and delete all my texts and the outgoing call to Jack. It's all I have time to do before the officer appears to take my phone.

"Not a big texter?" he asks as we walk back to my room. He looks at me skeptically

"Not really."

"Hmm… Who's Annie?" The officer looks over his glasses at me, and my heart sinks. He's going through my contact list.

"One of my friend's granddaughters," Grandfather says, and he seems pleased. He smiles at me. "I didn't realize you two swapped numbers."

I nod without speaking. I've never called or texted Annie. I only took the number because she gave it to me if I ever wanted to meet up at the country club to swim. She's nice, but calling people I barely know out of the blue is not anywhere within my comfort zone.

"Dr. Valerio?"

"Her therapist," Grandfather supplies. "She came from foster care, so I thought she might want to talk about it with someone."

It's embarrassing, the look of surprise mixed with

pity that the officer gives me. And it's the first time Grandfather's ever mentioned to anyone that I'm from the foster system. It hurts, deep down, though I know he's just saying it because he's trying to help the police. "Anyone from your foster homes you think might want to hurt you?" the officer asks.

"I don't think so." Those who tried to hurt me have moved on, and I don't want to bring up the past. Grandfather doesn't know much about what happened in any of my homes—not with Derrick, not with the ones before who bullied me or abused me. He doesn't even know about Bernadette—the one I thought loved me and promised to keep me forever, till she left me for Hawaii. I wouldn't have been able to stomach his pity. And what he knows about Bill Sykes was that he was a stranger who kidnapped me—not the crime boss of the guy he despises.

"Emerson?"

"My best friend." I glance at Grandfather, who's now preoccupied at the balcony door, staring at the roses. *Please don't be listening.*

My stomach clenches when he says, "Jack?"

All eyes look my way, but the only face I really notice is Grandfather's. His head rotates in my direction, his eyes wide with disappointment. It's a punch in the gut to him, I know, especially after our conversation yesterday. I keep my face even as I talk to the officer. "A friend from a school I used to go to." It's true—he's a friend from my last school, so it's not like I lied.

"A good friend?"

I shrug. "Not really. I haven't seen him in a long time." *Only yesterday.* "I've just had that number in my phone for a while and haven't deleted it."

"Well, maybe it's time to delete those old numbers you don't use anymore," Grandfather says, a slight edge in his voice. I avoid looking at him.

"Well, considering he's calling you right now, looks like he's not that old of a friend," the officer says, holding up my phone so I can see the incoming call from Jack.

Great. I laugh shortly and take the phone, using the auto reply that I can't talk. I silently pray for him not to call me again and keep my gaze on the officer. "He's an old friend, but I sent him a picture of the roses. I thought he'd find it funny."

"Funny?" The officers look at each other with raised eyebrows.

I swallow and nod, trying to smile. "Yeah. We did a project on *Romeo and Juliet* once and had a scene kind of like this one with the roses, so I thought I'd tell him about it. I...I didn't realize there was a knife in the roses when I took the picture."

Worst lie ever. I can see my grandfather shifting out of the corner of my eye. Now he knows I'm lying about not being in contact with Jack. I should've just been up front with him from the beginning.

"I can pull records of texts, of course, if you'd like me to." The officer addresses my grandfather more than me. Obviously, he knows I'm lying, too. Grandfather's eyes are still on me, and I'm silently pleading with him not to say anything.

"I don't think that'll be necessary just yet," Grandfather says quietly, and I breathe a little. His gaze is still disappointed, though, which tells me he didn't buy a word I said. "What about the bracelet, Olivia?"

"I'm not sure where I put it," I tell him. He shakes his

head slightly. I don't blame him for not believing me on that one, either. I suck at lying.

The policemen finish their search of my phone, do a few quick fingerprints, and leave with the usual "Call us if you see or hear anything" message. They give Grandfather the numbers for a few local private investigators for hire and he thanks them. His extreme politeness puts me on edge—I know he's upset, and the fact that my lie is the reason for it makes me feel horrible. But I can't have them going after Jack.

"I know what you're thinking," I start after he sees the officers out, but Grandfather raises a hand.

"Olivia, I've tried being patient with you on this, but the lies…"

"I know. I'm sorry. But I promise I haven't had contact with him before this week."

He shakes his head. "I want to believe you, but you have to understand how difficult that is. What I want to know is are you seeing him now?"

"No. I just talked to him about what's happening here. That's all."

"And why would you do that?" When I don't answer, he nods. "You thought he was the one doing this. Has he proved that he hasn't?"

"Jack wouldn't do this," I tell him firmly. "I know it. He's more upset than you are."

Grandfather scowls. "I doubt that. Olivia, whatever happened with that boy must stay in the past. I forbid you to have anything to do with him, do you understand? For the sake of your future."

"My future?" I ask, but he's already walking away. Final word is the final word, as far as he's concerned. But for the sake of my future—what does that mean? Is he going to disown me? Not help me get to Princeton? I've already been accepted—the letter came in December. But if he decides to cut me off, I don't know how I'll be able to do it.

I wrap my arms around myself, flashbacks of the foster life creeping over me. Things were always held over my head. If I needed new clothes, most of the time I had to hope my foster parents were in a good mood or I'd just get by wearing things that were too small. I thought the days of worrying were over, that I was with family who'd love me no matter what.

I don't blame Grandfather—he's only known me for a few months. I can't help but feel I'm here on a trial basis until he realizes I'm not going to run away pregnant like my mother did. No matter what he says about me being part of the family, I have a feeling I'll always feel like this— an outsider.

CHAPTER SIXTEEN

JACK

Everyone in the house is tense—including me, but for different reasons. The missing money is all they're talking about, and it's grating on my nerves. Not because I think they shouldn't be worried, but because all I hear is, "Who do you think did it?" Over and over. But nobody seems to actually be doing anything about it. I've combed through the house computer along with Micah, and we can't find any evidence that someone stole our money.

Nancy tries to keep the peace and refuses to look through people's computers. "Everyone deserves privacy," she says. "Unless we know without a doubt it was someone on the inside, we're not raking through one another's computers."

Some people have obviously already made up their minds. Jen's eyes accuse me every time she looks my way. Every once in a while she'll say something like "Whatcha gonna do with all our money?" when she passes me on the stairs or in the hallway, but I ignore her. It's not like I'm the only one whose bank account wasn't touched.

I have Bill's old detective contact, Jim Rush, look into Frank Jones, but he comes up with nothing illegal. The guy barely has an online existence. I even parked outside Frank's house while he was there but couldn't find an open wifi to hack into. Nancy refuses to talk about him. Well, mostly she just changes the subject and finds a reason for us not to be alone together. She's definitely hiding something, so I'm not letting her off the hook where Frank's concerned.

But it's not just the money that has me worried right now. I can't stop thinking about the picture of slashed roses on Liv's balcony, a knife buried within them. I can't text her or call her. Her auto reply message was enough to tell me police were probably going through her phone.

I tap my finger on the face of the phone, wishing she would let me know what's going on.

Micah calls me to his room and tells me he's found the footage I'm looking for in the security cam. He brings up the grainy black-and-white video from the jump drive he captured it on and lets me sit in front of the monitor.

"This is the only transaction that went down at the time stamped on your receipt. I don't think you're going to get much from it, though. Hard to see the guy's face with that hoodie."

The man appears to be lean and maybe around five foot ten. As normal as a person can get. Liv's right, there's no telling who the guy is from this footage. He could be Frank, but he could be a thousand other people, too. I try to see if I can catch a profile or anything when he turns to leave the store. His face is down, either examining his purchase or avoiding cameras. Considering all the trouble the guy went through to keep himself hidden, looks like he's avoiding security cameras.

"Did you get the pawn shop's external angle?" I ask.

Micah nods. He opens the footage up and plays it. "See? Same guy—but he's with a woman."

The quality is better on the pawn shop's camera, though unfortunately the couple walks away from the lens. The woman is much shorter than the man. She links her arm through his, cuddling up to him as they walk away. I rewind it and stare at the long blond hair.

"Is it just me, or does that look like…"

"Jen," Micah finishes. We look at each other.

"What would Jen be doing with a guy buying Liv a bracelet?" I ask.

"If that's even her," Micah says doubtfully. He rewinds the video, peering closely at the screen. "You can't see her face. Lots of people have blond hair."

"It makes sense, though. She's so pissed off about everything. Remember how mad she was when Maggie and the others moved in?" And she blames me for us not having any money. But who's the guy?

Micah shakes his head. "Dude, you better not accuse her without more evidence than this. Nancy will take your head off."

He hands me the jump drive. "They're both on here."

"Thanks for this. I owe you big."

"Hey, Z," Micah calls from behind me as I head toward the door. "Why do you think our accounts weren't touched? I mean, mine, yours, and Nancy's were the only ones left alone. And some of the girls from Bill's other house."

I lean against the doorframe. "Maybe the hacker stole from the people least likely to check their account balances regularly, giving him time to get the money offshore before the bank could stop it."

Micah frowns. "If that's true, it means he knows us well enough to figure that out."

I flip the jump drive in the air. "Exactly. For now, keep this to yourself, please."

Jen approaches me as I walk toward my room. "Crying because your girlfriend hasn't called you?" she asks, her face drawn into the usual sneer. "Guess you're too busy to worry about the little things. Like money being stolen from our accounts. Asshole," she adds as I pass by, her elbow poking me in the side.

"You know," I say, turning around to face her. "Interesting that you're gone all the time. I wouldn't be surprised if you were hooking up with whoever's doing this."

A tiny pinch of her eyebrows is the only sign of concern from her. "You just automatically assume I'm hooking up because I'm not around?"

I shrug. "Well, you'd have to actually be competent at hacking to steal the money yourself, so—"

Her mouth drops open. Then she straightens, her chin pressing forward. "You think you're so much better than everyone else. You'll get what's coming to you, too."

I cross my arms, frowning at her. "That sounds like a threat."

She smirks, trying to act unaffected, though I notice she moves back a tiny step. "It's just that I know people like you will eventually get what they deserve."

"Uh-huh." I keep my gaze on her, and it's only seconds

before she drops hers.

"You don't know anything," she mutters, turning and walking away. She goes into her room and slams the door behind her. Then she opens it again, her laptop in one hand and her keys in the other. "Try hacking my computer *without* my computer, asshole," she says as she walks past.

I have to give it to her—she's smart. I wouldn't hack Nancy's computer, but Jen is a different story. Considering her motivations have always been out of hatred for me, hacking everyone else's account but mine in order to point the guilt in my direction is something I could see her doing. I need to show Nancy this footage.

Nancy's talking to Sam when I walk downstairs. From the relaxed postures and smiles, I'm guessing it's nothing to do with the crap going on.

"What's up?" Sam asks as I join them.

"Not much. Hey, Nancy, can I talk to you for a sec?"

"I can't right now. I'm on my way out and will be gone for a while. Sam, you're in charge, okay?"

It's like I have some disease or something, as fast as she moves away.

"Nice going," Sam tells me.

"At least I'm trying to figure out what's going on instead of standing around goofing off."

"I *was* doing that. My way isn't like yours. Which is why I'm so much better at this than you." She winks.

She's got me there. "Did you get anything from her?"

"She won't hear back from the bank till tomorrow. We'll go from there, since she's not spilling on this Frank guy." She pauses as I get out a pan and the eggs from the fridge. It's my morning to cook breakfast, something I really don't mind doing. "Did *you* find out anything more about him?"

"Nope. Nancy won't tell me anything, either. And if it is him, I think someone might be working with him. Someone who wants to make it look like I'm the one stalking Liv." I stop as Dutch comes in to pour himself a glass of orange juice. I crack open the eggs into a bowl and whisk them as Sam moves to my other side.

"Okay. So who wishes you'd be out of her life for good?" she asks quietly.

"Where do I start? With you?"

She sticks her tongue out at me. "Funny. I mean who would stand to gain from pretending the giver is you? Like someone close to *her*."

I was about to say "Jen," but that last question throws me. Someone close to her who'd have it in for me? For some reason, Liv's grandfather comes to mind. He was kind to me when I first introduced him to his granddaughter, and grateful, too. But I know he links Bill's abduction to me. He made that clear enough when I showed up at his house.

But what would he gain by pretending to send gifts to Liv? Maybe he suspected she stayed in touch with me and was trying to figure out how to bring me out into the open so he could officially break us apart. And make me look like a jerk to Liv in the process so she'd never talk to me again.

No, Carlton Brownlow is a straight shooter and really cares about his granddaughter. He wouldn't pull this stalker crap.

"I was thinking it might be someone right here," I tell her. "Think about it. Someone knows enough about each of us to steal from our accounts. Except, conveniently, me." I pour the eggs in the pan and shove them around with the spatula. "Someone who hates me enough to make me look bad to Nancy and to Liv."

She watches as I sprinkle pepper and salt on the eggs. "So you think it's Jen."

"She's on the top of my list of suspects, yes. Can you keep an eye on her?"

"Sure. Where are you going?"

"Norfolk. I can't let her stay up there by herself while some asshole's creeping on her."

"That is so like you to be worried about Liv when our bank accounts are being hacked. I told you a long time ago getting involved with that girl was a bad idea." She half laughs, taking the spatula out of my hand. "Anyway, I figured you'd be going up there today. Go on. I'll cover for you here."

I put my hand on her arm, causing her eyebrows to skyrocket. I rarely show affection, but Sam's more like a sister to me than anyone. "Thanks."

She smiles, and it's a genuine smile without the usual snark. "Sure thing."

I borrow Sam's phone to call Liv, since Liv probably told her grandfather about the roses. Cops might've looked at the phone. Her voice is hesitant when she answers.

"Are you okay?" I ask softly.

"Oh, hey Marie," she says, her voice light. "Nothing much, just talking with my grandfather. How's it going with you?"

I hear her tell her grandfather it's a friend from school.

"Can you talk at all?" I ask, keeping my voice as quiet as I can.

"Not really. Just that history test on Tuesday."

"Okay, listen, I'm coming over today. Can you get out?"

"Oh, yeah, sure. I'm going to study with Emerson at her house today. You can join us. Hang on and I'll give you her address."

I can hear a deep voice in the background saying something, and Liv is saying something back, but she must've muffled the speaker, since I can't hear what they're saying. Her voice sounds higher, though. Agitated. Her grandfather probably doesn't like the idea of her going out with a stalker on the loose. Can't say I blame him on that one.

She comes back to the phone. "Sorry, Marie," she says. "Here's the address. I should be there in two hours. You might see someone following me so don't freak out—Grandfather hired a bodyguard."

In other words, get there before her. I stop in Nancy's office after I hang up with Liv, putting the jump drive in an envelope and a leaving a note for her to watch it as soon as she can. I wanted to show it to her myself, but I'm not waiting around for her to come back.

It takes me less time than usual to get to Norfolk—probably because I ride like a bat out of hell. It's colder than yesterday, too. But unlike the last ride, I'm dressed for it, the leather blocking the cold.

Part of me feels guilty for leaving right now when everyone in the house is so upset about the money being gone. It's not like I'm okay with it, but I'm a hell of a lot less okay with leaving Liv to fend off a stalker by herself. Jen's at the house, but whoever she could be working with isn't. And I'm not going to rely on some half-baked security guy to keep an eye on Liv rather than his tablet's Netflix.

When I get to Norfolk, my GPS takes me to a neighborhood with homes even larger than Liv's. Her friend Emerson's home is three stories tall, with a gate separating the street from her house. The gates are open, so I drive through. The grounds are pretty nice. There are gardens and a fountain in the front of the house. Sterile. I decide to park in back, just in case.

I knock on the kitchen door, and a large woman opens it, wiping her hands on her apron and frowning at me. "I'm here to see Emerson," I tell her.

The woman looks me up and down, her nose slightly pinched. "Is Miss Emerson expecting you?"

"Yes, ma'am, she is."

"It's okay, Tammy," a light voice calls from behind the woman. "I've got this."

"Your mother won't like it," the woman tells Emerson, her eyes still on me.

Emerson shrugs and grabs my arm. "So don't tell her, then. Or do. I don't really care."

She loops her arm through mine and smiles up at me as we walk through the enormous kitchen and into the dining room. "My, my. Aren't you a sight?"

"Excuse me?"

"Obviously you were trying to give Tammy a heart attack, looking like that." She releases me and her eyes rake over my black leather jacket and pants. But instead of the warmth I usually get from girls, her gaze is ice.

"It's cold outside," I tell her, tugging off my gloves.

"It's not that cold," she says, lifting her chin.

"It is if you're on a bike."

Her lips purse as she considers that.

"Is Liv here?"

"Not yet." She glances at the foyer. "In fact, I think you should go upstairs. Her grandfather's giving her a rough time so there's a possibility he could be the one dropping her off."

I follow her up the staircase. It's large and winding and reminds me of the one at Monroe Street, though it's much grander. She leads me into a library full of books, chairs, and a desk with a small lamp.

"Nice," I tell her, shrugging off my jacket.

"What are you up to, anyway?" she asks, crossing her arms and leveling a dark look at me. It doesn't bother me at all. This girl is obviously protective of Liv, and I'm grateful.

I tilt my head slightly. "What has Liv told you?"

"Everything."

I just keep my gaze steady on her, expression unchanging. It's the best way to ferret out the truth from a lie, and it works with Emerson, too. Her eyes flick away. "Well, not everything," she says. "But I know there's something about you that is just wrong. If you're trying to use Liv—"

"I'm not," I tell her. "I'm here because I'm worried about her."

"Yeah, well, I'm worried about her, too. Some weird guy is sending her cards and flowers and gifts, and how do I know it's not *you*?"

"You can't, but she knows it's not."

"Do you really care about her, Jack?" Emerson asks, and her voice is sharply accusing, almost daring me to say yes.

"I do."

"Then where have you been all this time? She needs to be normal, and you're keeping her from that. She doesn't even go out on dates like a regular person, and she keeps so many secrets that I have a feeling she's going to explode one day."

"I didn't want to stay away," I start, but then stop. I don't owe her any explanations, which are too complicated to justify anyway. This isn't just a case of a boyfriend who never called his girlfriend. I cross my own arms and ask, "Where can I wait until Liv gets here?"

"You can sit right here. Don't leave this room until I say you can, got it?"

I nod once and she leaves. I breathe out heavily when she's gone. Liv's clearly made a good friend here, but I wonder what she's told her. Probably not much to do with me, but that alone makes me both relieved and worried. Shouldn't she be able to tell somebody something?

CHAPTER SEVENTEEN

LIV

A week ago, my grandfather didn't ask me questions about where I was going or worry about me driving myself to school or a friend's house. Now, he's having security cameras installed on the grounds and a guy following me around. A sick feeling twists in my gut as I watch the men drilling holes for the cameras on the outside of the house. I know he would never suggest installing them in my personal space. He understands the need for privacy. But I can't help but remember what happened in my last foster home, when Derrick installed a camera to spy on me in my room.

It's been about two hours since Jack's call, so I head downstairs. Mrs. Bedwin comes out of the kitchen as I'm putting on my coat.

"I need to get out of here for a while," I tell her, picking up my car keys. "I'm going to study at Emerson's house."

She frowns. "I don't know. The weather's supposed to

get bad later, and I know your grandfather wanted you to stay close by. He ran to the office but said he'd be back shortly."

"He'll be okay with it. I need to study and stuff."

"Why don't you ask Emerson to come over here? I can make you both dinner. Tacos, your favorite."

She looks nervous, and I feel a little bad that I'm putting her in such an awkward situation. Unlike my grandfather, who can be swayed by a smile or a hug, the only thing that works with Mrs. Bedwin is total honesty. "It's only for a few hours, and I'll be home before ten. I'm sure the private investigator grandfather hired will follow me, so I'll be safe."

She opens her mouth to respond, but seems to think better of it. She nods. "Okay, but straight to Emerson's and back by nine, not ten. And check in with me on occasion, okay? A simple text works."

I head out the door and am in my car on the way to Emerson's quickly, before my grandfather can show up and decide I need to stay home. The drive to Emerson's takes about ten minutes, and the gates to her driveway are open, as she said they would be. Emerson's parents are out of town, so Emerson keeps the gates open when they're gone. She once joked that she'd be happy for someone to break in to steal something just so she could have someone to talk to. I wish she had someone like Mrs. Bedwin, but the staff in her house are coldly professional.

Emerson opens the door almost as soon as I press the doorbell. "It's about time. I thought for sure you weren't coming," she says, yanking me into the house. "Is that dude just going to sit there?"

I glance over my shoulder at the unmarked car with the

guy who's trailing me. With the tinted windows, I can't even see his face. "I guess so."

Emerson smiles so big her teeth show as she waves at the man. Then she pulls the door shut. "What a boring job."

"Yep." The house is quiet, with the exception of the occasional clink of dishes in the kitchen. "Is he here yet?"

Emerson nods. "Upstairs in the library. But hang on a sec." She grabs my arm and pulls me into the living room opposite the staircase. "Remember when I first saw that guy and thought he looked like trouble? Yeah? Well, I still believe that. What are you getting into with him?"

"I'm not getting into anything. He's just here to help us figure out who's stalking me."

She releases her grip, her face relaxing slightly. I can tell she didn't miss my "us" reference. I meant it, too. It's time I start confiding in my best friend.

"There's more going on, though," she says. "That guy—"

"Jack," I tell her.

"Fine. *Jack* has this look in his eyes that tells me he's about to kick someone's ass. You know I'm a good people reader, and he's definitely got something going on that isn't right."

"He's fine," I say lamely. "He's just…had a tough life."

"A tough life." She tilts her head to study me. I stare at her chin. I can't look into her eyes—she's right about being a good reader of people. She knows I'm hedging. She sighs. "Liv, you're my best friend, and I'm yours. I trust you with everything—all my weirdest ideas and craziest thoughts. I just wish you'd trust me back. There's something you're hiding, and I think it's something that could hurt you." She jerks her head toward the staircase. "Something to do with *him*. Now he's here in my house with my best friend, and I think you're going to get in even more trouble because of it."

"He's not the one stalking me," I tell her firmly.

"Do you know that for sure?"

"Yes."

She puts her hands on her hips. "Then who is?"

"I don't know. But it's not him. You don't understand."

"Then *tell* me so I do."

I glance toward the stairs. "This guy—Jack—we've gone through a lot together. As in life-and-death kind of stuff, and it's not even anything I can share because some of those secrets aren't mine to tell. For a while, he was all I had." I half laugh. "We're like a bad fairy tale turned upside down. For real. Though we're just friends now."

Emerson is silent, her eyes downcast. I can tell she's upset because she's worried, not curious. Because she actually cares about what happens to me. And it makes me feel like crap that I can't even tell her.

"Okay," she finally says quietly. "I'm sure you want to see him. Come on."

She leads me up the stairs, pointing to the library before turning to go back downstairs.

As soon as I enter the library, Jack stands up from the desk chair. I move toward him without thinking, my heartbeat quickening with every step, and throw my arms around his neck. His arms wrap around my waist, pulling me so tightly against him that my feet actually leave the ground.

"Are you okay?" he asks.

"Yes," I whisper. He sets me back down, his arms still locked around me. This look in his eyes—the soft gaze that stirs every cell in my body as if they'd been sleeping from the moment he left me until this very instant—this is what I was afraid of. How am I supposed to distance myself when all I want to do is wrap myself around him and never let go?

Thankfully, my common sense stays alert, if just barely.

At almost the same moment, Jack and I drop our arms and step away from each other. "Thanks for coming," I tell him. "I'm sorry I worried you."

"Liv, whoever's doing this—"

"Nothing's happened. I'm fine. Grandfather's even got a detective following me now. He'll make sure I'm okay. Thanks for coming, though," I say again. *Shut up already, Liv.*

He nods, though his eyes stay soft on me. He knows I'm full of crap.

"Really," I say, stepping back again. "I can handle this. You can go back to Richmond."

He shakes his head, his lips twitching slightly. "No."

Does he think this is funny? I wish he'd stop looking at me like that.

Em walks in then, and I've never been so glad to see her. I think she senses it. Her eyes are hard as she sizes up Jack. She sinks into a chaise lounge, crossing her legs and patting the space next to her so I can sit. "So have you solved the mystery yet? Didn't you say the card you got was from Richmond?" She looks at Jack accusingly.

"It had a Richmond postmark," Jack says quietly. He looks at me. "I took a look at the footage from the pawn shop next door. There's a blond woman with the guy who bought the bracelet—she looks a lot like Jen."

"Well, that would make sense," I say. "We just need to figure out who the guy is, then."

"Who's Jen?" Emerson asks.

I don't answer her. We probably should've waited to have this conversation in private. But Jack looks at her, his eyes wide in exaggerated innocence. "Ex-girlfriend who still lives with me. She doesn't like when I bring home new girlfriends."

"Shut up," I say, trying my best to laugh naturally. Em does one of those ha-ha-ha laughs that tells me she's not sure if he's kidding or not. Sad that he really isn't. I make a mental note to never bring up Maggie in conversation. "Jack's just messing with you." I look toward Jack. "Anyway, Jen is more of a 'key your car' person rather than a 'leave roses on the pillow' kind of girl, don't you think? And what would she gain from stealing from your emergency house account?"

"Trying to set me up, I think. But she's not working alone, and the only person I can come up with who's working with her—the guy in the video—is Frank."

"Who's Frank?" Emerson asks.

"This guy who worked for Jack's boss," I tell her without thinking.

"Boss?" Emerson asks, her eyes cutting over to Jack. Uh-oh, I know how that sounds.

"Yeah, at this company he works for. Or worked for," I say lamely. Jack's examining his fingernails.

"Uh-huh," she mutters, her eyes still fixed on Jack. "So why would this guy who worked for your *boss* be after Liv?"

Jack doesn't answer. I know what he's thinking. This isn't Emerson's business, and he has no intention of letting it be.

"Excuse me, Miss Emerson." A young woman peeks

into the library. "Ms. Gray said to tell you it's snowing harder outside and the roads are gonna be real bad soon. Your guests may want to think about leaving."

"Great," Jack says, moving over to the window and staring at the heavily falling flakes, looking more like white rain than snowfall.

"Thanks." Emerson turns to me, raising an eyebrow. I nod, and she sighs. "Cassandra, can you please make up the guest room? They'll be staying with me tonight."

Emerson looks at Jack. "Liv can sleep with me and I'll get one of the guest rooms all set up for you. It's far away from the one we're in."

"Thanks, Mom," I tell her as I text my grandfather. She finally cracks a smile. The doorbell rings and we jump.

"Stay out of sight," I tell Jack. I follow Emerson downstairs as Cassandra opens the door. It's the private investigator. He steps into the foyer, rubbing his arms briskly.

"Ma'am, I'm headed out, but your grandfather told me to do a quick check here to see if everything's as it's supposed to be."

I laugh lightly. "Of course it is. We're just doing homework and will probably be up late. Boring. You can go."

"Ma'am, it's not for you to tell me how to do my job." His voice is snippy. He takes another couple steps in and looks around, like he's proving a point. His eyes land on the staircase. It's all I can do not to turn and look, though I know Jack is hidden upstairs. "Mind if I take a look around?" he asks Emerson.

"I'd rather you didn't," she says brightly. "My parents don't like me to let strangers in the house. No offense."

"Your parents are away?" His eyebrow is raised like he

knows we're throwing a keg party the moment he walks out the door.

She nods. "On business. But some of the household staff lives here. We're fine." She flips her hair back and grins in a flirty way that is so not like Emerson. She's protecting Jack. Though I know it's for me more than him, I was right to confide in her.

The man stares at her, then me. "Okay, well, I want you to call your grandfather and let him know you're okay." I nod, but as he waits expectantly, I remove my phone from my pocket and call Grandfather. I explain to him the situation, relieved that instead of being upset, he agrees that I should stay put. I hand the phone over to the officer, who confirms that we're not out hitting the bars. After telling me he'll stop later if he can "just to make sure everything is as it should be," the PI leaves. Emerson shuts the door.

I give her the biggest hug I've ever given anyone. "Thank you!"

She squeezes me back. "That's what friends are for. We have our uses, you know. But man, that guy was intense!"

It's weird, being in this mansion with Jack and Emerson, like kids trying to play grown-up. The staff makes us dinner—stir-fry chicken and vegetables and chocolate fondue for dessert. Emerson puts on some music and breaks open her parents' wine cabinet, pouring us each a glass of red.

"This is the sweet one," she says, swirling the glass in the air as if to look at the color. "I'm getting a taste for it, actually. Something to do when the parents are away. Which is like, all the time."

"Your parents leave you alone a lot?" Jack asks her.

"Yep. But it's better this way. They kind of suck at being parents."

"I know how that goes."

I smile as the two banter back and forth. They may not be best friends after tonight, but it's a start.

"C'mon, let's dance," Emerson says, pulling me to my feet. I laugh as she swings me around, though after three rounds I start to get a little dizzy.

"Okay, okay," Jack says, removing my hand from hers. I lean against him, the wine making my head just slightly fuzzy after only a few sips. No more for me. "Are you okay?" he asks, tilting my chin up slightly. He's so close—a couple inches more and we'll be kissing.

"Jack," I say, and it comes out more like a sigh.

He stares at me.

"What?" I ask.

"It's crazy, the effect you saying my name has on me."

"What effect does it have?" I ask, trailing my fingers down his arm and noting that I'm not the only one with goose bumps.

"I think your grandfather would strongly disapprove of the effect it has on me," he murmurs, kissing my temple. He spins me around a couple of times, making me laugh.

"I love you." The words slip out of my mouth before I realize it. I stop, backing away from him and into a chair, almost knocking it over. *Crap.* "I…I didn't mean…"

We stare at each other for a long moment. His eyes are tight at the corners, and I'm sure I look completely freaked out. I don't even know if the words are true. Not anymore. But if they are, I certainly didn't mean to say them out loud.

Emerson clears her throat. "Just friends," she mutters.

My face grows hot as Jack says, "I think it's time we

called it a night." He looks at Emerson. "Maybe you should help her upstairs?"

"I'm not drunk," I tell him a little too loudly, jerking my arm away from him. Does he think that's why I said it?

Was it?

"And don't tell me what to do," I add loudly. The woman clearing the dining table looks over at us. I hope she doesn't tell anyone we were drinking wine, especially my grandfather. Emerson's parents probably wouldn't care.

I grab Emerson by the arm and pull her toward the staircase. "Maybe you should pull out the sofa for Z," I tell her, forgetting for a second that she had the guest room already made up for him.

"Who's Z?" she asks.

"Never mind."

The house is quiet. I've been in this room for two hours doing nothing but staring at the clock, the ceiling, the stuffed animals in their corner hammock. Emerson got Jack settled in his room with an extra toothbrush and towels and stuff, then came back to her room and went to sleep after grilling me for a while. Mostly she wanted to know about why I said I loved him. It really seemed to bug her. I told her I had no idea, that it must've been the wine. I pretended I was too tired to talk after that.

Truthfully, even though I know I shouldn't have said it, it hurt that he didn't respond at all. It made me feel like a naïve girl who put a note in his locker asking if he liked me, circle yes/no. I have to remind myself that he's been gone for eight months, only back now because I'm being stalked. Like last time, worrying about me when I was a lonely foster kid in a crappy situation.

Grandfather, Emerson, Jack—everyone's worried about me. But I'm tired of it. Right now, I just want to be wild and have someone to be wild with. Jack used to be that guy—the one who'd take me on long rides on his Ducati, kickstarting my adrenaline when he sped up to avoid cops. Really, I am glad he's deeper than that. But sometimes I miss the danger and excitement of being with Z.

I toss and turn for a few more minutes, then slide out of bed and slip on my shoes and Em's fluffy pink robe. I make my way to the balcony doors, opening them to the cold, quiet night. The white snow is now just a light, ghostly blanket. I walk across the balcony, letting my hand brush over the thin layer of flakes on the railing. Not sure why, maybe because it's so quiet, but I start giggling. Harder and harder, my laughter echoing through the darkness.

Eventually, the cold wins over, and I walk back in and pull the doors shut. I shrug off Em's robe and drape it on her desk chair, noticing my phone lit up with a text: **Why are you still awake?**

I text him back. **Because I am.**

Still mad?

Yeah. I have Grandfather, security guy, Em. Don't need another babysitter.

Definitely not here to babysit.

I bite back a smile. I can imagine him saying this, looking slightly pissed. I type, **Then why are you here?**

To hear you laugh.

I put the phone down and resolutely climb back in bed. It's no good, though. I'm wide awake, my mind full of *him*.

Before I know it, I'm standing outside Jack's door. This might be a very bad idea, but I don't care. For once, I'm going to do something without thinking it through. Just for me—just once.

I turn the knob.

Jack is standing by the window, shirtless, the paleness of his skin gleaming in the moonlight. He turns as I close the door behind me and walk toward him. His eyebrows twitch slightly. "What are you doing here?" he asks.

I stop a few feet from him, a little embarrassed now. I guess I'd pictured him opening his arms to me and picking me up and all the romantic crap you see in movies. This was a stupid idea. "Just checking to see if you're good here. Okay, so good night."

"Liv."

His voice is frustrated, tinged with something else I think I recognize. His eyes search mine for something he can't seem to find. Maybe he's afraid of being too close to me. That would make sense for the side of him known as Z, the boy who stayed tough on the outside and pushed everyone away so he didn't have to *feel*.

I walk toward him slowly. Something about his fear turns my steps from uncertain to confident, his eyes filled with something so much more than the desire I've seen before in his gaze. It's a real need that mirrors my own. He closes his eyes, swallowing hard as I reach him. I trail a finger down his arm and let my fingers slide through his. "Jack," I say softly.

He cups my face in his hands, the emotion in his gaze burning into my heart, a brand that's been there since the day I broke through the hardened Z to find the real Jack underneath. He leans forward, resting his forehead on mine.

"I don't think you—"

"You think too much," I tell him softly. I reach up to touch his cheek, letting my fingers explore the roughness along his jawline. I slide my hands behind his shoulders, trailing the lines of muscle in his back. His hands set me on fire as they brush over my curves. He lifts me as I sink into his kiss.

I don't come up for air until morning.

CHAPTER EIGHTEEN

JACK

The sun's barely cracked the sky and I'm already awake, staring at the sleeping girl next to me, wondering what the hell I finally did right to deserve this. To deserve her.

Maybe I don't.

I gently lift her dark hair over her shoulder. Her skin is so smooth, like pale satin. My fingers trail over a pink scar I've never seen that reaches from the base of her neck to her shoulder blade.

She stirs at my touch, her eyes flicking open to meet mine. "Hey," she says sleepily.

"Hey." I smile at her, probably the first real smile I've been able to manage in months. "You okay?"

She laughs lightly, blushing. "Yes. I didn't expect to spontaneously combust or anything."

I brush my finger along her arm, causing a deeper red flush to move across her cheeks. God, she's beautiful.

Which I tell her. I'll tell her all the time to bring out that smile. "Regrets?"

"No. You?"

"Definitely not."

She smiles, but it fades as she looks over my shoulder. "Shoot. It's six thirty. I'm going to be late for school if I don't get up now."

"Stay with me, then. I can help you change your grades later."

"Funny." She punches me lightly on the arm, then cuddles into my chest. "I know this doesn't change anything between us."

I don't say anything, though I wonder what that means for her. She's right about it not changing things for me—my heart was lost to her a long time ago. She told me after dinner that she loved me, and I never said it back. I don't even know why, except maybe it scares me to think I could hurt her again.

I stroke her back, my fingers once again finding the slight rise of the scar. "How'd you get this?" I ask.

She stills. "You don't want to know."

I get up on one elbow to stare at her. "Hell yeah I do."

"It was a long time ago. This lady I lived with got mad because I broke a piece of her good china. She had a really bad temper." She rests her hand on my waist, curving around it to pull me close to her again. "I don't want to relive all the old memories, Jack. I'm trying to stay in front of them."

I lean over to press my lips to her shoulder. She deserves so much better than what she's gotten. I hope she really is over all the shit in her life, but I doubt it. I know I'm not.

A knock sounds at the door, and Emerson calls out, "Wake up, lovebirds. Time for school."

"Jeez, Em," Liv says, and I smile as she scurries around to get dressed. "You have school too, you know," she adds, throwing a sock at me.

I shake my head. "I'll be doing some research today. Checking out Frank, talking to Jen."

She straightens, her eyes worried. "I know Jen hasn't been very nice, and if she did this, that really sucks. Just don't be too mean, okay? She hates you for a reason—just keep that in mind." She kisses me lightly.

I take longer than Liv to get ready, mostly because I know Emerson will have a million questions for her this morning, and I don't think she'd want me around to listen to them. It goes beyond that, though. Emerson doesn't like me. Not that I can blame her, but every time she looked at me yesterday, I could see she was judging me and I was falling short. I'm guessing her feelings about me will have deteriorated today.

I'm glad Liv has a friend like her, though. If she was too accepting of me, I'd be more worried.

By the time I dress and make it downstairs, I can hear Emerson and Liv talking in the dining room.

"I'm happy for you. Really, I am," Emerson is saying. But the flat tone in her voice says otherwise.

"You were okay with him yesterday."

"That was *before* he took advantage of my friend. I assume you were careful?"

"Em!"

"Well?"

"Yes, Mom." Liv's voice sounds muffled, like she's covering her face with her hands.

She sighs. "I just hope you know what you're getting into with him. I don't trust him."

"Then trust *me*," Liv tells her. "I'm one of the most skeptical people on the face of the planet, and I trust him. That should be enough."

Emerson sighs loudly. "Okay, fine. Now give me all the details." Her voice is lighter. *Whoa*, I do *not* want to hear this. I step around the corner and the girls both look at me, flushed.

"Good morning, Emerson. Thanks for letting me stay here last night." I walk over to give Liv a kiss on her cheek as I sink into the chair next to her.

"No prob. Roads are clear, so you can head back where you came from now."

"Em!" Liv says, frowning at her, but I laugh.

"I'll do that."

Emerson looks at Liv. "We're going to be late if we don't leave now."

"Oh, shoot, I left my stuff upstairs. I'll be right back."

When she's gone, Emerson turns a glare on me. I hold up a hand. "I know what you're going to say and don't worry, I'm not here to screw around with Liv. Trust me." I smile brightly, but Emerson scowls.

"You've already screwed around with her. And I don't trust you at all. If anything happens to her, I'm coming after you, got it? I have money so I can hire people to finish you off for me."

I raise my eyebrows at her threat. Impressive. "Got it."

"Breakfast?" She pushes a plate of toast at me but I shake my head.

"I'm good."

"Doubtful."

Minutes later, we're standing outside the back door. Liv will leave first, through the front door, so the PI can follow her, then I'll take off on my bike. Saying good-bye to Liv sucks, so I decide not to say it. "Be careful, okay?"

"You, too. If it's Jen, she could make trouble for you, too."

I grasp her fingers and kiss them as Emerson calls to Liv from inside the house. "I'll call you later."

During the entire ride back, Liv's face fills my mind, her eyes, her lips. With her, I'm a better person. I want to protect everything about her. But the idea of someone coming after her sobers me. Frank, Jen—whoever it is, I'll figure it out.

Except when I get home, everyone is standing in the living room, and in unison they all turn to stare at me when I walk in and drop my car keys on the side table.

"What?" I unzip my jacket. "School canceled today?"

"We got information from the wire rep at the bank," Nancy says. She glances around at all the grim faces, then looks at me. "I think we better talk in the office."

"Oh I don't think so," Jen says, her voice full of anger. It's nothing new, but looking around the room, I can see she's not the only one who's directing daggers my way.

"Jen, shut up," Sam says sharply.

"Why? This is about all of us." Jen crosses her arms, her lips rising to form a smug expression. "And I'd like to see exactly how he's going to worm his way out of this one."

"What the hell are you talking about?" I ask, nervous now. Even Dutch is staring at me weirdly, like I shaved his head or something. That one bothers me more than anything.

"Enjoy your visit to your girlfriend?" she snaps.

"Why don't you tell me?" I step closer to her. Jen stays where she is, though fear flickers in her eyes. I've never touched anyone in this house and don't plan to, but that doesn't mean I'm going to sit back and take it from her.

Nancy steps between us. "That's enough. Z, I'm afraid you have some explaining to do here."

"Since when do I have to explain where I go to anyone?" I ask.

"Since the IP address of the account all the money was wired into came from this house. And the activity was traced to your computer."

CHAPTER NINETEEN

LIV

It's hard to concentrate on anything at school. I find myself staring out the window at the bright sunlit day. If the windows weren't rimmed in white, I'd swear it was a warm spring morning outside.

Emerson is quiet at lunch. Kade even notices, poking her side and asking what's wrong. She just looks at me and tells him nothing. Qualities about Jack that I find intriguing, she finds questionable. The laid-back cynical attitude of his that disappears when he's with me doesn't do anything for her. And I know she's figured out he is, or was, involved in something illegal. She mentioned the fact that I said "boss" when we went to bed last night, but I pretended I was too tired to talk. She stared at his Ducati this morning and looked at me as if accusing him of stealing it. And she *really* hated that I told him I love him.

I don't know why I said it myself, except that it was probably the alcohol. Not that I don't love him. Deep down,

I know I do. But I am also realistic enough to get that it will never work between us. I'm sure he realizes it, too.

I smile slightly. Even knowing that after we figure all this out, Jack will disappear again, I wouldn't trade what happened between us for anything.

"Still walking around like a grinning idiot?" Emerson says, coming up behind me after school.

"I guess so."

"So what's this guy Jack's last name?" she asks.

"Uh-uh," I tell her. "You're not looking him up."

"Why not? Have you searched for him?"

"You can't. He's unsearchable." I say it without thinking, and kick myself after I do.

She stops, tapping her finger against her chin. "Unsearchable? The only people I've heard of being unsearchable are either spies or criminals."

I keep walking, my body numb. She catches up with me. "So he *is* a criminal? *Really,* Liv?"

"Shut up," I tell her in a harsh whisper. I glance around, but no one is paying attention to us. "Listen. I said things I shouldn't have, and I'm sorry about that, but you need to leave this one alone, okay?"

"You can't just pretend that everything is fine," she says. "He's going to screw up your life."

I stop and glare at her. "He's the one who helped me fix my life in the first place. You don't know anything about the way things were before."

"No, I wouldn't know because you never tell me anything."

"Well, maybe this is why," I tell her. Her eyes widen, and she opens her mouth. I hold up a hand. "I don't need you to be a mother, Em. What I need is a friend, but I guess that's asking too much."

I walk on, faster now, tears spilling down my cheeks as I push open the doors leading out of the school. My one friend here, the only best friend I've ever had, and I'm running away from her. I should've known, though. I let her too far into my life, and she couldn't handle it.

Best friends are highly overrated.

I look down at my phone, opening the single red heart emoji text again that sent my heart skyrocketing when I got to school this morning. But this time, it feels like a lead ball right in the middle of my chest.

Oh, Jack, why can't you just be normal? Why can't you get out of that life so you don't have to hide anymore?

There's a part of him—probably more than he'll ever admit—that wishes he could stop. That would love nothing more than to go to college and be part of the normal human world. He could do it. But the anger and resentment he's built up over his father—and his father's family—keeps him from taking those steps. Worse, he's terrified the part of him that *is* his father will come forward and turn him into the worst kind of person. Jack's generosity with money, his support of his family—in his eyes, he's robbing from the rich to give to kids in need; a modern day anti-corporate Robin Hood. Overcompensating to prove to himself that he's not his father. And while I get why he does it, I can't allow myself to get involved in his hacking schemes again.

His fear is real, though…and if there's anyone who understands this, it's me. Once my grandfather sees the side of me that lied and hacked into bank accounts for the fun of it, he'll realize there's more of my father in me than his beloved daughter. Then he'll be quick to disown me.

The PI follows me home. I wonder how long he's going to keep this up. At least there are no new roses or cards or anything to worry about today. I step into the house, glancing over my shoulder to see the PI parking behind my car. Even though I know Grandfather is paying him to watch me, it's a creepy feeling to have someone constantly *there,* staring over my shoulder everywhere I go. I find myself wanting to text Emerson about it, but then remember our fight. My heart breaks a little to think about it, something else I didn't know could happen with a friendship.

Mrs. Bedwin comes around the corner from the kitchen, carrying her iPad as usual. She smiles at me. "How was your day, sweetheart?"

"Fine, I guess."

She peers closely at me. "Are you okay?"

I shrug.

"Hmm. Did you have a disagreement with Emerson?"

"How did you know?"

She taps my arm lightly with her pencil. "You're very easy to read. Do you want to talk about it?"

"She just disagrees with me about…stuff."

"Stuff? Like a boy kind of stuff?" She laughs at my surprised face. "Oh, yes, I know about a certain handsome young man who came by the other day looking for you. I also happen to know this young man is not exactly in your grandfather's good graces."

"Please don't—" I start, but she holds up a hand.

"Don't worry, I'm not going to say anything about it, to you or to your grandfather." She sighs. "You know Mr. Brownlow is just looking out for you because of what happened to your mother."

"I'm not my mother, though." Will I ever be able to live here without being compared to her?

"I know that. He does, too, but that boy reminds your grandfather of another young man who'd come around on his motorcycle, asking for your mother. It's natural for him to worry. And you can't teach an old dog new tricks." Then her eyes widen. "Please do *not* tell your grandfather I referred to him as an old dog."

"I won't," I say absently. So my father rode a motorcycle, just like Jack. That explains a lot. "What was his name?" I ask her. "My father."

She stares at me like I just asked her to name all the stars in order from their proximity to the sun. "I don't know…"

"Please. I know nothing about him, and it would at least be nice to know his name."

Mrs. Bedwin looks around guiltily. "I guess just a first name doesn't hurt. His name was Van. Anything else and you'll need to talk with your grandfather."

I nod. "Thank you."

Mrs. Bedwin places a hand on my shoulder. "As far as Emerson goes, remember that good friendships are too rare to be throwing them away over a boy. You should call her and get past it."

"I will."

She nods and heads back toward the kitchen. I go upstairs, stopping as I pass my grandfather's office. Glancing around to make sure I'm alone, I turn the knob and slip inside, pulling the door shut behind me. The only time I've ever gone in here by myself is when Bill Sykes tried to get me to download Grandfather's information on a keylogger. Maybe he hasn't changed his password since then.

I sit behind the mahogany desk and type in my mother's name and birthday. I breathe out as the password is accepted. Not that I couldn't have hacked in without it, but why waste time? He really should've changed it by now, though. Maybe I should give him a quick tutorial on computer security. I go into his system properties and give myself remote access to his computer, then grab the port ID number and IP address. I head back to my room.

I open up my computer and remote into my grandfather's computer, conducting searches for anything labeled as "Van." Of course, a ton of files pop up. I grit my teeth. Apparently, there are a lot of documents that have the word "van." I change the search to Aggie, his nickname for my mother. I sort the results by type of file, most of which appear to be pictures. I open a few that have the latest dates, months before I was born and before she left home. There are none with my father, though I see a change in her appearance from the photos that hang in the hallway. She wears heavier makeup, black liner underneath her eyes giving her a Goth-like appearance. And she's not smiling, unlike all the other pictures I've seen. Except for her dark hair, I don't remember what she looked like so much as an overall sadness when she held me in her arms at the shelters we stayed in.

I move to the documents and open up one that looks like communication between Grandfather and a private investigator. A transcript of messages from my mother's phone. And some images embedded in the document, mostly of my mother at a couple different places, but there's also one of a guy leaning against a motorcycle.

I zoom in on the image. I can see why Mrs. Bedwin says Grandfather's nervous about Jack. Besides the motorcycle and the fact that he's wearing all black leather, Van holds his stance like he's going to kick someone's ass. With Jack, I know that's all show, but this guy—he gives me the chills. And half of me *is* him.

I stare at my father's face, and though he's wearing aviator sunglasses that hide his eyes, I can tell we have the same triangular face, the same slightly pointed nose. I scroll through the rest of the pictures, finding another that's at a closer angle. He's still wearing those glasses, though, so I can't get into his eyes. Eyes tell so much about a person.

I find another document from the same PI—this one a picture of my mother holding the guy's hand as they walk through what looks like a mall. My heart drops—this is definitely not the same woman I remember who hummed softly to me and read *The Little Red Hen* in the shelter. The kind woman who held me with soft arms before the streets consumed her. This is the kind of girl who'd scare the crap out of me—all hard angles, scowling, and looking for any reason to kick someone's ass. Holding the hand of a leather-clad guy with long dark hair sporting the same hard look. I pick up a mirror and stare at my own image. There are definite similarities that make me sick to my stomach.

Was he really a thug like my grandfather says and like these pictures suggest? Or was there a kinder, gentler side of him? There has to be. I'm not perfect, but I'm not a bad person. He couldn't be all bad, right? But then where did he go when my mother ended up on the street with me?

Mrs. Bedwin knocks on the door, telling me my grandfather is home. He never gets home this early, so I'm immediately worried. I dress as nicely as I can, pulling my hair up into a bun, then head downstairs for dinner.

He stands when I walk into the dining room, a tangle of nerves twisting in my stomach. "Olivia." His voice is formal, even stern, much more so than when he usually talks to me. He gestures to the chair next to him. I sit down, keeping my fidgeting hands in my lap as one of his kitchen staff, Sarah, ladles soup into my bowl. He's patient, sipping his merlot and watching me.

"Eat," he says briskly, nodding at the bowl in front of me. Maybe he's trying to wait me out on this one, to make me more nervous until I panic and say something that will give away whatever's on his mind. It's a tactic I've seen him use with some of his business people, though this is the first time he's used it on me. I'm not going to fall into his trap. I eat the soup and keep my mind focused on schoolwork. It's hard to stay calm, though, when all I can think about is my father's pictures and how often Grandfather remembers him when he sees me.

"How was your night last night?" he asks. Oh, no. The one question I'm not prepared for, worded exactly in a way that guarantees a blush. But I fight it and pretend a yawn. "Good. Emerson and I stayed up working on homework all night."

"Is that all?"

"Of course." My mind races. I wonder if the PI was around in the morning to see Jack leave on his bike.

"The detective passed a motorcycle on his way to the house."

Crap, I was right. I shrug. "Maybe one of the staff."

"Maybe." His eyes stay on me as he sips from his wineglass. He pats his lips with his napkin. "John Tate said he saw you at the café on Saturday."

"Oh?" It's at that moment that Mrs. Bedwin and Sarah

come back through the doors with dinner—steak, red potatoes, and asparagus—grandfather's favorite. There's no way I can eat right now, though. I notice Mrs. Bedwin giving us a quick, worried look. Even she can sense the tension just by walking through. By the time they leave, I'm able to look Grandfather in the eye. "Yes, Emerson wanted to stop for coffee, so that's what we did."

"Mmm-hmm." Another sip of his merlot. "Did you meet up with anyone there?"

Stay calm. "No. Well, I saw someone I used to know and asked him what he was doing in town, but that was pretty much it."

"Did you give Jack back that bracelet?"

I frown at him. His expression is passive, completely unchanged, and it unnerves me. "It wasn't from him. Though it looks like you've already arrived at your own conclusions no matter what I say."

He sets down his glass and folds his hands in front of him. "Olivia, if I can't trust you—"

"Then what? You'll kick me out? Is this how you handled things with my mother? No wonder she ran away."

My grandfather's eyes widen as I drop the napkin in front of me and push back my chair. Doing my best to ignore his hurt expression, I walk out of the dining room as fast as I can, mostly so he can't see the tears that are forming in my eyes. I can't believe I said such a terrible thing to him, knowing how much he suffered when my mother left. What kind of person am I, anyway? Especially after all the things he's done for me.

I must be my father's daughter after all.

I grab my coat and keys and head outside to my car. Nobody chases after me or tries to get me to stay. Probably because the detective assigned to me will follow me anyway, no matter where I go. Glancing at my phone, there are three texts with apologies from Emerson as well as two missed calls.

The drive to her house takes almost no time at all, and before I know it, she's flying out the door and hugging me.

"I'm so sorry I was rude," she says, her voice full of tears. "You were right. I should've been a better friend."

"I'm the one who should apologize," I tell her, gulping air between my own sobs. It's probably the first time I've openly cried in front of someone before. But with Em, it feels perfectly natural. "I should've been more honest with you."

"No," she says firmly, shaking her head. "You didn't have to. And I shouldn't have tried to force you." She wraps an arm around my shoulders as we walk into the house. "From now on, you tell me whatever you want to tell me, no more."

"I do want to tell you, though. That's why I came here."

She hands me a tissue and perches on the couch in the sitting room without saying anything, though her eyes are curious. I get the feeling she's being careful not to push for details. I sit next to her, the silence between us more comforting than awkward. And just like that, the rest of the defenses I worked so hard to build up start to crumble. I've never told anyone the full story—except Jack. It wasn't so hard to do with him. "I wouldn't know where to even start," I say softly, unaware until Emerson's eyes lift that I said that out loud.

"You said it was like a bad fairy tale, right? Maybe start with 'once upon a time.' If you want to, of course," she says quickly.

"Once upon a time?" I laugh shortly. Considering the

crappy early lives of almost every Disney princess, I guess it is fitting.

Standing up, I move to the window, my eyes on the oak tree branches bobbing in the wind. For some reason, it occurs to me that every house I ever lived in had at least one oak tree in the front yard. Horrible memories come to mind of crouching in the corner of a room as one foster mother pulled a switch from it, while others are wonderful—climbing up in the tree to investigate baby squirrels, for one. Funny thing is that I neither hate nor love oak trees now. But I don't think I'd want one in my yard when I have a house of my own.

I take a deep breath. "Okay, so once upon a time, there was a girl whose mother ran away from home when she was pregnant with her to live on the streets, buying and selling drugs, and even selling herself to get enough money for more drugs. She died in the middle of the street, right in front of her daughter, and the police came to take the little girl to foster care."

The story is actually easier told without using the word "I," as if it's someone else's story. I can even feel sorry for the little girl who'll never be able to erase the image of her dead mother crumpled on the dirty street. The picture of my mother holding her boyfriend's hand in the mall comes to my mind, but I force it away. I can't talk about my father—not when I haven't even absorbed it yet. My eyes stay on the bare oak branches, away from Emerson's gaze.

"The girl grew up in a lot of homes—too many to count. Some were good, and some were so bad that—" I shudder. Even in third person, I don't really care to relive the memories I've tried so hard to get past.

"Jesus," Emerson whispers behind me. I keep my eyes

from hers. Either she'll be pitying or despising me, and I'm not sure which is worse. I take a deep breath.

"Anyway, the girl met a guy at school who had it easy. Like, really easy—he rode a Ducati, and his friend drove a Camaro, and they lived in this gorgeous mansion with a bunch of other foster kids, but it wasn't like the usual group home. They were more like a family, and the girl found out that they were involved in some—well, some underground kind of things. Not drugs or anything like that," I add quickly, looking at Emerson. Her face doesn't change, though her jaw moves slightly forward.

"The girl found out the boy had just as horrible of a life as she did before he came to that home. Maybe even worse. Too many people had judged him for something they knew nothing about."

I don't mean it as a jab at her—well, maybe just a bit. But it doesn't matter. Emerson's attention is riveted. I take a deep breath. This is the part that keeps me up at night most, but I have to tell her. Right now, so that way I don't have to keep worrying about it. *Say it one time—pretend like you're talking about someone else—and then you don't have to ever say it again.*

"One night, the foster father the girl lived with, Derrick, attacked her. He had been watching her through cameras in her room and tried to—" The words get stuck in my throat. I stare at the window again, trying to focus on the reflection of my mother's locket rather than the evil face of Derrick.

"So anyway, the girl was able to get away from him. The boy found out and got so mad he wanted to kill the girl's foster father." I smile at the memory of Jack keeping me close to him those first days when I came to Monroe Street.

Now that the worst part of the story is over, I can breathe again. "They put the guy on the sex offender registry themselves, and the girl went to live at the boy's group home. The woman who ran the home wanted the girl to get involved with what they did. But when the boy found out the girl's grandfather was alive, he decided to turn her over to her grandfather so she could live a normal life. Then he left her, promising he'd be back one day. And now he is." *Even if only temporarily.*

I leave out the part about Bill kidnapping me, about escaping by almost drowning in the James River. It doesn't feel as important to tell her right now, and I don't have the energy for it anyway.

"Wow," Emerson whispers. I sneak a peek at her glassy eyes, and I wonder which part of the horror story that was my life she's thinking about. "I had no idea."

She probably thought I was going to tell her I didn't get along with my parents and that I'd run away or something. "Nobody here knows," I tell her firmly. "*Nobody.* You have to keep this to yourself."

Emerson nods, her lips tight. "I told you, you can rely on me." She hesitates. "Are you okay? I mean now—are things better?"

I smile. "Yeah, if you take out the part about me being stalked by some rose-crazy freak. Pretty much life as usual."

We both laugh, a ridiculous sound considering what I just told her. But it feels good. And as we laugh, for the first time, I think I can breathe easier.

"One more thing. I think I need a change in color," I tell her, gathering my hair in one hand. I don't want to remind Grandfather of my father—or my mother—when he looks at me. From now on, I want to know that he sees me for me and no one else.

Emerson's eyebrows rise in surprise, but then she smiles. "We can go see Dixon. He'll get you right in."

She gives me a hug. Emerson was right—telling her some of my darkest secrets is a huge relief, like breaking the surface after being held under water.

Mrs. Bedwin was right, too. A good friendship is much too important to lose.

CHAPTER TWENTY

JACK

For the first time in my life, I have nothing to say. No defenses built up, no alibi, nothing. If I'd really stolen the money, I would've been prepared to handle being caught with my hands in the virtual vault.

Being accused of something I haven't done by people I consider to be my family is infinitely worse, and I have no words. My own computer betrayed me—the proof is right there on my hard drive, showing a profile created for a Donald Smith, same as on the account the money was transferred into. I can't prove I wasn't online during these times.

I stare at the laptop as Jen takes it on herself to act as prosecutor, asking me over and over where the money went. And it doesn't help that money wasn't stolen from my account. If I didn't know better, I'd think I was guilty, too.

Except for one simple fact: I'm not an idiot. The transfer coming from our IP address means it wasn't encrypted. I encrypt *everything* I've ever done. I know how to use Tor to hide my tracks on the web. Hacking 101. If I were going to steal money from our house, I would've stolen from my own account to keep attention from being focused on me. Whoever did this should've thought of those basic things. Which tells me it was a setup, or that it wasn't done by the smartest person in the house.

I glare at Jen.

Nancy allows a few of the older kids in the office with us as she asks me questions, my laptop sitting on the desk as evidence. I know she's only letting them in because everyone thinks I get preferential treatment anyway. This way, they won't think she lets me off the hook easily.

But I know that I need to convince them more than Nancy.

I look around the room at my jurors. Sam and Maggie have both spoken up in my defense. They sit together on a credenza, also glaring at Jen on the opposite side. Micah and Cameron are sitting with them. Only Cara, Jen's roommate, is sitting next to her, though Cara doesn't look convinced, either.

"Okay, so stop and think about it," I tell them. "If I had created that account on my laptop, don't you think I'm smart enough at the least—the *very* least—to disable the cookies? And why the hell would I let it track me here? How stupid do you think I am?"

Jen goes off on how stupid she thinks I am as everyone else stares at me. I can see it in their eyes—this makes sense to them. After all, I'm Z, a leader here, one of the original Monroe Street hackers. I wouldn't have made so many careless mistakes. Again, if whoever did this was smart, they would've realized that and not left so many doors open.

"You do seem pretty quick to ignore what Z said about encrypting his activity. He wouldn't be so stupid," Sam says. Micah and Maggie nod in agreement.

"Obviously, *someone* is setting me up here, Nancy," I say, looking meaningfully at Jen. "Didn't you watch that video I left on your desk?"

"What video?" Nancy asks.

"Oh, don't even try that," Jen snaps. "That video doesn't prove anything."

Everyone stares at her. I cross my arms, hiding a smile. This is working out perfectly. "'That video,' huh? So you took it off Nancy's desk before she could watch it. What'd you do with it?"

"I don't know what you're talking about," she says, but her twitching hands give her away. "He's just trying to frame me for something he did," she says to Nancy in a pleading voice. "I know for a fact that he bought his girlfriend Liv jewelry. A bracelet."

"Bracelet?" Maggie asks, her eyebrows pinched slightly as she stares at me.

"How'd you find out about the bracelet?" I ask Jen.

Jen shrugs, struggling to maintain her confidence now that everyone is looking at her. "I overheard a conversation between Z and Sam." Her lips pucker into a smug grin. "He went to visit Liv as soon as he found out she got the bracelet, and Sam helped."

"Why don't you shut the hell up," Sam snaps at her as everyone's eyes swivel her way. Cameron puts his arm around her shoulders protectively, but she shrugs him off. "You don't know anything."

"Yeah. *You* seem to know an awful lot, Jen," Maggie says.

"So why don't you tell us, Jen," I say, noticing Jen's starting to lose her cool. "What made you think buying a bracelet for Liv with our house money would be a good way to set me up?"

"Z…" Nancy warns.

"Are you smoking something?" Jen screeches at me.

"I have it on video. Jen with the guy who bought the bracelets at Abbott & Peterson's." I wasn't planning on outing her before I talked to Nancy, but I'm also not going to sit around and let everyone think I stole their money. "Where's the video, Jen?"

"I…I don't have it."

Nancy stands and holds up her hand. "I'd like to see this video. Jen, did you take it from my desk?"

Jen's eyes cast around the room, finally glaring on me. "I was just curious. He's been trying to set me up for a long time because everyone knows he can't stand me."

Nancy takes a deep, concentrated breath. She's about to lose it on Jen, and glad as I am that the focus has changed, I feel a little bad. "Just get the video and show them. If it's not you, you have nothing to hide," I tell her.

"I said I don't have it. I threw it away when I saw what you were trying to do. It looks like me in the video, but it's not," she tells Nancy, her voice desperate now.

"I'd like to see it myself."

"Good thing I made a spare," Micah says. He leaves the room and comes back a minute later with a jump drive. I take it, nodding at him as thanks. I insert it into my laptop, and everyone gathers around. I notice Jen back away as the video plays, her face pale.

"It's not me," she says weakly as Nancy looks over at her. "I swear that isn't me! Lots of people have blond hair."

"It looks like you," Maggie says, her expression smug.

"Oh, shut up," Jen snaps at her. "You don't even belong here. You're just a stupid ho who can't even hack."

That's when the entire room loses it. Nancy and Jen are shouting at each other. Sam is alternating between flipping Jen off and yelling, and the others are trying to calm them down. Only Maggie is quiet, pulling up her legs and resting her chin on her knees. I make my way over to sit next to her, letting her lean against my shoulder; no one notices.

"Jen's a bitch. Don't listen to her," I tell her, tuning out the noise of the shouting. "Thanks for having my back."

"Anytime." She looks up at me. "Did you see that there's someone else in the video? A guy?" I nod, looking interested. As much as she's trying to be helpful, it's like someone telling me that the same sun that rises in the morning also sets in the evening.

"Whoever did this also crawled into Liv's room and left a rose on her pillow," I tell her.

"Like when she was sleeping?"

I nod. "That's why I've been going up there. To figure out who planted the rose so I can kick his ass. Not to take jewelry to her." I wave in disgust at the argument going on in front of us. "Jen's just looking for any opportunity to— Are you okay?" Maggie's face is pale.

"I...I just have had a bad experience with roses on pillows," she says, shivering slightly. "It wasn't really you, was it?" she asks meekly.

"Of course not!"

She relaxes against me again. "Good. Nobody deserves that creeper move."

I get the feeling she's shifted from hating Liv to feeling some sort of camaraderie with her. Shared creeper experience. Considering where Maggie came from, I wouldn't be surprised if some asshole customer hit her then left a rose for her on the pillow afterward. Everyone in this house has had a bad experience with something, like Micah and duct tape that bullies once wrapped him in when he was in fifth grade, or Dutch and his fear of water from the time his stoned stepfather tried to drown him. Or me and my hatred of Christmas—the night my mother killed herself. I awkwardly place an arm around Maggie's shoulders, causing her to look up in pleasant surprise. We're all screwed up in one way or another.

Nancy finally calls it quits, announcing that Jen isn't a suspect based on the video alone, since you can't see her face, and sends everyone out of the room. She holds me back to talk in private, ignoring Jen's protests that now I'm going to be off the hook as Nancy's favorite.

"Why'd you let her off so easy?" I ask as Nancy closes the door behind her. I can hear the others still arguing outside the office.

Her face is grim, her eyes set on mine. "I was hoping you would be able to tell me what's really going on."

"Nancy, you *know* I didn't do it. I have my own bank account—I would never steal from the others. Why would I?"

"I know. But—" She clasps her hands, her eyes still on me in a way that makes my blood run cold. "It's hard to believe everything you say when you've told me you stopped hacking and here I see a transfer from ICL account in your computer log."

"Nancy..."

"You *are* still hacking." Her face reflects crippling disappointment. "You stole money from that bank after we decided not to do that anymore."

I draw myself up. I'm not going to let her intimidate me—not on this one. "No, *you* decided we wouldn't do it anymore. Not me. I never agreed to that, and neither did the others."

"Don't speak for them."

"Why not? You did. I know that at least some of them aren't happy about the decision you made."

She sighs heavily, rubbing at her temples. "We've had this conversation already."

"And I told you then I disagreed with you. You brought us in for one purpose, no matter what you tell everyone else about caring for foster kids." I wish I could stuff the words back in once they're out. Nancy's done nothing but love and protect everyone in this house all these years. For me to throw that in her face is pretty low, especially considering it was Bill, not Nancy, who encouraged us to hack.

"That's enough." She stands up, frowning. "I *do* care about you all, more than anyone. You're my family, and I can't bear the thought of any of my kids ending up in jail. You are such a smart guy and could be anything you want to be. You don't need to be 'Z' anymore."

I glare at her. She says it like it's a simple choice for me—go back to being just any other kid who goes off to college and becomes some ladder-climbing corporate jerk— just like my father. Screw that.

"Don't pretend like you didn't know where the money came from that suddenly appeared in the house account a few days ago," I tell her. Her face stills; she knows exactly what I'm referring to. "You didn't have to use the money, did you? But you did because you care about us. I care, too.

That's why I think it's a mistake to stop."

"Yes, I allowed you to make that transfer. I should've stopped it. That was my error."

"Nancy—"

She holds up a hand. "Enough. You of all people should understand why I called an end to the business. All it would take is one slip. One person to get arrested. One to call attention to our business. All of you would end up in the worst kind of group home or juvenile detention. I will *not* stand for my family to be split apart like that. End of story."

Her expression softens, and she reaches for me. I back away. "You've been angry for so long, Jack," she says. "The hacking helped you cope with life when you were younger, but you're eighteen and an adult now. Don't you think it's time you let that part of you go? Live your own life and stop allowing your past to dictate your future."

I want to scream at her that this *is* my future, that I can't just stop because she says to. I don't want to stop. But her words wrap themselves around my lungs, suffocating me. The one person I thought was always in my corner has shifted sides.

"Think about it, at least," she says softly. "I can help you through this if you'll let me." She walks around her desk and places her hands on my shoulders. "As for this other nonsense, I don't believe for one second that you stole money from the others. You wouldn't do that to them."

Someone knocks at the door behind me. I move away from Nancy as Micah walks in. "Frank is here to see you," he says, his eyes flicking over to me. Nancy nods and ushers us out. But not before I press Sam's number and leave my phone on the bookshelf. Such a basic eavesdropping tool, but it's all I can manage at the moment.

She waves at Frank, who's standing in the foyer, shifting from foot to foot and looking uncomfortable under our gazes. He walks to the office quickly and she shuts the door behind them. Sam is in the foyer, her phone to her ear, confused. "Sam," I call to her. I put a finger to my lips and gesture for her to keep listening. We take the phone upstairs to my room and close the door.

"—don't understand the opportunity here," Frank is saying. "Bill would've wanted us to use the money."

Nancy groans. "I had this same conversation with one of my kids today. We don't need this, Frank."

"You may not, but I do."

"How much do you need?" There's a long pause, during which Frank is mumbling.

"Again?" Nancy asks, her voice exasperated. "When are you going to learn to stay away from those thugs?"

"When you wise up. What about that Z kid?"

"No." Nancy's voice is firm. "You will leave my kids alone. I'm sorry for your troubles. I really am. But stay away from my family, understand?"

Frank says something else, but so low that I can't catch it. Nancy says, "I don't care," a couple more times, then the door opens and slams closed.

I run downstairs in time to see Frank grabbing his coat from the rack and opening the front door. His eyes catch mine, and his frown deepens into a scowl. I don't have any evidence yet about Liv, but he's confirmed my suspicions about money.

As soon as he's gone I go back into the office, reaching over to grab my phone from the bookshelf. Nancy's staring at her computer, her eyebrows pinched. She glances up at me.

"What was Frank doing here?" I ask. "Stopping by to say hi?"

"Something like that."

I lock eyes with her. "So I have an idea about the man in the video. I think you might know who that is."

Her expression changes from curious to wary. She drops her hands. "It's not Frank."

"And you know this for sure because…"

"Because I do. Leave it alone."

"Nope. I'm being framed for something I didn't do, and according to the jewelry store, it was a blond guy who came in to buy the bracelets. You can even see him on the security camera's footage."

She raises an eyebrow. "Considering you can't see his face, if that's all you have, it's not enough."

"What's he wanting money for?" I ask. "And why does he want to use me?"

She frowns. "Eavesdropping is a bad habit and not one I'd have thought you'd stoop to in your own house."

"Only when I think it involves me or someone I care about. Someone's after Liv. So far, Frank is my best suspect, and you haven't convinced me otherwise. And someone is working with him—a blond girl who looks a lot like Jen."

"I can understand why you feel this way. But Frank's just a guy who needs help like everyone else. He lost a lot when Bill died and needed a handout. I gave him one from my own account. End of story."

"Why would you do that?"

"How about compassion? How about loyalty? Doesn't that mean anything these days?"

Her voice is agitated. Nancy is extremely loyal when it comes to any of us in the house. She always said family is the most important thing to her.

Family.

Suddenly, it clicks—the one person associated with Frank Jones, the one I could find nothing on for the past twenty years except the fact that he was from Pittsburgh. Same reason you wouldn't find anything on Jack Dawkins.

I take a deep breath and hope I'm right. At the same time, I don't want to be. This will complicate things a lot. "The salesman said he talked to the guy who bought it about how they both grew up in Philadelphia. Isn't that where you're from?"

She shakes her head. "Pittsburgh," she says. "I don't see why—"

She stops as I watch her silently figure it out, her mouth closing, then opening, then closing. *Gotcha.*

"You're Frank's sister." I shake my head. "And here I thought I had a lot of family secrets to hide."

Nancy's face pales, and she leans back against her desk. "How'd you find out?" Her eyes shift to her computer.

I hold up a hand. "I didn't hack your computer. I wouldn't do that," I tell her quickly. At the same time, I'm not planning on telling her how Sam and I hijacked her phone or Frank's. "Elizabeth is your real name, isn't it?"

She nods. "My mother used to call me Nancy, though. I'd rather you keep that information private."

"I'm not going to tell, if that's what you're worried about."

Then her face relaxes into a smile. "I know that. And of anyone, I'm not surprised you'd be the one to figure it out. How— You know what? Never mind, I don't think I want to know."

"Frank must've used your relationship to figure out his

way into our accounts."

"No, he's not the one doing that, I'm sure." She sighs. "Frank is my brother, but we've never been close. He's the one who actually introduced me to Bill a long time ago. He was Bill's driver for years, but he never did anything but drive. Maybe that's why he ended up in Bill's confidence." She says the last quietly to herself, like an afterthought.

"What did Bill confide in him about?"

Her eyes rise to meet mine, her face smoothing into a mask. "I don't know. I'm just assuming. Bill's death left a gaping hole in a lot of people's lives. Ours as well as his. Some just need more help getting back on their feet than others. Frank's one of those guys. But he's not stealing from us."

"How are you so sure it's not him doing this? If he needs money that badly, he might think about Liv in her big mansion. He's gone there before, when he was Bill's driver."

"Frank's not... Well, he's not exactly a mental giant. He dropped out of school when he was fifteen. Definitely not capable of working out the whole hacking thing. That's why he stayed as Bill's driver, nothing more."

"But what does he need me for?"

"He thinks he can get you to hack one of Bill's old accounts. We don't even know if it's available." She straightens. "I think that's about enough of this conversation, Z. Whatever he wants from you, he's not going to get it. I gave him enough to start him on a new path, and I hope he takes the right one. Just like I hope you do. End of story."

End of story for her, but someone stealing from our accounts should point the finger immediately to Frank. I don't know why Nancy turns a blind eye to that, brother or not.

The door opens and Jen walks in, holding—*shit*—a small white box. Her face is gleeful. "Hi, Nancy! Just thought you might need a little more evidence."

"Where'd you get that?" I ask her sharply.

"You know. I found it in your room." She opens the box and lets out an exaggerated gasp. "Wow, such a gorgeous bracelet! Who's the lucky recipient? Not like I really need to ask."

I look quickly at Nancy. "That was in my desk drawer. She's out of line."

Nancy walks over and takes the box from Jen. "Is this what I think it is?" she asks me.

"Yes. I got it from Liv last time I went up there. Sam and I took it to the jewelry store to find out who bought it. I don't know why Jen's looking so surprised when she obviously was involved."

Nancy hands it to me. I slip the bracelet into my jacket pocket and turn to Jen. "Stay out of my room or I'll kick you out of this house myself."

She looks to Nancy for support, but Nancy nods in agreement. Jen shakes her head. "Un-freaking-believable." She storms out, slamming the door so hard it shakes everything in the room. Sam and Micah walk in.

"What's up her butt?" Micah asks, looking at me.

"You know," I say, "I'm tired of talking about this. I'm going upstairs."

Maggie jumps up from the couch to follow me to my room. "I believe you, you know," she says, closing the door behind her. She sits down on my bed next to me. "And Jen is awful. She was talking the other day about getting back at you."

I look sharply at her. "She told you that?"

"Well, not really. She was talking to Cara. I walked by and heard her say it. She was so angry." Maggie picks at her fingernail. "I have to admit, she scares me a little."

Maggie's eyes flick up to see my reaction. I don't miss it, and I suddenly wonder if Maggie knows more than she's letting on. She and Jen don't get along, but they could've teamed up to get back at Liv…and me…

But I haven't noticed her missing recently. She's been at every dinner here, every breakfast. She's barely left her room since moving in. Jen, on the other hand, has disappeared for long periods of time—even Nancy has noticed. And I don't see Maggie managing to climb up Liv's balcony or figuring out how to hack into our accounts. Her mind barely seems functional, and she was terrible at hacking.

"I have an idea. Would you help me?" I ask. Maggie nods eagerly. "Let me know when Jen leaves again. I'm going to follow her and see what she's up to."

"I will!" Maggie stands, looking happier than I've seen her in a while. She's always been so eager to please. It makes me feel sick to think of how often people have taken advantage of that eagerness. Myself included.

As soon as she's gone, I sit at my computer. Nothing but hard evidence will convince Nancy of Frank's guilt. Evidence I don't have. I've looked through rosters of crime rings and wanted felons, but nothing with Frank's attributes shows up. And if our detective contact Jim Rush, who accesses the dark side of the web as much as we do, can't come up with any dirt on Frank, the guy knows how to stay clean. Nancy's claim that the guy is uneducated doesn't seem authentic to me.

Thirty minutes later, the door flies open. I grit my teeth, wanting to shout about lack of privacy in this house, but I can't do that to Maggie. "Yes?" I say as politely as I can.

"She's leaving now," she whispers excitedly. "Jen. I overheard her telling Cara not to wait up, and she was laughing."

"Thanks." Maggie doesn't leave. Does she think I'm going to take her with me? I think quickly for something else to give her as a job. "Okay, so now what I need is for you to see if you can get any information from Nancy on this guy named Frank, okay?"

"Frank?" she asks, her brow wrinkled in confusion. "That man who comes around to talk to Nancy?"

"Yeah. I think he's the one who's been stealing money from everyone."

She slowly nods like it all makes sense. "Okay, I will."

I breathe out heavily when she leaves. Having Maggie around is like having a kid sister always banging on the door. I wasn't planning on leaving here until after graduation, but it might have to be sooner than that.

Grabbing my keys and jacket, I head outside, grateful that it's not as cold as yesterday. It doesn't take me long to catch up to Jen's old pickup truck just ahead of me. Slowing down, I allow a car to pass me and stay behind it to follow her.

The blue truck turns onto a smaller road. I pull over to wait a couple minutes, then follow her, keeping the vehicle small enough in my vision that hopefully she doesn't notice. In my mirror, I can see another truck behind me. I slow down a bit to let it pass in order to keep it between Jen and me, but it stays on my tail. A couple miles later, I can see Jen slowing down, her right blinker on as she turns onto another street. I start to speed up to not lose her, but a glint of something to my left causes me to look around.

The truck that was behind me is now passing. It swerves quickly toward me. I jerk the handles to the right and apply my brakes as the truck veers sharply into my lane. The bike careens over the shoulder.

I can't get control.

I can't—

CHAPTER TWENTY-ONE

LIV

Jack hasn't answered his phone or returned my text. I stare at the last message from him that reads **Trouble here will call you later.**

Trouble? What does that mean? I tap my phone impatiently. *Jack, where are you?*

Grandfather is home having dinner with me tonight, and I really wish he wasn't. I apologized to him this morning for speaking rudely to him, and he told me to forget about it, though I'm sure he's still hurt. He looked shocked at my change in hair color, but he didn't say much about it. Mrs. Bedwin seemed slightly disappointed when she touched my hair, but then she nodded like she understood. Blond is not my mother, and it's not Van. It's Olivia.

Grandfather seems to be making an extra effort to be around. He tries to strike up conversation about school, but I'm unable to focus on what he's saying. The more time that passes, the more I worry. I finally push my barely touched food away at dinner and tell him I'm not feeling well. I head up to my room and try Jack one more time—again straight to voicemail. I call Sam but she tells me she hasn't seen him for hours.

"His last text said something about being in trouble," I tell her. "Do you know anything about that?"

There's a long pause. "Well, there's some money missing from accounts here, and he's been accused of stealing it."

"What?" Jack stealing money from his own house? Not a chance.

"I know. I don't believe it, either, but Jen put up a pretty good argument."

"What did she say?"

"That he was sending you gifts."

"You mean the bracelet? It wasn't him. He thought it might be Jen."

"I know," Sam says. "We saw the video." Sam says something to someone, but her hand must be over the speaker, since I can't make out what they're saying. "Sorry, gotta go," she tells me. "I'll have him call you when I see him."

I hang up with her. For Jack to be accused of stealing from the others is pretty extreme. I can't believe anyone would even start to think that would be true. I'd be shocked if Nancy actually believed that, either. I wonder, though, why he hasn't called me back or even texted me. It's been hours now. I get that he's preoccupied with whatever is going on there, but it seems like he'd at least say something.

I text him again. **You okay?**

Nothing. Again.

It isn't until early morning, when my ringing phone wakes me from a restless sleep, that I hear back from Sam.

"They found Z," she says, her voice higher than usual.

My throat tightens. "Found him? What do you mean?"

"He's at VCU Medical Center since last night. He was in a bad accident. I think he'll be okay. I'm not sure, though. Nancy's with him. I'm driving over there right now. My battery's dying but I'll try to let you know."

"Sam!"

"Don't worry about it. I'll call you later."

The phone disconnects. I call her back but it goes straight to voicemail. *Damn it.* They've found him—what does that mean? And does she think I'm going to sit here waiting for her to let me know if Jack is okay or not? What if he's really bad off? I look up the number for the VCU Medical Center. But I don't know what name they have him under.

My knees start shaking. I lean against my desk. *Oh, Jack. I still love you. I shouldn't have pretended I didn't care.*

My alarm rings, making me jump. Screw this. I switch it off and head to my closet, slipping into a pair of jeans and a sweater over my tank. The hospital will be cold, I'm sure. I pick up a duffel bag from the corner and consider my clothes. I may not have to stay, but I should be prepared just in case. I pull out another pair of jeans and sweater and stuff them into the bag.

A light tap on the door makes me jump. Mrs. Bedwin opens it, the usual cup of tea in her hand. "Good morning," she says, walking over to me. "What are you doing with that bag?"

"Huh? Oh, nothing." I drop the bag back in the corner of my closet, hoping she didn't notice the bulk of it. "Just thinking about giving away some of my old clothes."

"Oh." She tilts her head. "Everything okay?"

I nod and smile. Nodding and smiling are what I do best these days. I take the cup from her and sip the tea, unable to stop it from shaking slightly in my hands. I'm sure Mrs. Bedwin notices, but she doesn't say anything.

As soon as she leaves the room, I pull out my bag and continue packing. Since I know I can't exactly carry a duffel bag through the house without being seen, I consider dropping it over the balcony. But I need to be able to get out of the house without that detective following me. The way the he acted at Em's house, there's no chance he'd take my need to leave town seriously. Instead of tailing me, he'd probably lock me up so I couldn't go anywhere. Grandfather won't understand, either. But I can't stay here while Jack's in the hospital. No way.

A quick call to Emerson solves that problem. She arrives at the house after breakfast and follows me to my room to switch outfits.

"I wore the brightest hat and coat I could find," she says as I stuff my hair into the orange knit beanie. "It was a good time for you to go blond, huh?"

Still, her hair is a lighter, brighter blond than mine, so she tucks it into one of my cream-colored beanies.

"It's perfect," I tell her. We stand side by side to look in my full-length mirror—me in her orange coat and her in my navy duster. "Nobody could tell the difference until they're close up."

"One more touch." She hands me her white Prada sunglasses and I give her mine. "This is so exciting. Oh, sorry," she adds, dropping her grin. "I know you're worried about him."

"Yeah. Thanks for helping me like this."

"That's what friends are for." She places a hand on my arm. "Do you know when you might be back?"

"No. If he's okay, I'll be back after school lets out. If not...well, are you good with keeping this up till tomorrow?"

"Sure." She adjusts my hat slightly to cover more of the front of my hair. "You can keep my car as long as you need. I'll just take yours home with me after school. If you aren't back, then you can tell your grandpa that you're spending the night with me. Or whatever."

"Thanks so much, Em." My voice cracks, something she doesn't miss.

"He'll be okay," she says quietly. She gives me a hug, but I pull away quickly when I feel the tears inching their way forward. I put the glasses on so she won't notice and model a pose.

"Emerson Daly, at your service," I say, my voice light.

"Perfect." She reaches up to wipe a tear slipping out from underneath my sunglasses. "Absolutely perfect."

My phone buzzes then with a text. I almost rip off my sunglasses to look at the message, assuming it's from Sam. As soon as I open it, though, I wish I hadn't. It's the picture of my grandfather and me at dinner on Valentine's Day—the same one that was mailed in the card. I stare at the picture for a long moment, my brain slowly switching gears. Stalker.

The stalker who now has my phone number.

I take a deep, shaky breath, trying to get control of myself. He's sending me the same picture as I already have. He has my number, but he can't reach through the phone and hurt me. I have my location untraceable through my cell—I verified that before. He can't hurt me.

But why would the idiot send me the same picture from a phone number that can be traced?

"What's wrong?" Em asks quickly, coming to my side. She takes the phone from my trembling hands. "Oh, my God, Liv! He's texting you now?"

"It's fine," I say as bravely as I can. "This is the picture he mailed me a while back in that card I got."

Emerson's face pales. She looks slowly up at me, and my heart drops at her stricken expression. "Has he sent you *this* one before?" she asks quietly, turning the phone around so I see the new image. I inhale sharply, the breath getting caught in my throat. The photo reveals me lying asleep in bed, wearing my gray sleep T and shorts, one leg draped across the top of the sheets. And a long-stemmed white rose on the pillow next to me. Valentine's Day.

There are no words, just a scream that never escapes my lips. The sound of blood pounding in my veins fills my ears as my vision starts to darken.

Emerson grabs my arm to steady me, forcing me to sit down on my bed. I take several deep breaths to keep from throwing up. "This is crazy," she's saying, running to the bathroom to get me a cup of water. "What a sicko."

The water helps me get control of my shaking. "Why now?" I manage to ask. "Right now, when I'm about to drive to Richmond."

"Coincidence? He doesn't know you're leaving."

These days, I don't believe in coincidence. "Unless he assumes I'm already on my way because of what he did to Jack. Maybe he thinks I won't be able to turn this in because I'm at the hospital with him?"

But that isn't right. I could still give it to the police.

Nobody in his right mind—not even the stupidest criminal—would send a text from his phone if he didn't want to get caught. It's a Richmond area code, too.

"Liv, you need to show the PI those pictures. And you should probably stay here, too."

I nod slowly. The idea of being on the road alone when some crazed freak is after me is too much. I click the phone closed, not wanting to look at that picture ever again. My grandfather is going to freak out when he sees this.

"Come on," I tell her after switching coats and hats back to our own. "Let's go show the PI."

We head downstairs, but something about this bothers me. Almost as much as the creepy factor. I grab Em's arm on the last step. "Wait a second. Let's think about this. The guy is sending me pictures, probably from a burner phone that we won't be able to trace. Really, why at this very moment, when the pictures were taken a while ago?"

Her mouth twists as she thinks about it. "Maybe to freak you out so you'll stay here?"

I nod. "Exactly what I was thinking. If I stay here, I might be walking into a trap. To be honest, I'm not even sure that's it not a member of Grandfather's staff."

I whisper the last words to her. When I originally thought Theo was responsible for the rose, it occurred to me that maybe he paid one of the staff to leave it for me. Why couldn't someone have been bribed to take the picture, too, while I was asleep? Not Mrs. Bedwin, of course, but he's got others who work here.

"So what are you going to do?" Emerson asks.

I glance at my phone. Still no text from Sam about Jack. If I drive to Richmond, I'll be alone. Hopefully disguised enough as Emerson to throw the guy off, but that's no guarantee. If I stay here, I'm a target waiting for the next bad thing to happen.

I look at Emerson and she rolls her eyes. "Fine. Just be careful." She hands me her keys, but I push them back at her.

"There's no way I'm taking your car. If they think I'm still here, they'll follow you. I'm not risking your life."

She crosses her arms. "But you'd risk yours? That's no better."

"It is for me. If something happened to you because of me, I wouldn't be able to live with myself. I'll be fine."

My words sound braver than I feel at the moment, but I'm not sticking around to see if the stalker would like to climb his way up the balcony again.

I start to walk toward the door but Emerson grabs my arm. "Liv, take my car. I'll have Kade give me a ride home from school so nobody will have to drive your car around, okay? It'll just stay at the school, and you can call your grandfather later to explain if you aren't back by then. Please. If you don't, I'll tell the PI what you're planning, and he'll stop you from leaving."

I hug her as tightly as I can. "There will never be a better friend than you," I say softly. She hugs me back even tighter, and I know she's afraid for me.

Emerson and I go outside to show the text to the PI. He heads to his car with my phone to make notes and take pictures, then tells me to call him immediately if there's another incident. He also insists on driving me to school himself. I glance at Emerson, who shrugs. I guess it doesn't matter whether my car is sitting here or at school.

He drops me off in front of the school. I go inside and

walk to the back door, which leads to the student parking lot. Emerson is waiting for me next to her car. She hands me her keys and insists on swapping hats, coats, and sunglasses again, just in case.

"You sure Kade will be able to take you home?" I ask her.

She nods. "Be careful. Let me know what's going on when you can. And if you aren't back before school's out, you can always text the PI that you're riding home with us or something. Maybe I should go with you."

"No, you need to be here." I hug her again, as tightly as I can. "I love you, Em. I'll be careful. I promise."

By the time I'm on the road, it's almost eight o'clock. Even though I'm in Em's car, wearing her sunglasses and hat, I feel exposed. The image of me in bed asleep is fixed in my mind, and I find myself jumping at every stoplight when another car stops next to me.

It's almost ten when I pull into the VCU Medical Center in Richmond. I find Sam wandering the halls on the third floor. She stares at me for a second, and I remember I probably look very different to her with my new blond hair.

"Liv?" She runs to me, wrapping me in her arms. For the first time since I left Monroe Street, I remember the warmth of the friendship we had, even if it was brief and for a purpose that wasn't really honest. "I'm so glad you're here."

She pulls back and smiles at me, but the smile doesn't reach her eyes. "He's okay, don't worry. Got some bruised ribs and is pretty banged up, but he'll live." She shakes her head and laughs shortly. "The guy drives me crazy, but he's like my brother."

Sam takes my hand and walks me to a room. The first thing I see when she pushes open the door is the bright blue dress of a woman standing between the bed and me.

"Nancy," I say quietly.

She whips around, her red hair flying around a half second after. "Liv?" She hugs me, but my eyes move to the sleeping boy in the bed. My throat tightens—he looks so vulnerable. A bruise trails along his jaw, but otherwise I don't see anything scary. I walk to the opposite side and take his limp hand, noticing another large bruise on his exposed shoulder.

"He's okay," Nancy says. "The doctors say he'll make a full recovery in a few weeks. The helmet and his leather protected him for the most part. But he'll need to rest to heal. He stayed last night, and the doctors don't want to release him just yet."

"What happened?" I ask.

"We don't know." She touches his forehead, brushing strands of his hair back. "He was found next to his motorcycle. His head hit a large rock, which seemed to have knocked him out for a bit, but thank God he was wearing his helmet. He also got a sliver of metal from something on the ground buried in his side, so they had to remove that."

"Has he said anything about what happened?"

She shakes her head. "He can't seem to remember much." She sighs heavily, which ends in a choke. "Maybe it was a drunk driver or something. I don't know."

"I'll stay with him," I tell her. "Why don't you go get some food or something?"

She smiles sadly at me. "I don't think I ever told you how grateful I am for you, Liv. I've never seen him happier than when he was with you." She fondly touches his cheek. "Did he tell you we've stopped hacking?"

I nod, even though I know he hasn't. I wonder if she suspects this, too.

"Well, it's partially due to your influence. The light in his eyes when he was with you, and the lengths he went through to shield you from the business—it was the first time I thought there could be something else for all of us." The smile fades as she looks at Jack. "He doesn't think he can quit. I know he can, though. Maybe you can help him see reason?"

I don't answer. I refuse to be used by Nancy to get Jack to do anything, even if what she says makes sense. Jack is the only one who should make that choice, not her. For the first time, I see it through his eyes. Hacking has been his life, and just telling him he should drop it isn't going to cut it. He has to come around on his own terms.

Nancy leaves, and I sit in the blue vinyl chair next to him, still holding his hand. My eyes focus on his closed eyes, mostly in an attempt to avoid staring at the IV needle coming out of his arm and the beeping machines that won't shut up. "Jack," I whisper. "I'm here."

My phone buzzes in my pocket. I take it out to see a text from Emerson: Is he ok?

I text her back: Sitting next to him. Bruised up but will be fine.

Good. Everything fine here don't worry. If you stay late maybe text grandpa.

Good idea. I text my grandfather that I'm staying after school, and after a few back-and-forths about this morning's awful pictures, he tells me to be careful and call the PI to pick me up as soon as I'm done. Perfect.

Except I don't feel perfect. Regardless of how important it is for me to be here in Richmond, it doesn't feel good knowing that I've lied to my grandfather more this week than I have the entire eight months since being there. He trusts me right now, even if just barely. If he finds out what I'm doing, he'll never believe me again. And could I blame him?

I wish he didn't hate Jack so much. He should be concerned for him, too, instead of worrying about me falling in with "the wrong crowd." For my grandfather, and for those like him, the wrong crowd includes people who didn't grow up privileged. Like Jack. Like me.

And maybe even like my father.

I lean back in my chair and take out my phone, staring at the strange number from the text. I look online, but there's no record of it, of course I'm sure it's a prepaid burner phone with no way of tracing it. I just don't get why someone would use it to send me pictures that were taken days ago, unless he was trying to get me to stay in Norfolk out of fear.

Jack stirs and his eyes flutter open, and for a moment we make eye contact before he falls back asleep. I lean forward to kiss his cheek, the emotions swelling over me. I'll never let my grandfather or anyone else hurt him—this guy I know I love.

CHAPTER TWENTY-TWO

JACK

The drugs allow me to fly in and outside of myself.
There are many faces to look at—

Nancy

Sam

Micah

Doctors

Nancy comforting a sobbing Maggie. Did I die or something?

Nurses

Liv

She doesn't notice I'm awake, watching her as she stares out the window. Her hair is different. The room is dark but her hair is lighter. Blond?

The drugs are still in my system, which is great for the bitch of a pain in my side but sucks because I can't trust myself to speak. The nurses have me propped up to where I'm almost sitting. Uncomfortable doesn't even begin to describe it.

"Hey," I say to Liv, and the word comes out muffled, like I'm speaking through cotton.

She turns to walk over to me, her warm hand sliding through my cold one. "Hey." Her eyes are puffy, and maybe it's the drugs, but it makes me feel good that she cares that much. Maybe even more than Nancy. Which I think I tell her because she smiles.

"Of course I care about you," she says. Her voice sounds far away, and I reach out—or don't, I'm not sure.

Minutes or hours later, I wake again. Liv is talking to the doctor. Or listening. Nancy is there, too. And Sam. They both look at me as I stir. I hate this. I hate feeling exposed and everyone looking at me like I'm some lost puppy. I was begging for the drugs when I first got here, as much pain as I was in, but now they're annoying the hell out of me.

"How are you feeling, sweetheart?" Nancy asks, coming to my side to take my hand. I appreciate the irritated look Liv gives her on my behalf.

The doctor asks me several questions, repeating himself a few times as he stares into my eyes. More concussion questions. I think I answer okay, though his eyebrows pinch slightly a couple of times. If I screwed up, I blame it on whatever drugs they're giving me. He checks the bandage on my side, smiling and nodding.

"Well, the good news is that we should be able to release you tomorrow morning," he says briskly, pulling up my chart and making some notes. "You'll have to take it easy for a few weeks, though, until your ribs heal. Get your homework sent home from school." He nods at Nancy. "And definitely no more hot-rodding."

Hot-rodding? "Someone ran me off the road," I tell him. And just like that, the memory washes over me, though I can't remember much past seeing the truck sidle up next to me.

He raises an eyebrow at me. "Uh-huh, are you sure? The roads were awfully slippery that day."

"Yeah, pretty sure I'd know if someone ran me off the road." He's still looking at me skeptically, like I'm just making excuses for "hot-rodding." Judgmental asshole.

"Who was it?" Nancy asks. At least she's taking me seriously. "What'd the car look like?"

"It was a truck. Maybe black. That's all I could see." I don't remember if the truck was black for sure, but it was dark. I keep my eyes on Nancy to see if she realizes a connection with Frank's truck, but she doesn't flinch. I try to sit up straight, but the pain in my side forces me back. The agony must show in my face as Liv hovers over me.

"Can't you do anything for him?" she asks anxiously.

"Not for another couple hours," the doctor says cheerfully. Enjoying my pain. I'm sure he's one of those doctors who thinks this injury will teach me a lesson.

Suddenly, there are too many people around me. I'm not claustrophobic by nature, but everyone staring at me is really starting to grate on my nerves. I want to be able to jump out of this damaged body and get away—run from everyone on my Ducati. I can't, so I do the next best thing: I close my eyes, pretending to sleep. I keep my hand clamped around Liv's. Everyone leaves, and now the only voice speaking is the only one I need.

"They're gone," she whispers, her lips pressing against my cheek. "You can stop pretending to sleep."

I open my eyes.

"What was that about?" she asks.

"Just needed some space. You dyed your hair."

She nods and sits back. "I needed a change. Now who is the jerk who ran you off the road?"

"I don't know. Really. It was a guy in a truck that was dark, either black or blue or something."

"You sure it was a guy?"

"Yeah. Well, no, but…"

She nods. "You're thinking it was Frank, aren't you?"

"Maybe. I don't know. I couldn't find much on him, but I overheard a conversation between him and Nancy about him wanting to use one of us for something. A bank job, I think."

"Did you ask Nancy about it?"

"Yeah. She still says he's not involved with all this. I'm not so sure. But you know, whoever is must be working with someone in the house."

Liv taps a finger to her chin. "I wonder if it could be Nancy herself."

I level a gaze at her. She smiles sheepishly. "Sorry. Jen?"

I nod. "I was following her when I got hit. And Maggie overheard her telling someone that she was going to get me back. This would be the perfect way."

"Jeez, she really needs to get a life. I'm going to work on this while you're laid up," she says.

"What?" I stare at her, and suddenly the fact that Liv is in Richmond registers in my mind. "Wait a minute. You shouldn't even be here."

She smiles and brushes her hand over my hair. I reach up to wrap my fingers around her wrist and firmly push it away. "Liv. Go home."

"Not a chance," she says grimly.

"There's someone after you, and you being here is going to make it easier for him. I don't need you here. I need you in Norfolk where you're safe."

"Safe?" She pulls out her phone, opening up a text and almost shoving it at me. "This is what I got this morning—a souvenir from that Valentine's Day rose on my pillow. Clearly, staying in Norfolk is not making me safer."

Whatever I was going to say is lost as I stare at the image of her lying in bed. My stomach twists as an overwhelming fear takes over my body. I swing my legs to the side of the bed, grabbing her phone from her hands.

She snatches it back. "I showed the PI the text this morning and he's already investigating. Lie down, Jack, before you hurt yourself." Almost as if on cue, the pain comes rushing back in waves. I wince as I let her help me back.

"Don't you see?" she asks, her hand brushing my hair back gently. "I can't just stay in Norfolk hoping that the police eventually figure it out. Every day that I stay there allows whoever is doing this a chance to attack me when I'm at a stoplight, or when I'm walking in between classes at school. And every day is another chance that someone has to finish the job on you. You wouldn't stay put if our situations were reversed. Why do you assume that I could?"

"At least give me a day or two so I can join you," I beg her. "Please."

Sam walks in as I finish speaking. "Easy, cowboy," she says, laughing lightly. "I think Liv and I are going to handle this one without you. And don't even try to tell us we can't because we're just girls or we'll kick your ass."

Even though I'd never say or even think that, I keep my mouth shut. There's nothing I can do now that they've both made up their minds. I squeeze Liv's hand. "Be careful. And stay together."

"We'll be fine." She leans over to kiss me lightly. "We'll let you know what we end up with."

She and Sam leave, already making plans and way too excited about all this. As soon as they're gone, I call our detective contact, Jim Rush, and leave a voicemail begging him to put surveillance on Frank. Then I close my eyes, hoping he'll get the message in time before Frank figures out Liv's here. Regardless, I'm going to be worried constantly about Sam and Liv until they're back safe.

CHAPTER TWENTY-THREE

LIV

"**S**o what first?" Sam asks as soon as I get out of my car at their new house. It's not as impressive-looking as Monroe Street—more like a big house instead of a lavish castle. I wonder whatever happened to the Monroe Street house.

"I don't know. Look for this Frank guy? Talk to Jen? Ja—" I catch myself, remembering that no one here except Nancy knows Jack's real name. "Z says he was following her when he had the accident."

"Yeah let's start with Jen," Sam says. "She should be home from school."

A thin girl with curly dark hair approaches us as soon as we walk into the house. At first glance I thought she was maybe thirteen or fourteen, but as she gets closer, it's obvious she's much older.

"How is he?" she asks Sam in a shaky voice.

It's the voice that I recognize. Holy crap—this is

Maggie? She barely resembles the pretty girl I saw only briefly one day at Monroe Street. The dark circles under her red eyes make her look almost ghoulish. Jack said she was having a hard time transitioning here. Understatement of the year.

She only addresses Sam, not even looking at me, reminding me of the cold treatment Jen gave me when I moved into the Monroe Street home. Another ex-girlfriend with issues.

"Oh, you know," Sam says, shrugging. "Broken ribs, concussion. An inch from death. The guy's lucky he didn't bite it."

Maggie gasps at that and runs up the stairs, sobbing.

"Jeez, I was just kidding," Sam mutters. "Come on, let's go find Jen."

Jen doesn't answer her door when Sam knocks.

"Maybe she's not here," I whisper.

Sam raps on the door again. "Come on, Jen, we know you're in there. We're not here to blame you for anything."

The door opens then to an angry Jen, her nostrils flaring as she looks at Sam. As with Maggie, she doesn't even look at me. "Blame me? And what exactly would you blame *me* for? Z's accident?"

"Should I?"

I almost elbow Sam hard at that. She'd be terrible in a hostage situation.

"Nobody thinks you're responsible for his accident," I tell Jen, but she turns her scowl to me.

"*Nobody?* Are you considering yourself *somebody* as it pertains to us? Because let me fill you in on something—you aren't. You may be the one he's—"

"Okay, stop right there," Sam says, holding up a hand.

"Are you screwing around with Liv by sending her shit? And do you have anything to do with what's been going on around here?"

I have to admit, I admire Sam's frankness. She says it in such a way that allows for no BS-ing. Jen seems kind of shocked, actually.

"No, I'm not. Just because I can't stand the guy doesn't mean I'm trying to kill him. And I'm definitely not bothering with you," she says to me, her nose wrinkling as if I rolled in *eau de skunk*.

"Then where are you going every day?" Sam asks.

"None of your damn business. That's where." Jen folds her arms and nods at me. "Why would you look here for someone who's stalking you? You lived with us for all of two seconds, and you didn't impress anyone long enough for us to give a shit about you."

"Come on," I tell Sam, tugging at her elbow. "Obviously she's not going to say anything." I pull her down the hallway, stopping to look at all the doors. "Um, I don't know which one's your room."

"Right here," she says, pointing to the room I'm in front of. She pulls the door closed behind us. "I don't think we should've let her off that easily."

"We're not. But she's not going to tell us anything from us just asking. Can't you remote into her computer?"

"Nope. She locked it down fast. Z tried." She tilts her head. "You said Z was following her when he got run off the road?"

I nod. "So we wait until she leaves and then follow her."

"Exactly."

I pull the door open again and sit in the desk chair to keep an eye on the hallway for when Jen leaves. Sam's room reminds me of Jack's—utilitarian for a bedroom. There are no posters of hot guys or pink flowered wallpaper like in Emerson's bedroom. Just a plain black and white comforter on the double bed and a large Ansel Adams of mountains and a lake on the wall. I'm surprised—I would've thought she'd have some funky art print or cool design everywhere.

"Yeah, my room's pretty boring, isn't it?" Sam asks as I look around.

"Not boring, just—black and white."

She shrugs. "I was hoping we'd move back to Monroe Street. You know, like if I made it look too awesome or got too comfortable, we'd end up staying."

I can understand it. This house is big—really big, by most people's standards—but it's not the fairy-tale castle of Monroe Street. "Do you think you'll go back?"

"I doubt it." Her face droops as she looks around the small room. "At least I have my own room. Nancy let Z and I have our own. Micah and Cameron do, too. But they're small like this one." She sighs loudly. "Really, it shouldn't matter. I turn eighteen in a couple months and will be ready to move out anyway."

"What are you going to do when you graduate?" I ask.

She looks at me for a long moment. Then she reaches over to open her desk drawer, pulling out an envelope and handing it to me. The return address in the corner has a James Madison University seal. "College?" I shouldn't be surprised. Sam is ridiculously smart. It's just that she's always looked down on the "regular" academic path, so I guess I thought she'd want to continue hacking when she graduated.

"It's stupid, I know, but Cameron talked me into it."

"Cameron?" I say teasingly, grinning.

She groans as her head falls into her hands. "*Oh my God.* I know."

"Sam, I think it's the best thing in the world."

She peeks through her fingers. "Really?"

"Definitely. You're ridiculously smart. You're going to be amazing in college."

"Thanks." She lies back on her bed and throws an arm over her eyes. "Sometimes I think I'm just the biggest idiot. I'm going to major in business. *Business.* After I spent the last few years hacking into them."

I laugh. "Makes sense, in a way."

"I guess. But they have this study abroad opportunity there, too. It might be cool." She gets up on her elbows and winks at me. "I always have my fallback career if this doesn't work out."

I ignore that. "Is Cameron going there, too?"

"Nope. He's going to UVA. We can still hang out on the weekends, but I figured I needed to be in a place where no one from here is going. Fresh start kind of thing."

"What's he think of that?" Sam shrugs and doesn't answer, but I know. Cameron is so into her that it probably kills him that she's going to a different college. Knowing Sam and her need for independence, though, I'm not surprised at all.

"So what about you?" she asks. "With Daddy Warbucks paying your way, I'm guessing Harvard?"

"Princeton."

She whistles through her teeth, cocking her head at me. "You know, I'm really glad things worked out for you. You never belonged in this life. Or even the foster kid kind of life."

The way she says that makes me wonder if she thinks

she belonged in the foster care life. "Neither did you, Sam. Nobody deserves that."

"I used to wonder all the time what I'd do if my life were different. Like how I'd end up if I wasn't here." She rolls her eyes. "Probably be some dorky cheerleader with a football player boyfriend, like Cameron, if someone had given two shits about him at home."

I laugh. It's hard to picture Sam in a uniform of any kind, much less cheering happily with a squad.

She jumps to her feet as we hear a door slam down the hall. We look out her window and soon see Jen walking toward the cars. "Let's go!"

A couple minutes later, Sam and I are following Jen's old truck as it pulls out of the driveway. Hopefully, she won't recognize us since we're in Emerson's car.

"Z said he turned on a couple roads before he got hit," Sam says after about five minutes. "See? There's the first."

I make the right turn and stay back as far as I can without losing her. There's less traffic on this road, but that doesn't prevent me from looking in my mirrors every five seconds. The road curves a lot, but then I notice the blue truck turning right again.

"Where the hell is she going?" Sam murmurs as we slow down to watch her pull into a high school entrance.

"Does she go to this school?" I ask Sam.

"Nope. Look—school's letting out. Pull in."

I turn into the school driveway and wave cheerfully at the security guard. "We're new students. Going to register."

He waves us toward the front of the building as I keep an eye on Jen's truck. We park in the visitors' lot on the other side of the drive from Jen. A stream of kids heads down the stairs and veers off in various directions. We watch as the number dwindles. Jen gets out of her truck and leans against it, her foot kicked back casually like she's waiting for someone.

"Maybe she's dating one of the boys here," Sam says. "I don't know why that's a secret, though. I'm sure everyone in the house would be thrilled that she's finally— Oh! Holy hell." Sam starts giggling as we watch a man with light brown hair in a tie approach her, setting down his briefcase to wrap his arms around her. The intense way he kisses her, not to mention the fact that his hands curve along her hips, tells me they've probably been at it for a while.

"Well, you go, Jen," Sam says, still laughing. "Hey, where are you going?"

I slam the car door behind me and lean down to look through her window. "Getting this sorted out. I think we need to know if this is all Jen has on her agenda, or if I should still be looking for knives on my balcony."

Sam is quick to follow. Jen's face freezes when she sees us headed her way. She says something to the man, who turns around to look at us. Older guy for sure. He looks like he's well into his forties.

Jen walks toward us. "What are you two doing here?" she asks, her words coming out more like a hiss.

"Well, well," Sam drawls. "Seems like now I know why Miss Unsocial is sneaking out all the time. Wonder what Nancy would think of your new, um, boyfriend? Or should I call him Sugar Daddy?"

"Shut up," she says, scowling, but I can see the worry in her eyes.

"So he's doing a little extracurricular teaching?"

"He's not that much older."

"Not at all. And I'm sure those are laugh lines next to

his eyes, right?"

"I'm almost eighteen," she says weakly.

"But not quite," Sam adds.

Jen's face is drawn in anguish as she glances back at the worried-looking teacher. Interesting choice she made—the guy actually looks like Jack might a couple decades from now, though with brown hair.

"Listen, he thinks I'm older. You won't say anything, right?" she asks Sam.

Sam smiles brightly. "Of course not. But I need to know something, and if you bullshit me, I will ruin you both. Got it? Good. Now, have you sent anything to Liv? Flowers, cards, gifts of any kind? Or visited there yourself?"

Her eyebrows pinch. "Are you kidding me? Why would I send her anything?" She wrinkles her nose at me in disgust. "And I didn't have anything to do with what's going on in the house. I know that's your next question."

"Do you know who did?"

Jen glares at me but I lift a hand. "Don't even bother saying Z. It's not him."

She glances around nervously. "Look, I don't know who did it, and I really don't care anymore. Just don't tell Nancy about this, okay?"

"Let me see your laptop," Sam says. Jen argues, but finally goes back to her truck to get it. Jen stands over Sam's shoulder, watching carefully as Sam checks the computer's logs.

"Nothing here," she finally says, and her voice is almost disappointed. Me, too, honestly. I thought for sure it was Jen.

"Now get off my back," Jen says, taking the laptop back.

"You'll lay off Z from now on, right?" Sam asks.

I want to hug Sam for having Jack's back like that. Jen doesn't answer right away. The man calls to her. "So this guy doesn't know you're a minor, huh?" Sam asks casually. She takes a step toward him.

"Fine," Jen says hastily. "I'll leave Z alone. I promise."

"Good." Sam cocks her head curiously. "Are you going to tell Nancy about this at some point? You know, you kind of suck for making her worry about you always being gone."

"I will...eventually." Jen blushes, a first that I've seen. "Evan asked me to move in with him over the summer."

"Well, more power to you. I'm glad you're finally happy."

Jen nods and walks away toward the teacher, who takes her in his arms and hugs her, whispering in her ear and making her laugh. Probably something comforting, like Jack would do for me. Sam's right. If Jen's finally figured out how to be happy, maybe she can be less of a bitch to the others, especially Jack.

As if she read my mind, Jen turns around, still clasped in the guy's arms, and looks at me. Her face isn't as full of anger as it was before. "I stand by what I said," she calls out to me. "The business is the only thing Z cares about. He's incapable of anything else."

I deliberately turn my back on her. "Do you believe her about not being involved?" I ask Sam when we get to the car.

She shrugs. "Well, there was nothing on her laptop, so yeah. I hope she does something other than sit around the house being Evan's little woman." Sam feigns gagging on her finger.

"Agreed." I start the car. "But now we're back at the beginning." I glance down at my buzzing phone and open up a text from my grandfather.

The PI traced the phone to a Frank Jones in Richmond and is headed there. I'll pick you up from school at 3.

"Sam, Frank's last name is Jones, right?"

"Yep." She takes my phone to read the text. "Well. So that's that." She hands the phone back to me. "No surprise, though. We figured it was him. You know they won't be able to do anything to him. Not for a while, at least. It takes forever to open a case."

I nod slowly, my eyes still on the text. "I don't get it, though. Why would Frank Jones use his own phone to text me when it'd be so easily traced?"

Sam shrugs. "Why do some people try hacking into banks from their own server? Because they're idiots."

"I guess." It still doesn't sound right, though. I don't know how smart the guy is, but anyone who worked with Bill Sykes in any capacity had to at least know the most basic rule—conceal your identity.

"Are you heading back to Richmond, then?" Sam asks.

"I don't think so," I tell her. I text my grandfather my plans to stay after school and catch a ride with Emerson. "We still have to track down the girl he was working with."

"I still don't completely believe that it's not Jen," Sam says.

"What about Maggie?" I ask. "I notice she didn't look at me at all when we were at the house earlier."

"Maggie?" Sam snorts. "Maggie's afraid of her own shadow."

"Would she steal money from the house?"

Sam shakes her head. "She wasn't good at hacking when she first came to Monroe Street. I'm sure she sucks even more now that she hasn't done it for a while."

One person I haven't considered is Sam herself. She wanted Jack to break up with me, thought he wasn't serious enough with me around. But then, there'd be no reason at all for her to try to stalk me. I'd point the finger at someone from *my* past if it weren't for the fact that whoever it is was stealing from the Briarcreek family.

Something about the Frank thing still bugs me. I purse my lips. "Sam, what would anyone get out of sending me hacked-up roses and texting me creepy pictures?"

She shrugs. "Make you panic. Could be money. Like maybe he's toying with you so he can freak you out, then kidnap you to get a ransom from it. Your grandfather would take him seriously at that point, I think."

"But he would've had plenty of time to kidnap me before my grandfather hired a private investigator. And why would they go after Z, too?" I shake my head. "Whoever did this has something against us both."

"Well, Frank would make sense, since you guys killed his employer."

Her words send a chill down my back. "True, and that's what I thought before. But again, does it make sense for him to text me from his own phone? And who would he be working with? It's two people we should be looking for. Him and a blond woman."

"We already tried Jen," Sam says, waving a hand toward the window. "Who else?"

I take out my phone, hoping I don't regret doing this. "Do you mind if we don't go back to the house just yet? I have an idea."

CHAPTER TWENTY-FOUR

JACK

I've never been hospitalized before and never want to be again. The nurses come in to administer pain medication like they're doing me the biggest favor and that I should be happy. I can't stay awake, and the fact that different people are in my room every time I open my eyes and that I never know what time it is is pissing me off. I can't be groggy while someone's trying to kill me. And Liv and Sam are scouting around. If something happens to them—

"Oh just deal with it," Nancy says when I try to convince her to talk to the doctors on my behalf. "They're taking away the pain, so let them. Stop trying to be in control all the time and just focus on healing. You're lucky you didn't end up with a concussion. I'm going to run home for a bit. Want me to bring you back anything?"

"My laptop."

She shakes her head. "You'd never sleep, then. We'll take care of everything, okay?" Nancy's lips press lightly against my forehead. She's never kissed me before, so it feels weird. "Hit your call button if you need the nurse."

As soon as she leaves, one of the doctors comes in, followed by a group of interns. One of them—the blond one—catches my eye, shocking me so much my body jerks. The pain responds accordingly, but no one seems to notice. Even if it weren't for the fact that he resembles me so closely, I've seen enough pictures of my half brother to recognize him immediately. The doctor examines my side and talks to the interns, but there is no flicker of recognition in Jeremy's eyes as he looks at me. He's not wondering who this guy is who looks so much like him. I'm just another patient. I start to laugh—what are the chances we would've ended up in the same room together? The laughter makes my side hurt so badly that I groan. Only one of the interns, not Jeremy, looks at me. Everyone else is tuned out.

Two minutes later, Jeremy's moved on with the group to another patient's room, and my chance to say something has walked out with him. What now? Obviously, the two of us being in the same hospital at the same time is too big of a coincidence to blow off. I make a promise to myself to find him later and confront him about our father. He deserves to know the truth, for his sake.

I ignore the twitch of guilt inside—it's for my sake, too.

I call Jim Rush again, this time getting through. Although he expresses concern that I'm in the hospital, he doesn't say anything other than he'll look into Frank. Says he'll need evidence, since the guy has no record. I can't be too mad. Staying off the grid is something the Monroe Street kids were trained to do, and now it's coming back to kick me in the ass.

As soon as I hang up with him, a text from Liv pings my phone.

PI thinks Frank Jones is the stalker and is going after him. We are still investigating. My mouth drops at the smiling emoji in her message. Like this is just a fun afternoon game she and Sam are playing. I have no chance to respond before a soft knock sounds at the door. Maggie walks in, tears running down her cheeks as she looks at me in the bed. Great. Just what I need. She mouths an *Oh my God*.

"I know you were here before, so don't look so surprised," I tell her. I reach over to grab my cup of water and wince at the responding jab in my ribs.

"Are you okay?" she asks, coming quickly to my side. "Can I get you anything?" She tries to take my hand, but I pretend I need both hands to hold the cup. Another nurse hovering in the form of Maggie is not what I need.

"Yeah, I'm fine. You don't need to stay." I realize when Maggie's forehead scrunches how that sounded. "Sorry. Rudeness is a side effect of whatever drug they're giving me," I tell her, motioning to the IV drip.

"I'm sorry this happened to you," she says, her eyes glassy again.

"Why? Did you do it?"

"Of course not! I would never hurt you!"

"I know." I close my eyes, this time hoping Maggie gets the picture and leaves me to sleep. She doesn't say anything for a while, and when I pop an eye open, she's lifting up my sheet and staring at my ribs like I have a hole in them. I tug the sheet from her hands. "I'll be okay, you know."

"Do you think whoever did it is the same person who stole from the house?" she asks, moving my phone to the side table so she can sit next to me on the bed.

"Probably."

"I wonder…" Maggie puckers her bottom lip with her fingers, her eyes fixed on the IV drip.

"Wonder what?"

"Well, you said someone's been giving your…um…Liv gifts, right?"

"Yeah?"

"And sending her roses and acting all like a stalker? Well, maybe he's someone who'd be mad at you because she likes you." She blushes as I stare at her. "Never mind, it's probably a stupid idea."

"I'm sure it's not stupid. Go on."

"Maybe it was an ex-boyfriend of hers. Or at least someone on her side who could have a motive. Something against her."

There's no ex-boyfriend as far as I know. The only one who could possibly have an obsession with Liv is that shitty excuse for a foster father Derrick Carter. It'd be a long shot, though. The guy has no record other than the one Liv and I slapped him with after he attacked her. And he wouldn't have access to my bank account or anyone else's at Briarcreek. Still, I'm glad to see Maggie's at least motivated to do something other than sitting around the house acting sorry for herself.

"It's possible," I tell her. "Good idea, actually."

She smiles then, the lines in her forehead relaxing. I return the smile. Maybe we haven't lost Maggie after all.

"So do you want me to follow up on that?"

Whoa. "No. I'll take care of it." I jerk up too fast, groaning as the pain cuts me in half.

She shakes her head, pressing me back with a gentle

hand. "With a broken rib? Don't think so. You stay here and get better." She kisses me on the forehead—as motherly as Nancy, weirdly.

"Hold up," I say as she turns to leave. "What are you going to do?"

She smiles, and the steel of her smile scares me. "I'm going to take care of you." Her voice is light, as if she's talking about going downstairs to get ice cream.

"Wait, come back!"

She ignores my calls and leaves me chained by my injuries to the bed. *Great.* I text as many people as I can to keep an eye out for her. Maggie going rogue is not what we need right now.

The nurse comes in then. "The young lady who was just here advised me that you're in a lot of pain, young man." She's all smiles as she checks my IV drip, ignoring me as I tell her I'm fine. "It's about time for your medicine anyway," she says, looking at the chart.

"I don't want any medicine," I tell her, which she ignores as she changes out the bag.

It's not long before I drift into sleep again, finding Maggie in the dreamworld, standing over Frank. "I'm taking care of you," she whispers as she holds up the knife. "Always have, always will."

CHAPTER TWENTY-FIVE

LIV

What the hell? "Great, now we have Maggie to worry about," I tell Sam, reading the text from Jack. "She's going all vigilante, apparently."

"She might have better luck than us. Trying to find Denise is like a needle in a haystack," Sam grumbles, scrolling through her phone. We already drove to the house where I lived with the Carters, my previous foster parents, just to find out from the new homeowners that the Carters left months ago after getting a divorce. I thought it'd be easier to start with Denise. The idea of finding Derrick again gives me the chills.

"You'd think in this town there'd be at least one Denise Carter." We've already followed up on the two generic *D. Carter* listings, one of which was a single man, the other, an elderly woman.

"Maybe she dumped her last name when they got divorced?"

I remember on the foster care paperwork there was a record of Denise's past history. Her maiden name was on the form, but I can't remember it. The only name on the form that I *do* remember is Alejandro Santos—the name of her husband who died with their little boy in a car accident. It was the first time I realized there might be reasons other than Derrick for Denise's drinking problem.

"Look up Denise Santos," I tell Sam. She types into her phone and scrolls through the results.

"There's one Denise Santos in Richmond," she says. "Lives on Victory Street." She grins at me. "That's only like a minute from here."

But when we get to the address, I groan. "It's an apartment complex. How do we know which one she's in?"

"Okay, okay, no worries." Sam closes her eyes for a moment to think. "Okay, so park at the main building. If it's a guy in here, we're good to go."

"He's not going to give you her apartment number just because you're cute, Sam."

She winks at me. "Wanna bet?"

She's right. As usual.

The guy inside the sales office is young and good-looking and totally falls for Sam's act. She should've been an actress, as good as she is about making up stories. She pretends like we're Denise's out-of-town college friends who are surprising her. Which is hilarious because although we could pass for college girls, if this guy saw Denise he'd see she's clearly older than that. Watching Sam's light-hearted, flirty manner as she talks to the guy reminds me of how she was Jack's right-hand person to recruit lonely foster kids who had a knack for hacking. She did make me feel like I was special, cool, fun—everything a good recruiter should do. I know I should be past that, but the feeling is still a bitter knot in my gut.

Denise's apartment is within walking distance, just on the other side of the pool. The place is nice, with flowers lining the walkway and bright white iron gates surrounding the pool area. Quiet. Kind of has a retirement village feel and, considering Denise's love of roosters and quilts and need for peace, it fits perfectly.

Number 226 is on the second floor, overlooking the pool. I hope she didn't notice me walking here, or she might not answer the door. Of course, she might not be home, either.

Sam gestures grandly at the door, and I use the brass knocker. About a minute later, the door opens and Denise is standing there looking pretty much the same as she did when I lived with her—mousy brown hair, a passive, slightly put-out expression on her face. Her eyes widen when she sees me.

"Olivia?" she asks. "What are you doing here?"

I think it's the most she's ever said to me at one time. "I'm not here to bother you. I just wanted to ask you a couple questions."

"I don't know…" She looks at Sam with a raised eyebrow.

"This is my friend Sam. We're looking for Derrick and hoped you could help us track him down." I didn't want to say it before she let us in, since I had a feeling she might close the door on our faces, but I have to take that chance.

Her nostrils flare. "Why are you of all people looking for him?"

Of all people? "Because I think he might be stalking me, and I need to know for sure."

Denise jerks the door all the way open and backs up. "Come on in," she says, frowning.

"Thanks." Sam and I follow her to the couch in her small living room. I look around and notice the rooster décor from her house has made it here, too. Rooster pillows, clock, canisters on the kitchen counter. Even more roosters than before, or maybe it just appears that way in a smaller place. I guess an obsession is an obsession.

Denise sits across from us in a formal-looking white armchair, her fingers interlaced across her lap. "How are you doing?" she asks, and I have a feeling it's more out of politeness than real concern.

"I'm fine, thanks."

"Your new home okay?"

I nod. She doesn't know about my grandfather, and I want to keep it that way.

"Good. I always wondered why you left, though I can probably guess. He was way too obsessed with you when you lived with us." Her lips twist in disgust.

"What do you know about it?" I ask her, trying to keep my voice even.

"Mostly what I guessed. Found a camera setup installed over your room after you moved out, too. I'm sorry things didn't go well at our house," she says stiffly. "Derrick was... well, he wasn't the person I knew in school. I guess I didn't know him enough when we got married. When I noticed things he looked up online..."

She shakes her head, not finishing that sentence. So not only did she not bother to look for me after I ran away, she ignored the warning signs from Derrick. I've never blamed Denise for anything, but at the moment, it's all I can do to not jump up and scream at her for pretending to be oblivious to his creepiness while I lived there. Of course, now I remember the handwriting on the foster care paperwork wasn't hers. She never wanted to be a foster parent in the first place.

"Do you have any idea where he is now?" Sam asks.

Denise shrugs. "He was fired from his job and is now working at some restaurant on the other side of town. The Burger Box, I think it's called. I have his address around here somewhere," she says, walking into the adjoining kitchen to get an address book. She writes something down on a yellow sticky note and hands it to me. "He's probably living with one of the hookers he screwed around with. Oh yes, he did that, too." She smirks at our stunned faces. "If I were you, I'd leave well enough alone and move on. Did you know he has a *record*? He can't even hold down a regular job." She huffs, scowling at the thought. I can't stop my face from burning. It's my fault he has a record, and for a weird, completely uncalled-for moment I actually feel guilty. I do *not* need to feel guilty about anything to do with Derrick Carter.

"Thanks for the information," Sam says, glancing at me with concern. She reaches over to squeeze my hand, which Denise sees and raises an eyebrow, clearly taking it the wrong way. Her head moves in a barely perceptible shake of disapproval. Obviously, nothing's changed with Denise.

"Liv, did you want to ask her anything else?" Sam asks.

"No, that's it," I say, though I have a thousand questions. Not the least being why she allowed him to take me in if she knew he was a sleazebag in the first place.

Sam and I stand and walk to the door, followed by Denise. I turn as we step outside. I don't know what I expected. Definitely not a hug or anything, maybe just a sad look or a commiserating smile. But Denise has nothing but quiet disinterest on her face. It's too much like the expression she had when she first opened the door to allow me into her home almost a year ago.

"Take care of yourself," she says, and I could be a pizza delivery girl for as much warmth as she puts into the words.

"You, too," I tell her. "I'm glad you're doing okay. I'm glad you left him."

Her eyebrows twitch, and I swear the corners of her lips tug up slightly. She nods and closes the door.

Sam breathes out loudly. "Damn. Still an Ice Queen. Are you okay?"

"Yeah." I'm not. Not really. But I don't want to tell her that seeing Denise again released the demons in my head that I'd tried so hard to bury. It makes me childishly wish that if I had one superpower, I'd fly around rescuing all the kids in bad foster care situations.

Sam and I look up Burger Box on our phones. It's five o'clock, so the drive will be even longer across town. An incoming call rattles my phone. Shoot, it's Grandfather.

"Hi, Grandfather," I answer casually.

"Hello, sweetheart. When do you expect to be home?"

"Sam and I are studying right now. I'll text you and let you know when we're done."

"Sam?"

"I mean Emerson. Sorry, we're in the middle of a history project. Did the PI find Frank Jones?"

"He's sitting in front of his house right now. The neighbor said he was around earlier, so he probably just went out for a bit. Sounds like he's still in Richmond, though. How about I come pick you up and we have an early dinner?"

I swallow hard. "I can't right now. But I'll call you when I'm on my way home, okay?"

"I'd really like to pick you up, just in case Frank decided to make another trip to Norfolk."

"It's okay, really. I have to go. I'll call you soon."

"But—"

I hang up. "Worst granddaughter ever."

"What's wrong?" Sam asks.

"I absolutely hate lying. Hate it."

"Me, too." I glance sharply at her—is she kidding me? "I'm serious," she says. "I do a lot of things—steal, cheat, whatever. But not lie. Think about it. Didn't I tell you when I was recruiting you that the company I worked at was going to offer you a job?"

"Monroe Street wasn't exactly a company, Sam."

"I didn't say I don't flex my truths a bit."

I glance at the clock on the dash. "I need to get back to Norfolk before my grandfather catches on. Let's go."

It doesn't take long to get to the Burger Box, and it's not until I see the building in front of me and realize Derrick Carter might be inside that I start to panic. Sam touches my shoulder. "Do you want me to go scope it out?"

I shake my head. I don't want her to go in and be exposed to that creep. And I definitely don't want to be sitting in Emerson's nice car, in this bad part of town, waiting for Derrick to walk up and recognize me. Sam waits patiently for me to get my tongue working again.

"Wait till he comes out." I manage to say.

"Are you sure? That could take forever?"

I nod. I don't care. I can't go in and face him. He'd just lie, anyway, and then he'd be so mad we showed up here, jeopardizing his job, that he might try to kill me next time.

Or even if he didn't stalk me before, he might start.

This was *such* a mistake.

I should've asked Jack to call his detective contact and follow up on Derrick instead. If Jack knew what we were doing right now, he'd be upset. As it is, he's already texted me to ask for an update. I had no idea what to say, so I haven't replied at all yet.

"There's no dark truck in the parking lot," I tell her. "That's something, at least."

"Uh-huh," Sam says. She nudges me. "Give me your hat. I'm going in."

She doesn't bother waiting for me to give her my beanie, taking it off my head and pulling it down on hers. She puts on her sunglasses and pulls her coat on. "He doesn't know me, don't worry." She jumps out before I can grab her, slamming the door behind her. Damn it. Sam is going to get in serious trouble one of these days.

She returns in about a minute, sliding into the seat. "He's off today. I asked what kind of car he drives and the guy in there just looked at me like I told him his momma smells bad."

I breathe out a sigh of relief.

"So let's go to his house," she says.

My stomach clenches. "No, let's go drive by Frank's instead."

"But the PI is at Frank's house."

I'd forgotten. Sam's staring at me like I should be more worried about the guy who's been stalking me than my last crappy foster parent. She has no idea.

"I know you're freaked out about it," she says quietly. "But Derrick won't hurt you. I promise."

Right now, I'm not worried about him hurting me. I'm

worried all the horrible memories I've worked the last eight months to get over will float up to the surface and smother me. But…if I turn away now, the helpless fear that nearly paralyzes me whenever I think of him won't stop.

I start the car. No way in hell do I want to have to do this again.

"Excellent," Sam murmurs, shifting in her seat like we're in a race car. Derrick's house isn't far, maybe five minutes. It's a run-down duplex next to an adult superstore. Figures.

"So what now, Captain?" Sam asks as I pull into the duplex parking lot.

"I don't know." Honestly, I'd only gotten this far in my head. But now that we're here, I realize I don't want to go up and ring his doorbell and confront him. Derrick isn't Denise. As cold as Denise is, she's still a normal person. Derrick is evil. A pervert. A rapist. Who could very well be my stalker and the person who tried to kill Jack. I can't take in enough air to keep up with my pounding heart.

Sam places a cool hand on my arm. "Breathe, Liv. You're not alone, you know. I'm here with you. I'm not going anywhere."

I nod, closing my eyes briefly and taking deep breaths. Calmly, calmly. *You promised yourself you wouldn't let him get to you again. You're the girl who bested Bill Sykes, remember?*

I'd rather drive off the James River Bridge again than go up and face Derrick.

"The good news is that there's no truck here," Sam says. In fact, there are only two other cars in the parking lot. As we watch, an older man and woman walk out to one of them and drive away. That leaves a beat-up silver minivan.

"I don't see Derrick driving a minivan, do you?" I murmur.

"If he did, wouldn't he park it in front of his own door?" She points at the door on the far left. "That's number four. Dude's not home."

I look again at the clock on the dash. If we're going to do this, it's now or never. "Can you pick a lock?" I ask Sam.

She grins.

Five minutes later, we're climbing into the side window of Derrick's duplex apartment. The lock on the window was obviously cheap and worn—it took us seconds to break it.

"Hurry," I tell her as Sam crawls through the window after me. I peer back through the panes but don't see anyone watching us. In this neighborhood, maybe nobody would care.

"Stinks in here," Sam says, wrinkling her nose. The apartment reeks of moldy soccer cleats that have been locked in a hot trunk for a week. I flip on a lamp sitting on a side table in the living room. My heart is beating so hard I wouldn't be surprised if Sam can hear it. And I wonder if she's as scared as me. Doubt it, the way she's wandering around, poking at the dirty dishes in the sink and the open bottle of ketchup on the table. I'm actually shocked at the mess. When I lived with the Carters, Derrick was always dressed in pants and tie for work, and their house was perfectly clean. I guess Denise enforced that rule, because this one is anything but clean. The dingy tan sofa looks like it might've been white a long time ago, and several water rings scar the cheap coffee table.

"How could someone this nasty be a foster dad?" Sam asks in disgust, flicking a finger against a glass with the remnants of something like whiskey on the kitchen table. It reminds me of the short glasses Denise used to fill with her vodka every night.

"Yeah." I grit my teeth and step into his bedroom, trying not to gag at the idea of being in here. A computer is set up in one corner. I turn it on. "Maybe you should keep an eye out for him," I tell her. We ended up parking at the unit behind his so he won't see Emerson's car if he comes back, but I have no desire to hide in his nasty closet if he suddenly shows up.

"Okay. I'll go back into the living room and look around for clues," she says.

"Thanks." I bypass his security and start searching through his computer, looking for documents or images that may have my name on it. I breathe out when I don't find any. And in his browser history, there's nothing that indicates a search for me at all, nor anything that involves the jewelry store or even Norfolk. I feel like crying, I'm so relieved.

"Anything?" Sam calls from the living room.

"Nope. Thank God. Because I was really— Ew!"

Sam runs to my side, her face screwing up at the porno sites that fill the history. Yeah, apparently Derrick doesn't look for me online, but he sure loves looking up smut. I remember seeing that magazine with a naked woman in his closet when I was looking for my laptop...yuck.

"Guys are so gross," Sam says as I close out the window.

"No one's as gross as Derrick."

"He has a lot of random shit. Who even uses blank CDs anymore?"

My eyes immediately flick up to the CD Sam is holding. There's no label on it. Just like the one I found in his closet—the one that showed me walking around my room in my underwear. My blood turns to ice. I take the CD from her and shove it in the disk drive on the computer. The whirring of the system matches the whooshing of my pulse in my ear.

A window pops up and I press play. *Please, please don't be me. Please.*

The video is shaky at first, like someone's holding a camera. I breathe out, my muscles relaxing in relief. It's not from an overhead surveillance camera like the one he'd installed in my room.

"Who is that?" Sam asks, pointing at the person in the background. I peer at the monitor. It's too dark to see many details except that it's a woman's figure lying on a bed. I wonder if she's aware of the camera. She leans up on her elbows and I catch a glimpse of dark curls before the person who set up the camera blocks her. Derrick is still the world's worst pervert. And hopefully, whoever this is isn't some teen who's been drugged, like he once tried to do to me. I eject the CD and look at the others lining the bookshelf. Could there be any of me?

"Hey, didn't you want to at least see who he was with?" Sam asks.

"No, thanks." I freeze as someone coughs right outside the door. I can hear voices and something jangling—keys! *Shit!* I hold down the power button to do a hard shut-down as Sam rips the CD from my hand and shoves it back on the shelf.

"Come on," she hisses, running to the side window. I follow, slipping out behind her and pulling down the window. It gets stuck an inch from the bottom. "Forget it," Sam says, tugging on my arm. We take off at a crouching run toward the parking lot behind the duplex.

"Crap," she mutters. "I forgot to turn off the lamp."

"Too late now," I tell her as we get to the car. "He'll probably think he left it on."

We yank open the doors and lock them as soon as we're inside, slumping down in the seats and looking around to see if anyone noticed us. No one seems to be around. We both start giggling hysterically out of relief.

"We suck at this," I tell her, starting the car.

"That is one creepy guy. Did you find anything else on his computer besides porno sites?" she asks as I pull away.

"Nope." Glancing over at the parking lot in front of the duplex, I see a white car, a green car, and the silver minivan. No black truck. Sam laughs as I whoop loudly. I give her a high five.

"Thank *God*," I say, relief swimming over me and making me feel almost dizzy. I'd rather deal with someone trying to get money out of me than Derrick stalking me, putting roses in my bedroom.

I drop Sam off at Briarcreek, noticing that Jen's truck is still not at the house. "You're not going to tell Nancy about today, right?" I ask Sam.

"No. She'd be pissed about us breaking into Derrick's house, and it didn't give us any new leads anyway. Keep me updated if you hear anything on your end and I'll do the same."

I promise to do that, then head to the hospital to see Jack before I go back to Norfolk. I'm definitely not looking forward to telling him about breaking into Derrick's and almost getting caught. I know exactly what he'll say about that.

CHAPTER TWENTY-SIX

JACK

Lying here waiting for Liv and Sam to come back is more torture than the pain in my ribs. The last text was vague enough to tell me they're probably doing something I'd disagree with. Not that it'd stop either Sam or Liv. A million things go through my head, and none of them are acceptable.

I also text Maggie, but all I get is a smiley face in return. I'm worried about her. She's getting weird on me, more so than normal. I start to wonder again if she knows more than she's letting on.

The nurses come in to help me walk around the hallway. It hurts like a bitch but they say it's to keep me from getting pneumonia. I ditched the hospital gown for a pair of black pajama bottoms and long-sleeve T-shirt Micah brought me. At least I don't feel like as much of an invalid now. As soon as we get back to my room, I notice a bunch of people gathered around the nurse's station, including a photographer.

"What's going on there?" I ask the nurse.

"One of our interns' father is visiting. He's a big deal, I think."

Without even seeing him, I know who it is. My father, here to show off his successful doctor-in-training. More of the "family values" promotion for his campaign. I step into my room, staying by the door to see if I can hear his voice.

"Let me help you into bed," the nurse says.

"I'm fine. Can you just leave me here? I want to hear the senator," I add. My father isn't senator yet, but at this rate, I'm sure he will be.

"Senator? Oh, my. Okay, well, I'll be back to check on you in a few minutes."

I nod as she leaves. I press my hand to the doorjamb. Just a few steps out and to the left and I'll be in his view. I force one foot out.

I can see him now: tall, blond, bright smile for the camera. His arm is wrapped around his son Jeremy, who looks slightly put out. The annoyed expression on Jeremy's face is like a shot of courage. I can do this.

A little boy runs by me, almost knocking into me and making me jump back. "Watch it, kid," I say, grabbing my side and gritting my teeth at the pain.

He skids to a halt. "Sorry." He tilts his head and stares at the side I'm holding. "What happened to you?"

"Motorcycle accident."

His eyes light up. "You ride a motorcycle? That's so cool!"

"Yeah. Except when you're flying off it. Then it's not so great."

"Do you crash a lot?"

I shake my head. "Where's your family?" I ask him. I need to refocus before my father leaves, and this kid's not helping. "Aren't they wondering where you are?"

"Nah." He waves toward the nurse's station. "My dad's busy taking pictures. So what kind of motorcycle do you drive?"

I don't answer him. I remember now—a picture of John Winslow's family posted in the *Times*. Older son Jeremy, younger son... "Caleb," I say softly. He can't be older than seven. Same age I was when my mother killed herself. Was I once this happy, too?

The boy's eyes widen. "How'd you know my name?"

"I...I think I heard someone calling you," I tell him.

He looks over his shoulder. "Guess I better go back. If I see you again, will you give me a ride on your motorcycle?"

I smile at his enthusiasm. "Sure." I hold out my hand and he slaps it, then runs back to his family. I take a shallow breath and start forward again. *Just get it over with, then all the pain will be gone. You won't have to think about your father again.* I can destroy John Dawkins Winslow III. Family, reputation, shot at the senate—all gone with one word from me. The moment I've waited for almost my entire life.

But my steps stall as I watch Caleb swing into his father's arms, laughing as his father kisses his cheek. Their affection looks real, not the kind put on for the cameras. It hurts worse than the pain in my body. If I do this, if I out my father's true shitty self, I'll not only destroy him, but his family, too. Caleb would learn that the world sucks like I did, though without the added horrors of foster care. He would no longer be this happy little kid running around asking about motorcycles. He'd hate his father as much as I do. He'd hate me, too.

Caleb points me out to his father, who glances over. His smile slowly drops as recognition dawns in his eyes— he remembers me. And there's something else—fear. It's gratifying to see that fear. The one time I went to confront him at his New York office, years ago, he pretended like he didn't know me. He didn't acknowledge how much we looked alike, and the only thing I walked away with was confirmation that he was an asshole.

I step back into the cover of my room as other eyes turn to see what he's staring at. The last thing I notice is Caleb's grin. I don't care about my father or Jeremy, but I can't do that to Caleb. He deserves the childhood I never had.

I climb back into bed, knowing my father won't show up at my door. He won't be curious as to why I'm in the hospital. He won't wonder how I've been all these years.

And for the very first time in my life, I'm finally cool with that.

A half hour later, when the excitement around my father has dwindled and a nurse comes in to check on me, Liv walks in, a white sack tucked under her arm.

"That looks really painful," she says, her eyes on my bruised torso.

"It is. They're making me get up and walk and cough and do all sorts of stupid sh—stuff."

The nurse clicks her tongue at me. "You'll be fine,"

she says, pulling my shirt back down. "You don't want pneumonia to set in." She adjusts the pillow behind my back. "Are you in any pain?"

"No, not at all," I tell her. When she leaves, I roll my eyes at Liv. "It's like having a bunch of grandmothers around, the way they click their tongues and disapprove of anything I do. What's that?" I point to the bag under her arm.

"For you." She hands it to me, looking pointedly at the untouched cardboard meat and carton of gelatin at the side of my bed. Hospital food deserves its reputation. "Thought you might be hungry." Inside are—hallelujah—two beef tacos.

"You're the best," I tell her, biting into a taco with a satisfactory crunch. I offer her the other one but she tells me she already ate. She sits on the bed next to me. I shock her with the news about my father's visit.

"Are you okay?" she asks.

"Yeah, I am. Surprisingly." I hesitate for a moment. I want to tell her that I'm not tied to my father anymore. But I can't say for sure that I'm over everything that happened, that I can leave it behind. "I think things will be better for me from now on," is all I can say.

She nods, smiling, though her lips seem to struggle to lift. I put the wrappers in my bag and take her hand. "You're exhausted."

She nods. "Long day, and I'm not looking forward to the drive back."

"Did you find Jen?" I ask.

"Yeah. I don't think it's her, though."

"What makes you think that?"

"Well, we followed her to a high school where she met

up with this guy. That's why she's always sneaking out. She doesn't want anyone to know, especially Nancy."

"Sam actually bought that?"

Liv smiles. "Yep. We both did."

I wait, but she doesn't say anything. I get the feeling she's toying with me. "That makes no sense. Why would Nancy care if she's seeing someone?"

"Well, the guy probably wouldn't meet Nancy's standards."

I grit my teeth. "Liv, I swear, if you don't tell me the damn story, I'm going to push this call button and have the nurse kick you out of here."

She laughs lightly and kisses me. "I doubt you'd do that." She leans back and threads her fingers through mine. I notice how warm they are, a welcome contrast to the cold room. "Jen is sneaking around with this guy because he's not just older like college older. I'm talking forties or fifties. He's a teacher."

I bark out a laugh, wincing when the pain shoots through my side. Liv jumps up, her face full of worry. "I'm sorry, I didn't mean to make you laugh."

Which makes me laugh again. "I'm fine," I gasp. "I guess I can see why she'd hide that. I hope she'll be happy now." I say that last part with sincerity. Hopefully, it means Jen is finally moving on. Though she's still not off my list. "Did you hear from Maggie?"

"Nope. We were busy tracking down Denise," she says. "Trying to figure out where Derrick was."

My heart sinks. The last thing I wanted her to do was track down the asshole who turned her last home into a nightmare. "What made you do that?"

She strokes her thumb along the outside of mine.

"Don't get upset. I thought there's a possibility he could be stalking me."

"He doesn't know where you live or your new last name."

She shakes her head. "I'm as smart as you are, Jack. You know you'd track him down, too. I know you're trying to keep me from getting hurt, but I'm not going to let him. And Sam was with me."

"So you found him?"

"We found Denise, who didn't seem surprised that he might be stalking me. I guess she'd caught him looking up stuff on the internet and hiring hookers."

"Hookers?"

She nods. "What a scumbag."

I close my eyes for a moment, and the image of Liv's teary face after Derrick hurt her comes to mind. The pain in my ribs is nothing compared to the pain I felt the day I found her crumpled on the bathroom floor at school, crying from what Derrick had done—or tried to do. She's right—I would've gone after him myself. And I wouldn't have let him walk away this time.

"So did you go to his house?" I ask, hoping the answer is no.

"Um, yeah." She toys with the blanket on the bed, not meeting my eyes.

"And?"

"He wasn't home, so Sam and I broke in and—"

"You *broke in*?" I jerk up, the pain jabbing again at my side. I try to ignore it. "What the hell did you guys do that for?"

"To see what he's up to, obviously. I needed to rule him out."

"I want you to stay away from him," I tell her firmly. "At least until I can go with you."

"Jack." She slides off the edge of the bed, her face looking like mine probably did after being interrogated for stealing money from the house—mad as hell. "I care about you more than anything. But you don't get to tell me what to do. And you have *got* to trust me. If you don't, I'm going to leave you here in the hospital, continue my own investigation without telling you anything, give my findings to the police, and only come back when it's all over. Got it?"

I reach for her hand but she steps away. "I don't want you to get hurt."

She huffs. "Because I'm a girl? *Really?* Do you remember who drove that car off the bridge and killed Bill? Not you."

I sigh. It's a losing battle, arguing with her. Liv's still the amazing, kick-ass girl I fell for, though, and I'm glad of that. "Fine. I'll keep my mouth shut."

"Good."

She smiles then, and my heart immediately responds, lifting in my chest and numbing all the pain around my ribs. Who needs painkillers when she's around?

"We figured if he knows that you and I put him on the sex offender list, then he'd be mad enough to come after us. But I found nothing on his computer. No searches that related to me, nothing at all. Except porn." She screws up her face in disgust.

"You aren't planning on going back there, right?" I ask nervously.

"Of course not. I'm done with him." She smiles a little. "It's weird, but I'm actually relieved to have done it. Like breaking in to his apartment helped me see he's just a pathetic person. Not a powerful monster who can hurt me, like in my dreams. I think all of that is behind me now."

I slide my fingers back through hers and pull her closer. "Just try to take Sam with you whenever you go investigate anything, okay?"

She cocks her head. "If you'll promise the same." She pops a carrot into her mouth from my untouched tray of food. "So the next step is figuring out who was with Frank."

"Look, I'm getting out of here tomorrow. We can do it together." I pause. "What's wrong?"

"Tomorrow's too late. If I don't get back soon, my grandfather will freak."

"Stay with me," I tell her. "Frank might be in Norfolk, waiting for you."

She smiles, which fades as she looks at her phone. "Crap. Emerson says Grandfather came by her house, and she told him I left already. I need to call him." She slumps back in the chair, her eyes on the ceiling. "He'll guess that I'm here. Maybe he'll kick me out. Send me back to foster care, since I suck as a granddaughter."

I carefully swing my legs over the side of the bed. "Liv, come here." I pat the space next to me, and she comes to sit at my side. I take her hand and hold it tightly. "He's not going to send you to foster care. You're every parent's and grandparent's dream, believe me."

"He doesn't tolerate lying," she says, the tears in her words rather than on her cheeks. "He'll know I'm a liar, just as terrible as my father. He's going to cut me out of his life, and I deserve it."

"No. You don't deserve that. You'll never deserve that. If he doesn't appreciate you for the amazing person you are, then something is wrong with him, not you. And you are *not* your father." *Like I'm not mine.*

She sighs and leans her head on my shoulder. Her phone buzzes, and she looks at the text. She holds it up to me so I can see the message from her grandfather. **You need to come home right now.** "I should've called him earlier."

She presses the contact for her grandfather, lifting the phone to her ear. A couple seconds later I can hear her grandfather answer.

"Grandfather, I—"

He's loud enough that I can hear him telling her to come home right away. She starts to say something else but he interrupts her, telling her again he'll talk with her when she's home. I hear the click on the other end. Liv stares at her phone. "I need to go," she says quietly. "I hate leaving you like this."

I squeeze her hand. "I'll be fine, don't worry about it. So will you."

She kisses me briefly, then she's gone. As glad as I am that she's not going to be tracking down some deranged stalker now, I have to admit I'm nervous for her. Annoyed, too. I know her grandfather doesn't like or trust me. He thinks I'm responsible for her getting kidnapped by Bill. Nothing I can ever do or say will change his mind, I'm sure of that. As much as I'm glad Liv found family—one that actually wants her—I hope she won't put up with that. She's strong, but if he pulls out the family card, or dangles Princeton in front of her, how much will she be able to take?

CHAPTER TWENTY-SEVEN

LIV

It sucks knowing that I screwed over the only family I have in the world. The guilt fits uncomfortably, yet familiarly, like an old shoe that's a size too small.

I wait for the truck in front of mine to move out of the parking lot so I can leave, but it doesn't budge. I press the horn, but the rear lights turn off. It occurs to me that the truck is dark—black or blue. *Does everyone drive a truck these days?* I can see the driver's door swing open and—crap—the guy is getting out. My heart is now playing a snare drum in my throat. I put my hand on the gear, ready to throw it in reverse. Could it be Frank?

As the person comes closer, I can tell it's not a man, but a woman bundled up in a coat and hat. She waves, her face apologetic. I take a deep breath, feeling like an idiot for freaking out like this. I roll down my window as she approaches.

"Do you need to call someone?" I ask.

"Already did," she says, waving her cell. She pulls her coat tighter. "I need to get a vehicle that doesn't collapse every time the temperature drops. Either that or move to Florida." She laughs, her breath coming out in huffs of smoke barely illuminated by the overhead lamps.

"Is someone coming to pick you up?"

"My son-in-law should be here in five minutes. He lives just a few blocks over. The car just needs some antifreeze and she'll be good as new. At least for a couple days." She nods toward the hospital. "My husband's in the hospital recovering from surgery. Thought I'd get him a real meal instead of the hospital food. Know of a burger place around here?"

Burgers? The only place that comes to mind is Burger Box. The very thought of it gives me shivers, even knowing Derrick's not the guy stalking me. And here I am, freaking out at the sight of a truck. This trip was supposed to help, but I have more anxiety than ever. Am I going to panic every time I see a dark truck from now on?

"You okay?" the woman asks.

"Um, I think there's a Burger King on the next street." I have no idea, but it's a busy street. She should find something. I'm already throwing my car into reverse. "I forgot something inside," I tell her. She wishes me luck and gets back into her truck while I return to the parking space I just vacated.

For a long moment I stare at my phone. If I do this, I'm probably wrecking any chance to patch up my relationship with my grandfather. But if I don't, if I go back, I'll end up sitting around the house all day, hoping the bad guys don't come in. Hoping they don't attack my grandfather or Mrs. Bedwin.

The idea of someone hurting either of them—

My chest tightens. Forget it. While this asshole is on the loose, I'm not allowing myself to be locked up at home, doing nothing.

I call my grandfather's number and wait.

"Olivia," he says gravely when he answers. "I assume you're calling to tell me that you are going to be detained in traffic for a few hours. Am I right?"

I take a deep breath. "No, but you're right about me not coming home just yet. I'm not going to lie to you about it, though."

"I fail to see the difference. I know you are in Richmond right now with that young man you already know I disapprove of. And driving your friend's car without regard to the fact that someone is trying to find you, possibly kill you."

I cringe at his businesslike voice. I may as well be one of his office staff. I've heard him do this on the phone when he's talking business. He's trying to scare me into saying something incriminating. It doesn't matter anyway. "I'm in Richmond, like you guessed. But I'm not here just for fun. One of my friends is in trouble—"

"Trouble as in drugs?"

Seriously? I keep my temper in check. "No. Trouble as in someone ran him off the road this morning, and he's in the hospital. That's why I came here."

"He can recover without your help. Have you forgotten that someone slashed up roses with a knife on your balcony? Yet you decide to pull one over on the detective who is trying to protect you and go hang out with your friends instead. This isn't a game, Olivia."

"Believe me, I know that. I told you, I'm not here to

goof off. I'm here because my friend is in the hospital."

"I know your friend is Jack, the very same boy who has come up here at least once before and whom you pretended not to have anything to do with. I'm not a fool, Olivia. I won't be lied to again. What exactly are you doing in Richmond?"

"I know it's hard, but you'll have to trust me," I tell him. "I can't tell you anything else."

"Olivia. if you want me to have even the slightest bit of faith in you again, you need to come home right now."

The words burn into my heart. I almost put the car in reverse and head back to Norfolk, tail between my legs. But images pop into my head of someone creeping around my house, waiting in the shadows until I fall asleep, or deciding to go directly to the source of my fortune—my grandfather—and holding him at gunpoint. Or shooting Mrs. Bedwin to get her out of the way—

I steel myself. "I can't. I'm sorry you don't trust me, but I can't just sit around the house, Grandfather. And Jack's family—"

"I'm thinking the word *family* is more like *gang*, am I right?"

My blood rushes faster through my veins at that one. "No."

"I think I'm going to launch an investigation into—"

"No, you will not do that," I tell him sharply, trying to keep the panic out of my voice.

"As your grandfather—"

"You should love me enough to understand that I can't just wipe away my past." My voice is rising, and tears are sliding down my cheeks. I'm losing control, but I don't care. "I know you think I'm acting like my father would, and that

I'm a bad person because of it. You think that the only thing that could possibly redeem me is the half of me that is my mother, but you didn't know much about her, either."

"Olivia…"

"Do you know what happened to me when your precious daughter Aggie died?" I continue relentlessly. "She collapsed in the middle of the street in the worst part of town, with her pimp standing over us, watching her body convulse with drugs. I remember crying over her dead body, begging her to wake up. I was in foster care for *years* after that. You have no idea what that's like. I've lived through more hell than I will ever tell you or any lame therapist. I'm your granddaughter, but that doesn't mean you know everything about me. And it doesn't mean you own me."

I brush the angry tears from my cheek. I hate reliving those memories as much as I hate throwing them in his face. "I love you, Grandfather. If you love me like you say you do, you'll let me do this. I'm not here partying or getting into trouble. I'm here with one of the very few people who actually gave a crap about me in my life, okay? The one who turned me over to the only family I had when I didn't even know it existed. It's because of Jack that I came to live with you in the first place."

Another pause, and this time his voice is subdued. "I don't think there's an easy answer to any of this, Olivia. For either of us. I want what's best for you, and I don't believe this is it. We will continue this discussion when you are back home." He pauses for a moment. "I do love you. Be safe."

He hangs up. I drop the phone in my lap, leaning back on the headrest and letting the tears fall freely. The conversation didn't go exactly as I expected, and I don't know if that's a good thing or bad. He won't send the PI after me, I don't think. But this wasn't the end of it as far as he's concerned. In my mind, I picture armed security guards outside my window and door day and night as well as my car keys being locked up. At the very least, he'll set a strict curfew, which is fine with me. Not like I stay out late partying anyway.

Guilt jabs at my gut, but with it comes a strange sense of relief. I've always let him think the best about his daughter. I never wanted him to know the real story of how I ended up in foster care. I never intended to make him feel bad about what happened when my mother ran away from home. But now that he knows, maybe he'll understand I'll never be the perfect angel granddaughter he hoped I'd be. But neither will I be the thug troublemaker he thinks of my father as.

Maybe eventually he'll learn to appreciate that I'm just me, Olivia.

I swallow the bitter taste from the conversation and start to get out of the car, then stop. Jack can't help me from here. All that I'll accomplish by going upstairs is to get him worried again about my investigation.

Instead, I drive to the house on Briarcreek. Sam is waiting for me when I arrive. Many of the other kids are home, too, staring at me like I just flew in from Mars. "I told them you were on your way over," she tells me in a whisper as she takes my coat and hangs it on a hook next to the door. "They want to see what you're planning to do."

"Do?" *Uh-oh.* Dutch is staring at me with wide eyes. Remembering his close relationship with his "big brother," I smile at him. "Z is doing fine. I think he'll be able to come home tomorrow."

Dutch smiles, relieved. In fact, the entire room relaxes. A glance at Sam's approving face tells me that was the perfect thing to say. I know how much Jack means to everyone here, and the words coming from me probably mean more than from Nancy, who'd say anything to keep them from worrying. I gaze around the room and notice Maggie sitting next to Micah on the sofa, her arms around her legs. Instead of looking at me like everyone else, her eyes are focused on the ground. She reminds me of Eponine when Grandfather took me to see *Les Miserables*—thin, sad, and lost.

She looks up and sees me staring at her. Immediately, she stands and heads upstairs.

"Want to go to my room?" Sam asks. I nod and follow her upstairs. She stops in front of one of the first doors. "I'll go see if we have any spare toothbrushes. You can look in Z's closet for a T-shirt to wear. And in his dresser for underwear."

She giggles and opens the door for me. Jack's room is small, very much like the one at Monroe Street, with the scent of spice and leather that makes all my nerve endings go on high alert. I sit on his bed and run my hand along his rumpled bedspread, wishing more than anything that he were here. The guy I should've known better than to trust is the one I ended up trusting more than anyone. Funny.

I text him. I'm sitting on your bed.

His response is almost immediate. You're killing me.

Grinning, I put the phone away. Sam comes back with a brand-new toothbrush and hands it to me. I notice the sound of sobbing coming from down the hall. Doesn't take a genius to know it's Maggie.

"Does she cry like that a lot?" I ask Sam, who rolls her eyes.

"Like all the freaking time. She's been a total zombie since Z got hit. Nancy's worried about her. I think we spend half our time these days worried about Maggie."

"I wonder if there's anything else going on that we don't know about."

Sam's eyebrows lift. "Like…?"

I lean back on my elbows. "She's that upset all the time but more lately, right?"

"Yeah, but you aren't suggesting she was in on the plot to run Z off the road, are you? She's all about that guy."

I shake my head. "But maybe she knows who did. Or maybe she knows who broke in to your bank account here. Maybe someone's blackmailing her, and she can't say anything."

Sam tilts her head, thinking about that. "It's possible, I guess. Sometimes she looks like she's dying to say something. But she's not close enough to anyone here in the house to spill secrets to. Except Z."

"Maybe we should try talking to her," I suggest. I know I'm not Maggie's favorite person, but could it really hurt?

Sam nods slowly. "We have to be careful, though. Nancy thinks Maggie's on the verge of a breakdown. Her roommate Sunny told Nancy she wants to move out because she's sick of Maggie crying all the time. I think she might snap if we so much as look at her funny."

Sam gestures at me, and I follow her down the hallway to Maggie's open door. She's sitting on her bed, her forehead scrunched as she stares at her phone. The room is pretty and clean. It reminds me of a little girl's room, pink and ruffly with stuffed animals on the bed. Well, one side does. The other side is more normal for a teen, with a red and gold bedspread and a lava lamp. Interesting contrast.

I wonder what Sunny thinks of all the ruffles and stuffed animals.

"Hi, Maggie," Sam says brightly. Maggie's eyes snap up to meet us, her face grim.

"What do you want?" she asks, her voice tinged with both tears and suspicion. She shoves her phone under her legs.

"We just wanted to see if you're okay." Sam walks in and perches on the other bed, opposite Maggie. "Is there anything we can do for you?"

Maggie doesn't say anything, but her gaze moves to me. A weird sense of recognition jabs at me, like I've seen her somewhere recently. And unlike Jen's icy glare, Maggie's eyes are empty, like her soul has already fled her body for another host.

I think I prefer Jen's glare.

"Z's going to be okay," I tell Maggie, and it sounds weak and lame.

"Well, that depends on the MRI," Sam says. I look sharply at her. Why would she give Maggie more grief?

Maggie's face pales. "MRI?"

Sam nods. "I mean, hopefully he's okay, but I don't know…"

Maggie looks down at her lap, a tear slowly rolling down her cheek. The girl is a tear factory, that's for sure. "I have to go see him," she says so softly, I wonder if she's talking to us or herself. She wipes the back of her hand across her cheek. "Right now."

Sam nods and stands, patting Maggie's shoulder. "I'm here if you need me."

She steps out, and I follow. As soon as we get to Sam's room, I turn to her but she holds a finger to her lips. About two minutes later, Maggie walks by. The sound of a motor starting outside draws us to the window, and we watch as her little white car drives away from the warm lights of the house.

"Why did you do that?" I ask Sam, expecting Sam to laugh as she usually does. But Sam's expression is unusually serious.

"I didn't mean to hurt her," she says calmly. "But if I didn't say something drastic, she would just sit there forever, drowning in her tears. Nancy's at the hospital still and can keep an eye on her. Z needs us to figure this out before someone ends up killing him."

That one word shocks my heart into action. "So now we check her room?"

She nods. "Exactly. Sunny isn't home right now, either, so this is probably the only chance we'll get."

Sam takes my hand and pulls me down the hallway, keeping her back against the wall like we're sneaking up on somebody, *Mission: Impossible* style. We couldn't look any more obvious if we tried. Thankfully, nobody walks by.

Sam opens the door and pulls it closed behind us, locking it quietly. She flips on the light and goes to Maggie's desk while I move to her dresser. The only contents in the drawers are clothes, neatly folded and stacked. I run my hand along the bottom of each one, fully expecting to find a diary and kind of hoping I don't, but there's nothing. Sam closes the desk drawers and heads toward the closet while I get on my knees to look under the bed. In the far back corner are three boxes. I lie flat on my belly and pull them out. They're all shoeboxes. I open the first to see a pair of sandals. This search is going nowhere. I flip the lids off the next two.

One has a pair of strappy silver heels. The other has a layer of tissue paper, and underneath are— *Oh, boy.*

"Um, Sam, get over here."

Sam kneels next to me and stares at the assortment of pictures in the box. They're all of Maggie, taken at a time when she looked a lot better than she does now. One in particular catches my eye—Maggie is leaning against a rail, wearing a blue knit hat and gray coat. Beautiful face full of life, her curly hair shining, her eyes glowing and happy. Her gaze is on whomever had an arm around her, but the photo has been cut down the middle and only the arm is showing. I pick up another photo and another—in all of them, the person on the other half is missing except for the occasional hand or glimpse of clothing.

"Where are the other halves?" Sam whispers. She brushes the tissue paper aside and lifts out a long white jewelry box. I take it from her and open it. "Holy shit," Sam whispers, giggling nervously. She lifts the stack of half-pictures that are tied with a pink ribbon. The one on top is Jack, wearing dark aviator glasses and looking like he's kicked back in a chair. I untie the ribbon and fan the pictures in my hand, my stomach churning at the sight of Jack in each one. All different pictures taken on different days.

"Obviously, we can see which half Maggie values most," Sam says quietly. She fits two halves together— Maggie perched on Jack's lap. My stomach churns to see it. "Creepy," Sam adds.

But it's not the picture that has my attention now.

Familiar gold swirling letters line the inside of the empty jewelry box: *A&P.*

CHAPTER TWENTY-EIGHT

JACK

Something's been chewing at the back of my mind ever since Liv left, but I can't figure it out. I run through the conversation with her, but it slips around my mind.

Maggie shows up a few minutes after Nancy left for the night.

"Hey." I put my phone aside and turn off the TV. With as much technology as they put into hospitals, you'd think they'd offer more than three network channels plus the Home Shopping Network.

"How are you feeling?" she asks quietly, not moving from the door.

"I'm okay. Didn't Liv and Sam tell you I'm going home tomorrow?" I cough and groan as the pain shoots through my side. The more I try not to move or cough, the more my body decides it must.

She moves closer. "They told everyone that, yeah. But—" A tear runs down her cheek as she stares at me.

"But what?"

"Sam told me about your MRI." She sniffles, taking a tissue from the box next to my bed to blow her nose. "I am *so* sorry."

MRI? It's on the tip of my tongue to tell her Sam is full of it, but then Sam wouldn't have said it if there wasn't a good reason.

"Why are you looking at me like that?" she asks, her hands twisting. I notice her chest is moving faster. *Oh, shit. Maggie, what are you up to?*

I smile at her and pat the side of my bed. "Nothing. Come sit down."

She perches on the mattress, her eyes fixed on my T-shirt. I lift it up to give her a full view of the horrible-looking bruise on my ribcage and the bandage that covers my surgery. She reaches out with a finger as if to touch it, but I drop the hem back down. "That looks really bad." Her voice is shaking.

I wince, pretending the pain is getting worse. "Yeah, it is."

Another tear. I take her trembling hand. "You look worried."

"I don't like to see you in pain." Her gaze drops, her eyebrows pinching slightly.

"I know you don't," I tell her. "You would never hurt me. But it'd be really helpful if you could tell me who did."

Her lips part slightly as she stares at me.

"You can tell me, Maggie," I say softly. "I won't hurt you or yell at you, I promise. Who did this? Frank?"

She gasps slightly at his name, but she doesn't take her watering eyes off me. I reach up to wipe a tear with a finger. Her eyes widen, and she lifts her own hand to touch mine.

The moment feels so sappy, but so necessary.

"Someone almost killed me." I wince again, grabbing at my side, causing her to gasp. "And whoever it is won't be happy that I'm alive. He might be outside the door right now, waiting for me to fall asleep so he can strangle me."

Her hand lifts to her mouth, her eyes wide with fear. Her sweater sweeps back on her arm, and I notice a flash of jewelry on her wrist. My attempt to be the pathetic patient fails as I reach out to clasp her hand. "Where'd you get this?" I ask, unable to stop the rough words once they've escaped my lips.

She yanks her arm away. "Nowhere. I've had it."

She's a terrible liar. "Maggie," I say in a calmer voice. "Did you go in my room to get that bracelet?"

"No! I didn't steal this from you. It's mine."

"Who gave it to you?"

Her eyes skip guiltily away.

"That bracelet is the one that was sent to Liv," I tell her. "Maybe you found it on the floor in my room or something—"

"No!" She jumps to her feet, her chest moving quickly now. "It's not yours. It's not *hers*." She almost spits the last word.

My heart is racing as fast as my thoughts. Maggie's totally gone off the deep end. I wouldn't be surprised if she pulled out a doll with Liv's face and a pin in it.

The nurse walks in. "Everything okay?" she asks, noticing the tension between Maggie and me. "Young lady, visiting hours are about over. You can come back in the morning."

"Yes, ma'am," Maggie says contritely, backing away as the nurse comes to my side and checks the machines behind me. "I'll see you tomorrow," Maggie tells me from behind the woman. It's like we were just talking about the weather, as calm as her voice is.

"Maggie, wait." But she's gone. Dammit. This is ridiculous—I'm stuck in this bed while Maggie goes crazy.

I tell the nurse I'd like to discharge myself. She tries arguing with me, then tells me her hands are tied until the doctor comes in again to sign off on my paperwork, which won't be until morning anyway. Great. She putters around checking my vitals for way too long. I pretend to fall asleep as she moves about. As soon as the light in the room darkens and the nurse leaves, I'm up again, flicking on the light and considering the IV. I grit my teeth and rip the tape off my arm, then slide out the needle. It doesn't really hurt. Even without the IV, it takes me longer than I thought it would to get into the change of clothes Nancy brought me—moving around with a bruised rib hurts like a bitch. I hate sweatpants, but at the moment, I'm glad for them.

I pull on my jacket, kind of sad to see it so scratched and torn from the accident. I've had it for a long time. I put my hands in the pockets, noticing something hard. I take a sharp breath as I pull out a bracelet—Liv's bracelet. Now I remember—I'd put it in my pocket after Jen showed it to Nancy.

But if I have the bracelet…

Two bracelets were purchased. Two—one for Liv, the other for Maggie.

Shit.

I move to the side table to get my phone. It's not where I left it.

I glance around quickly to see if it fell off the table or onto my mattress. No sign of it.

Maggie took my phone.

The world swirls around, and everything slowly falls into place. What an idiot I am. Maggie always in my room, pretending to need comforting when she was probably digging up whatever she could on Liv. She might've even stolen my debit card information to buy the bracelets. Put a wig on to make it look like she's Jen. I can't see her climbing up the window to Liv's room, but I bet she knows who did it, and I bet I know who it is, too.

And she could've been the person on the inside of the house, helping Frank figure out how to hack into our accounts. That could make sense as to why mine was left alone, too.

My heart nothing more than a brick in my chest, I pick up the hospital phone and call my cell, but no one answers. It doesn't go straight to voicemail—I'm sure Maggie can see I'm calling it. I dial it again and again, but she doesn't answer. I don't know Liv's number from memory, so I call Sam instead.

"I need to talk to Maggie," I say before she even says hello.

"She's not here. Why, what happened? And what number are you calling me from?"

I look at the clock on the wall. Maggie left about twenty minutes ago. It only takes ten to get to Briarcreek from here. "Maggie stole my phone. Listen, I'm coming home now. As soon as Maggie gets there, you and Liv don't let her leave. Keep her distracted or something. I'm going to call Nancy, too."

Dead silence on the other end. "Sam?"

"Liv's not here." Her quiet voice makes my throat tighten. "She…she said you texted her to meet you."

All the pain in my ribs disappears as my body goes completely numb. I lean against the bed. "Where?" I manage to choke out.

"I…I don't know," Sam says. "She just said you texted her to come see you alone, so I assumed she was going up to the hospital to be with you and *ohmygod* are you saying you didn't? Z, are you there?"

"Tell Nancy," I finally manage to say. "Have her call Jim and run a trace on my phone right away."

"What are you going to do?" she asks quickly. "Do you want me to come get you?"

Good question. I have no car, no phone, and no way of knowing how the hell to find them. "Stay there in case she shows up. I'll figure out something. You still have Liv's number in your phone, right?"

I write down Liv's number and hang up, then call her. It goes straight to voicemail. I leave a frantic message, begging her to call Sam and to go back to Briarcreek. I dial her again and again, but it goes straight to voicemail. I slam down the phone, jerking my hand back when it rings.

"Hello?"

There's a long pause. Then, "Z?"

"Maggie, where are you?" I try to keep my voice calm but it's damn near impossible when all I want to do is scream at her.

"You know I wouldn't hurt you."

"Maggie! Where's Liv? Where are you?"

"Don't be mad at me, please," she says, each word shaking like she's already been crying.

I take a shaky breath. "I'm not mad at you. Where are you?"

"You can still save her," she whispers. "You need to

come back home. Where we were happy *together*."

She hangs up. I call back, but now my number goes to voicemail. *Damn it.* I call Nancy myself and warn her about Maggie, asking her to get a hold of Jim Rush. Like Sam, she begs me to wait so someone can pick me up, but I don't have time for that.

I've never sneaked out of a hospital before. Unfortunately, the nurse's station is between my room and the exit. Several nurses are gathered around the desk, chatting casually. The fact that they're laughing while Liv's life is in danger makes me want to throw something. I look around and see another patient walking toward me. An older hippie-looking man with a long beard and a scarf around his head. I reach into my pocket and pull out my wallet. "Hey," I whisper, waving a hand. The man moves his walker my way. "Want to make a quick twenty bucks?"

Two minutes later, the man is screaming in pain at the opposite side of the hall, causing all the nurses to run to his side. I move quickly out the double doors, trying not to look like I'm anything more than a visitor here. Nobody stops me, and I'm soon outside the hospital, sliding carefully into the cab that I'd called earlier.

I can feel the nerves pinching around my ribs as I give the driver my Briarcreek address, but only barely—fear really does dull pain. I don't know what Maggie's up to. She's not capable of murder, I'm pretty sure, but whoever she's working with might be. I replay in my head every conversation I've had with Nancy, with Liv, with Maggie. And there's something that nags like a tiny marble rattling around my brain. Something Liv said she heard when she went to visit Denise about Derrick seeing hookers.

I jolt upright, ignoring the pain. The pieces finally join

together to form an evil picture in my mind. How did I not figure this one out before?

Immediately it hits me—*home where we were happy together*—for Maggie, that isn't Briarcreek. "Turn around," I tell the driver sharply. "We're headed to a different address."

CHAPTER TWENTY-NINE

LIV

The huge Monroe Street house looms in front of me, nothing but a shadowy outline set back too far to be lit by the streetlights. It's abandoned and has been for eight months. Makes me sad to see such a beautiful house reduced to shadows. Even though there are dark memories, too, I can't help but remember the warm laughter and family I found in this place, even for a brief time.

A soft glow comes from the front of the house. As I approach, I can see it's from large white candles set on either side of the steps. The text from Jack at first said to come alone to the hospital right away, but halfway there I got another text telling me he'd checked out and to meet him at 1605 Monroe Street. I shiver slightly. What is he thinking, getting out of the hospital early just to meet me here? If this is his attempt at a romantic gesture…just, no. Something stirs inside me, a warning, where I can almost hear spooky music playing before the masked murderer comes around the corner with an ax.

"Don't be ridiculous," I say aloud. Saying it does nothing to keep the goose bumps from popping up all over my skin.

I step between the candles, noticing the door is already slightly open. A soft light spills out through the crack. Pushing the door wider, I notice a line of candles leading from the foyer and around to the living room. A little farther in and there are white rose petals scattered along the line. My heart beats uncomfortably fast, my steps echoing in the empty house as I move around the pillar to see where the candles and roses end. But it's not Jack standing in the ring of candles.

Maggie is holding a single rose, smiling sweetly at me.

Oh, shit. "Maggie. What are you doing here?"

"Being romantic." She waves her arms at the line of candles and roses. "Don't you like it?"

"Sure," I say as calmly as I can. The girl is clearly out of her mind. "It's very nice. But where is Z?"

"He'll be along soon. If you have to know, this wasn't my idea." She kicks at the trail of rose petals on the floor, her nose scrunched in disgust. I notice her voice is stronger than before when I saw her at the house. She isn't looking as meek and afraid as she did before, either.

"Whose idea was it?" I ask.

Maggie cocks her head to one side. "I am curious about what they see in you. You're not *that* pretty. Are you smart?"

They? I shrug. "Not that smart. You say this wasn't your idea?"

"I always thought you were just Z's rebound after Jen. Did you know she was his rebound from me?" She sighs, staring at the rose in her hand. "I told him if he stayed with me I wouldn't go with Bill. I would've been his forever. I think his feelings for me scared him. That's why he broke up with me."

"That makes sense," I say carefully, pulling my phone out of my pocket. I unlock it with my thumb and glance down to press the call button.

"Don't bother," she says. "Your signal is jammed."

Of course. "Does Z know you set up these candles for me?"

"Like I said, this wasn't my idea." She narrows her eyes. "Z doesn't love you, you know. He doesn't love anyone. Not even himself. How could he love us if he can't even love himself?" she adds softly, her fingers fiddling with something around her wrist. I stare at the familiar gold band, emeralds glinting softly in the candlelight.

"Maggie, is that the bracelet that was sent to me?"

She presses her arm to her chest. "This is *my* bracelet. Yours was nothing but a means to an end."

"And what's the end?" I ask. "Are you planning to kill me?"

Her face clouds over, and for a moment my heart plunges to my shoes. Then she shakes her head. "I thought about it, you know. I was supposed to just leave the rose and the bracelet and go, but you were just *there*, sleeping. I couldn't figure out why Z wanted *you*. I hated you right then more than I've ever hated anyone, even Jen. He used Jen as much as he used me."

"So why didn't you?" The words come out almost strangled-sounding, probably because I'm sure I haven't swallowed since the moment I stepped into Maggie's crazy trail of candles.

"I can't kill somebody. Even if I do hate you," she says. "You were supposed to think it was Z after you. You were supposed to turn him in to the police, start the paper trail against him. You're an idiot for not doing that, you know."

This is making less and less sense. "How did you get into my car and into my house?" I ask.

"Climbed up the vines to your balcony. It was easy. And amplifiers work wonders for getting into fancy locked cars."

She laughs then, a strong, proud sound, and I can't help but admire the front she put on this whole time. She had everyone fooled, especially Jack. I'm pretty sure the whole plan wasn't just about turning me against him. The paper trail—she's trying to frame him for something, but what? What would she gain from setting up the guy she obviously loves?

"Who are you working with, Maggie? Frank?"

She laughs again. "That was an easy one to set up. Sort of an afterthought once I found out you guys suspected him. You're too easy to fool."

I stare at Maggie's curly hair, bouncing on her shoulders as she laughs, and suddenly everything clicks. I know where I've seen her recently.

God, please no.

"Maggie, this guy who tried to kill Z is someone you knew when you worked for Bill, isn't it? A customer?"

Her smile grows across her face slowly, a Cheshire cat's grin.

He's here. I can see it in the lift of her chin.

The cold confidence that someone's got her back.

Running away isn't an option for me—even if my feet weren't rooted to the ground, my knees literally knocking against each other in terror, I wouldn't make it very far before he'd catch me.

I can't let him catch me.

This girl might be my only chance now.

"Maggie." I force my feet to rise and fall until I'm standing in her circle of candlelight. She stares at me, her face void of emotion. "Listen. You said it yourself—you're not a killer. You're not a bad person. The person who's making you do this is no better than Bill Sykes. He's using you to get to me."

She scowls at that. "What do you know about it? You, with your privileged life and perfect house. You don't know what it's like to have nothing and no one, even in your crappy foster life. I found one person—*one*—who wants me for me. Who treats me like a real person, even a friend, instead of a whore. So I'll go where he goes and do what he wants because he at least treats me like a human being. He needs me. We'll go live on a beach in Mexico together with the money from those jerks over at Briarcreek."

"I wouldn't count on it," I say, trying a different tactic. "He tried to kill Z by running him off the road. Z almost died." She flinches at that. Jack is still her weakness, no matter what she says. "If you think that Derrick will let him live, you're wrong. And if you think he cares more about you than himself, you're wrong again. I lived in his house, remember? I know."

Maggie doesn't say anything, just holds the rose between us, the stem clenched in her fist like it's a weapon. I hear a slam behind me and whip around to see Jack walking toward me quickly, his jaw set so hard I know he's clenching his teeth. I don't remember him ever looking this mad. I breathe out, both relieved and worried that he's here. He's a target, too, and now that we're together, who knows what she and Derrick will do. I hope he called the police before he came here, but Maggie has his phone, and in the state he's in, I could see him just rushing here without calling anyone.

"Z," Maggie says sweetly. "Come in."

"Maggie, what are you doing?" he asks, his voice shaking with anger. "This shit needs to stop now."

"Shut up," she says harshly. "You've never, ever believed in me. Do you remember when you first brought me to Monroe Street? I had already hacked into two banks. You told me I was as good as you. You don't remember that, do you? All you remember is sad, crying Maggie, who was nothing but a joke to you and Sam. I heard you talking about me."

"We talked about you because we were worried about you," he said, his voice crisp.

"You used me, pretended to love me when the whole time you thought I was just a stupid, pathetic girl who couldn't hack. I showed you. I showed you all."

"Maggie—"

"Actually," she says in a lighter voice, "you should be grateful for me. I'm the reason you're still alive, you know."

"I almost wasn't," he says, placing a hand on his ribs.

"That wasn't my idea," she mutters.

"Where's Derrick?" Jack asks.

"Right here," a chillingly familiar voice says before I have a chance to wonder how Jack knew it was Derrick. My entire body trembles as I turn to face the most horrible person in my life. This man, who once welcomed me into his home when I was a hapless foster kid, is now pointing a gun at me. Derrick looks so different from when I lived on Green Valley Drive. His hair is longer, pulled back and tied behind his neck, and he's got scruff around his face like he hasn't shaved in a week or so. But the worst part is the look in his eyes. Once kind (or so it seemed), his hard gaze cuts me. And when he turns his eyes on Jack, they go flat entirely.

"Well, well, well, if it isn't the infamous Z, the whiz kid who thinks he can ruin a person's life with one keystroke," Derrick croons softly.

The revulsion rises into my throat.

"Maggie," I whisper urgently to her. Her eyes flick to me, void of any emotion. "Derrick isn't kind. He's a monster. He tried to rape me. He'll do the same to you."

Maggie's hand flies toward my face, smacking my cheek hard enough to make me stumble backward. Jack starts forward, his jaw set fiercely. I have to grip his arm to keep him from losing it. "Don't." No way is he playing the protective hero, especially when I'm pretty sure that Derrick would rather kick his ass than mine. My face burns where she made contact, but I don't reach up to rub it.

Derrick laughs. "That's my girl," he says fondly to Maggie. She beams back at him. Derrick waves his gun toward us. "So let's start by separating you two lovebirds." His eyes rake over me, and a horrible sensation of loathing slides through me.

"I'll take her," Maggie says quickly, and I wonder if she senses his ulterior motive. Maggie grabs my arm and pulls at me, forcing me into a chair inside the ring of candles. I don't fight and neither does Jack—what can we do when a gun is pointed directly at us? And the police—they thought it was Frank doing this. Sam will send them directly to his house. I'm guessing Derrick and Maggie forged a phone under Frank's name to set him up.

"Derrick, let her go," Jack growls as Maggie ties my hands behind my back with a cable. She pulls it tight, but I press my fists together hard to keep my wrists as far from each other as I can. "You've already stolen money from our house, so what's the point?"

Derrick laughs. "The point? Well, for one, you haven't paid *your* debt to me. Putting me on the sex offenders' list— pretty ingenious. But considering it's opened up a whole host of problems for me, I thought I'd return the favor."

Jack looks over at Maggie. "You did this from my computer in my own room so everyone would think I did it, didn't you? When I trusted you more than anyone else." His voice is surprisingly soft, though his eyes flash with anger. As Maggie starts forward, it's obvious Jack knows how to get under her skin. She jerks to a stop when Derrick barks at her to stand still.

"It was the only way I could do it," Maggie says, and now her voice has a slight pleading tone to it. "The only way it couldn't be traced to him. You understand that, right?" After all of this, she's still looking for Jack's approval.

"That's enough!" Derrick backs his way over to me, keeping the gun pointing straight at Jack. He then presses the cold barrel to my temple. My eyes stay on Jack's, watching as his anger turns to fear. I can see his chest moving rapidly now. *Don't panic,* I try to tell him with my gaze. *Please don't panic and do something stupid.*

"Put the cuffs on him, Maggie," Derrick says. "In front."

Nodding, Maggie takes a pair of handcuffs from a bag on the floor and walks back to Jack. He's saying something to her in a soft voice, but I can't make it out. His wide eyes stay on me, though, and the gun pointed at my head.

"No talking," Derrick snaps. Obviously he doesn't trust Maggie around Jack. As far as Maggie trusting Derrick, that doesn't surprise me. I did for a while, too.

"How did you even end up together?" I ask, though I already know. At this point, with our cell phone signals jammed and no one knowing where we are, I can only hope to stall whatever he's planning. Maybe he'll say something that will turn Maggie against him. I still think that, given the choice, she'd rather be with her beloved Z than Derrick.

"Maggie and I have been friends for a while," he says. "She took care of me when Denise wouldn't."

I bite my lip to keep from gagging. "How did you know Maggie knew Z?"

"I dropped her off one day and saw his bike in the driveway. Recognized it from before, when you lived with me. And Maggie told me all about how he helped you find a new life with your sugar grandpa. And then all of a sudden, I have a sexual predator knock against my record. Didn't take me long to put two and two together."

"You deserved it," I say.

"My beautiful, smart Maggie," he continues as if I hadn't said anything. Maggie looks over at him, beaming. "She stopped by my house earlier today. Said it looked like someone had been in there. Know something about that?"

The white car parked in front of Derrick's duplex when we left—it was Maggie's. And we were so caught up in being relieved there wasn't a black truck that Sam didn't even notice. "I know you're a scumbag, addicted to porn," I tell him. "I saw a video that you took of Maggie, too."

Maggie laughs. "If you think you're outing him, you're not," she says.

She knew she was being filmed—great. There's got to

be something that will turn Maggie against Derrick. "You know, Denise knew about you cheating on her," I tell Derrick. "She knew what you were up to with the cameras you installed in my room, too."

Maggie looks sharply at me, then Derrick. She's not laughing now. "Cameras?"

"He was spying on me, watching me undress when I—"

"Shut up," Derrick says, pressing the gun against my temple so hard that I have to squirm away to relieve the pressure.

"Stop, Derrick. Leave her alone, and I'll do whatever you want," Jack says sharply, his fists clenched through the handcuffs. I can tell he's trying hard not to lose it. I try to look calm, for his sake as much as mine. Easier said than done.

"Maggie, get the laptop," Derrick orders.

Of all the possibilities swimming through my head, this is the last thing I expected to hear. Is he wanting Jack to transfer money into his bank account? That would mean he'd have to shoot us both, since it'd be easy to stop the transfer before it goes through.

Maggie brings a laptop and a tray table over and sets them up in front of Jack. His brows pinch together in confusion. "You brought my own laptop here?" Then his jaw sets as he stares at me. I get it, too. They want him to break into a bank account from his own computer so it traces back to him.

"I've got an account pinpointed right here." She smiles at Derrick as she flips open the top. Jack's face pales. "You've been looking at this ICL page a lot. I'm sure no one will be surprised when a million dollars goes missing."

"Derrick, the police will be here any second," Jack says

calmly, though I can tell by the quick rise and fall of his chest that he's nervous. "You can take what's in my wallet, leave right now, and no one will find you."

"Your wallet?" Derrick snorts. "Right. And I know they won't find me, *Jack*. Oh, yes. I know your name. I've been tracking your conversations for a while. I'm just as clever as you."

"*We're* just as clever," Maggie pipes up, glaring at Derrick. "I'm the one who did all the work. And it was my idea to disguise ourselves at the jewelry store." She smirks at me. "They totally thought I was Jen."

"Right, you wore a blond wig. That made *all* the difference," Derrick says in exaggerated praise, rolling his eyes. "But if you'd done like I told you and hidden that bracelet, they wouldn't have suspected you in the first place."

"If you hadn't run Z off the road," Maggie yells, "we could've followed the original plan and gone through ICL from his computer ourselves. *She* wouldn't even be here right now. You've screwed everything up, and now look where we are!"

I watch their bickering like a tennis match, the entire time working at the cable holding my hands captive behind my back. My arms ache, and my wrists are sore and probably bleeding, but I keep them moving.

Derrick holds up a hand. "This is getting us nowhere. Party time, tough guy," he says to Jack.

"You are insane if you think this will work," Jack says. "They'll track you down right away and stop the transfer."

"You mean they'll track *you* down." Derrick sighs. "Which will be really sad, especially because you won't be able to defend yourself after your little accident."

"Derrick," Maggie says sharply. "You promised."

Derrick shrugs and smiles at her benevolently. "I promised I'd do everything I could to protect our future, sweetheart. And that's what I'm going to do." Derrick gestures at the laptop screen.

Jack stares at it, his eyes flicking to catch mine as Derrick backs up toward me. I close my eyes as a series of clicks sounds next to my head. Derrick strokes the gun against my head in a caressing way that makes me choke back a gag. He's really loving this. All I can hope is that he wants to make this moment last as long as possible. Long enough for us to figure a way out. "It'd be so easy to pull the trigger. Just the slightest twitch and our beautiful Olivia will be gone."

"Okay, okay," Jack says quickly, his hands shaking as they move to the keyboard. It doesn't do anything for my nerves. I swallow hard, imagining what the bullet would feel like when it punctures my brain. The pain will be sharp and fast. Like ripping off a Band-Aid, except when the Band-Aid is gone, I'll be dead. I work at the bindings around my wrists, keeping each movement tiny so as not to attract attention.

Jack's fingers move slowly over the keys. He's sweating now, even in the chill. He must know as much as I do that there's no way Derrick's going to let either of us live after this.

Maggie bites her lip nervously as she stares at Derrick, obviously thinking the same thing. She doesn't care about me, but killing Jack wasn't in her plan.

"Why did you buy me a bracelet?" I ask, trying to buy time.

"Figured you'd suspect your ex-boyfriend. Get the police on him. Easy as cake." Derrick doesn't take his eyes off Jack. "The police will have no trouble buying in to the fact that he stole this money. It'll be too late by the time they find you both here. The ex-girlfriend he was trying to lure here and shot when she realized what he was up to. Just before he killed himself."

My wrists are painfully raw now from trying to slide out of my bonds, but I finally manage to slip one hand over the other. Keeping my hands behind me, I wait until Derrick and Maggie are both completely caught up with whatever Jack's doing. I slide out of the chair and put my hands on the back, lifting it as quietly as I can.

Unfortunately, Derrick sees my shadow and whips around, his eyes widening to see me holding the chair. Without getting the momentum I need, I swing the chair at him as hard as I can. He doesn't fall, but the gun does. He dives for it even as I bring the chair down again on his back. Jack lunges for him at the same time, his hands still handcuffed in front of him. Unfortunately, Derrick's foot makes contact with Jack's ribs, sending Jack howling in pain to the floor. Everyone scrambles—a confusing mess of chairs and bodies. Derrick manages to pin me down, his elbow pressing hard into my shoulder. His breath is stale, making my stomach lurch. Jack shoves him off me, and Derrick turns on him, his hand wrapping around Jack's throat. I throw myself at Derrick, trying to wrench his hands from Jack's neck.

A shot blasts the air above us. "Stop," Maggie calls out. She points the gun down at us, her hand shaking so hard I'm pretty sure one of us will end up with the bullet.

"What are you doing, Maggie?" Derrick growls. Jack rolls to his side, gasping, his face screwed up in pain. I crawl over to him quickly. Maggie backs up and turns the gun on

Derrick, then on me, then back to Derrick. *Oh, lord. Pick a person.*

"Give me that gun, Maggie," Derrick says, his voice coldly calm. She keeps the gun fixed on him.

"We were supposed to get the money and tie them up and leave. That's what you told me," she says shakily, tears rolling down her cheeks. "Not kill him."

"It's okay, sweetheart," Derrick coos softly. He reaches for the gun but drops his hand as Maggie backs up, her gun firmly pointed toward his heart. "It's gonna be okay. I'll take care of you. Didn't I promise you that? Haven't I been there for you when no one else was? Z's the one you hate. He's the one you said you wanted to get back at."

"I didn't want him to die."

"I'm so sorry, sweetheart," Derrick says, like he's really torn up about it. "There's no other way,"

"No." Maggie's eyes flicker to Jack. "I loved you," she whispers through the tears. "Now I'll always haunt you." She turns the gun toward her mouth.

"No!" Jack and I shout at the same time as I lunge toward her. But Derrick gets there first, wrestling the weapon from her grip. He shoves Maggie to the ground and turns the gun on Jack.

Jack holds his bound hands up in the air. "Derrick, I just have one button to press to get this transfer to go through. You'll get a million dollars and you screw me over in the meantime. That's what you want. But if you kill us, it's not gonna happen."

Derrick grins, showing more teeth than a person should be able to. "You know, there are a lot of things that I want right now." His eyes linger on me. "Let's see how long you can hold off pressing that magic button while I work over our girl Olivia here." His grin widens at my obvious panic. I get the feeling he's saying it more to mess with Jack's head, but it still makes me feel like I'm going to throw up. "This will be fun."

Jack propels himself toward Derrick, his face screwed up with rage. Derrick smiles, raising the gun as his finger tenses on the trigger. Maggie flings herself toward him, yelling "No!" Derrick's finger presses the trigger and I scream as the shot blasts the quiet in the house. I grab the laptop from the tray table and swing it as hard as I can at Derrick's back. He falls forward, pressing Maggie and Jack under him.

For a long moment, no one moves. Nothing except a trickle of blood between the bodies that becomes a small stream. *No!*

"Jack." It comes out like a strangled whisper. Movement, then, and Derrick stands, staring at the blood covering his shirt and the floor, at the gun in his hand. Then at the unmoving bodies below him.

"You should've stayed out of this," he says to me hoarsely. He points the gun at me, but I'm no longer afraid. Now that I know I'm going to die, all that's left is clarity. The smooth black metal of the gun, the round barrel that is now awake and ready for its next victim: me. I've rarely gone to church, but I find myself praying that there is a heaven and that Jack will be there.

Derrick shifts slightly, muttering something. The movement pulls me out of my trance.

"You will rot in jail for this," I tell him. "And it was my idea to put you on the sex offenders list, you disgusting pervert. *Mine.*"

His eyes narrow as he raises the gun. I close my eyes.

A single blast of fire shatters the silence, and I stagger backward, ending up on my butt.

Something's wrong. Or right. The pain that should accompany the bullet is not there. I open my eyes to see Derrick kneeling on the ground, the gun hanging limply in his hands. He falls forward. Bright lights spill into the room. I shield my eyes as there are suddenly voices—police—everywhere.

The relief I should feel isn't in me. I crawl over to pull Maggie off of Jack. Blood is everywhere. Maggie's body is heavy and limp. I lay her gently on the marble floor and turn back to Jack, who's groaning, his face drawn in pain. *Oh, hallelujah!* I lift his shirt and gently run my hands along his stomach, his chest, to make sure the blood isn't coming from him. His bandage is red—his stitches must've bitten it when they fell on him.

"Liv!" Sam's voice rings out. I look up to see her and Nancy pushing past the suddenly full foyer, ignoring the policemen's shouts. Nancy gasps at the blood, tears streaking down her face as she falls to the floor at Maggie's side. I tug my arm from the policewoman whose trying to pull me away. I won't leave Jack.

He coughs and groans, his eyes tearing up in pain. But he's alive.

Gloriously alive.

CHAPTER THIRTY

JACK

With the knife-sharp pain throbbing in my torso, my first thought was that Derrick's aim was true and that I only have minutes or seconds left. Liv's face looms over me, outlined by a ridiculously bright light. This is dying, I guess. Then I realize the pain is coming from the earlier injury to my ribs. But who took the shot?

"Z," Nancy says, sweeping my hair back over my forehead. Nancy? Sam is next to her, peering over her shoulder at me. Cops are moving around everywhere. I notice Derrick's still body nearby.

"Liv?"

"I'm here," she answers, stroking my face. I relax. Nancy and Sam and the cops are here. And Liv is unhurt. And—

"Where's Maggie?" I ask, looking around.

"Rest," Nancy says. She presses on my shoulder but I sweep her hand away. I grit my teeth as the fire in my side flares with the movement. Liv and Sam pull me into a seated position.

"Where is she?" I ask again. Why is Liv not looking at me? Why is Nancy crying? I look around, focusing on the second group of policemen near me. Surrounding a body.

"Maggie?" I choke out.

I crawl over to her limp body, almost screaming with the pain, but I press on. Maggie's eyes are closed, but what gets to me is her face. She looks so much younger now, her face full of the peace she wanted but never had. It's not fair. I press my hand on her cheek, sweeping the curls back from her face.

Arms wrap around my shoulders. "It's not your fault," Liv says quietly, as if she can read my mind. But it *is* my fault. Images of Maggie assault me—the first day I met her in school, a foster kid who looked like she was ready to take the world by storm. She had so much hope, so much excitement in her. She thought we'd be Bonnie and Clyde, and now that I think about it, I'm sure she wanted to use the feeling of power to get back at the foster care system she was trying to escape. Unlike Liv, it never got better for her. It only got worse.

I remember her face when I brought Jen home, the asshole that I was, thinking it was all fine because I'd already broken it off with Maggie. Her expression was like I'd used a jackhammer on her heart. She ran to Bill because of me. Then ran to Derrick. Looking for one person who'd love her, because I sure as hell couldn't.

My body shakes as the sobs rip free from my body. I ignore the angry response from my ribs. I'm broken, but Maggie's dead. And she had no one there for her at the end. Not even Derrick, the scumbag she thought loved her.

Liv presses her cheek against my shoulder, holding me.

Nancy joins us, taking one of my hands as Sam takes the other. Connecting our messed-up little family. But at least we are a family.

More people arrive, including paramedics who examine my side. They tell me I should go to the hospital to get my stitches looked at, but I refuse a ride in the ambulance. Soon, policemen come over to take our statements. One of them—a detective—introduces himself with a sly wink and tells them he'll take over. Jim Rush, a man I've worked with many times but never met in person. He's smaller than I expected, a few inches shorter than me and wiry. I guess I pictured a big burly guy for someone who dealt so much with Bill Sykes. Some would call him crooked, but I'd call him a hero for as many times as he's bailed us out.

We cover all the bases, that Derrick was some jealous psychopath Liv stayed with in her foster care days who started stalking her at her new home and going after me because he was jealous. We keep Maggie's part a secret except to say she was another one of his victims.

Liv and I sit on the staircase as the CSI unit arrives, their cameras and pads in hand. A couple of them talk to Nancy. I see Sam disappear with my laptop in her bag. I'll have to thank her for that later.

"Derrick said you'd been looking at the ICL account a lot. Why were you doing that?" Liv asks me, her arms wrapped around me as I lean back against her, finding a position that isn't agonizing.

"The ICL account is my father's. I used to pilfer from it in the past. I'd decided not to do it anymore, so poetic justice, I guess, that he wanted me to break into it."

Her fingers weave through mine. "And the transfer didn't go through?"

"Nope. I knew Derrick would never let me live if I completed the transfer, so I tried to hold on to that leverage as long as I could. I knew we'd end up fighting for our lives, though."

I just didn't expect Maggie to die.

"I've screwed up so many lives, Liv. Now Maggie's dead because of me."

"You aren't responsible for what happened to Maggie," Liv says firmly. "Or to me or Jen or anyone else."

She tightens her arms around me, holding me together. "I know you think you're not worthy of a happy life. All the crap your father put you and your mom through was horrible. But every time you broke in to a bank account to get back at him, you were letting him control you. I've told you before you're better than Z, but you have to believe it yourself. And you have to forgive yourself, too."

"I know," I whisper hoarsely, though the scars go too deep to forgive myself for the things I've done. For Maggie's death and for all the kids at Briarcreek who look at me as a role model. For Liv's never-ending parade of nightmares that I'm partly responsible for. For my father's family that I stole from in retaliation for something that I should've gotten past a long time ago. She's right. Being top criminal hacker Z fed my need for revenge, but it did nothing to fill the emptiness inside me.

No, the only one who does that is sitting here with me.

The flash of the cameras pull my attention toward Maggie's body. In different circumstances, Maggie could've been Princeton-bound, just like Liv. If she was dealt a better hand, she could've had a family who loved her and sent her to the best schools. If she'd never met me—

Nancy gestures for us to come with her. Liv helps me

stand, and I turn to look at her. "I'm a mess, Liv. I can't just snap my fingers and be over this. I'm not good for you or anyone else right now."

She smiles gently. "I know. One thing at a time, Jack. Get through your senior year. Take care of your family. Once you're ready, I'll be there for you." She leans forward to press her lips against mine.

I kiss her back. It doesn't feel like the last time I left her. Then, I really wasn't sure if a future for us was possible. As hard as it is to quit being Z, being Jack for Liv is more important. The girl hacked her way right into the center of my heart, and nothing will remove her from it.

CHAPTER THIRTY-ONE

LIV

Nancy, Sam, and I go to the hospital with Jack for a reevaluation after the scuffle at Monroe Street, but surprisingly, he's no worse off than he was before. He begs me to stay in Richmond for the night since it's so late, but I can't think of intruding on his family's mourning time. Maggie may have been crazy, and she did participate in Derrick's scheme, but she was still just a sad, messed-up girl who got dealt a really bad hand in life. It's something only another kid who's been through the system could understand, I think.

The police call my grandfather, who leaves Norfolk immediately to come pick me up. I want to argue that I could drive myself home, especially considering I'm responsible for Emerson's car, but since I'm a minor, I can't fight it. The police agree that I can wait at the hospital for him, since I'm being evaluated for trauma anyway. I have a feeling I'm in for more therapy sessions with Dr. Valerio when I get back to Norfolk.

I call Emerson to give her a very brief rundown of the last twelve hours. After a lot of "are you *serious*" comments, she tells me how glad she is that I'm okay. She asks about Jack, too, with real concern in her voice. The conversation is warm and friendly, even with a couple laughs. The years that I spent without a best friend are being made up for in spades by Emerson. I'm grateful to have her in my life.

Jack points out his half brother to me when the intern isn't looking. I'm shocked to see the resemblance. And I'm proud of Jack for not making an issue of it. It's a solid first step.

Jack seems different now, too. His voice is lighter as he talks to Nancy and the doctor. Z may always be a part of him, but now that he's letting go of the anger that gnawed at his heart for so long, he can be free to make choices that don't relate to his father.

If he can do it, maybe I can, too.

Nancy offers to wait with me for my grandfather. Jack does, too, but I tell him that's not a good idea. Not when my grandfather blames him for most of what's happened.

Jack and I don't drag out our parting. A quick kiss and overly cheerful good-bye masks the heartache. The break is necessary, though. Jack has too much to sort out here, and I need to focus on graduating and moving to New Jersey for summer orientation at Princeton. I know he'll find me when he's ready.

I know I love him enough to wait.

The adrenaline fades before my grandfather gets to the hospital, and I'm both exhausted and nervous. Nancy keeps an arm around my shoulders as we wait, but it does nothing for the nerves doing battle in my stomach. I'm not looking forward to seeing the disappointment in my grandfather's eyes. Or the anger. Either he's going to yell at me and tell me I can never leave home again, or he'll have that cold, calm businesslike air and tell me I'll need to make other living arrangements because he can't handle living with a teenager. I wouldn't blame him for either.

The doors to the ER finally slide open, and Grandfather strides through, his eyes searching. He looks so much like he did the last time I was in a hospital, after Bill Sykes kidnapped me and I ended up swimming for my life. His hair is mussed, the wrinkles in his face deepened, and he's wearing a green sweater instead of the usual button-down. But what gets me is the look in his eyes when they finally land on me. There's no anger. No judgment. Just concern and overwhelming relief to see me alive.

I release myself from Nancy's protective arm and walk toward him. All the pain that I've caused him, all the horrible things I've gone through, the emotions that have been building in me come rushing out through my tears. I start sobbing. He pulls me to him, holding me and stroking my hair. I can't even get out the apology that's lingered on my tongue for days out.

Then he says the words I've longed to hear from a parent my entire life. From someone who loves me and always will.

"Everything will be okay. I promise."

EPILOGUE

NINE MONTHS LATER

I pick up Jack at his apartment after packing up my dorm. The finals at Princeton are no joke, and I'm glad it's the holidays. Jack, on the other hand, would probably rather take ten more final exams than deal with what's coming this evening.

"You sure you want to do this?" he asks me. "I don't mind staying here for Christmas by myself, you know."

I curl my arms around his neck, kissing him lightly. "Grandfather will accept you. You're part of my life, and he loves me. Besides, I think it's time you have a nice Christmas." *No more escaping on your bike to hide from the memories of your mother's death.*

He heaves a sigh and buries his face in my hair. "Okay. Just remember that this was your idea."

It takes about six hours to get to Norfolk. Jack is quiet for most of it, and I wonder if he's trying to figure out a way to get into my grandfather's good graces. The truth is that I worry about it, too. Grandfather would be a lot happier if I brought home practically anyone else. I kept it a secret that Jack had enrolled at Princeton until very recently, so maybe he hasn't had enough time to let that sink in.

When we arrive, the house is decked out inside and out in white twinkling lights, and one of the house's three large Christmas trees gleams brightly in red and gold in the foyer. Presents wrapped in foil are stacked underneath—these are the ones that will be shared at a Christmas party my grandfather and his business associates host for kids from local group homes. It's something he instituted after I came to live with him. I tried to get him to dress as Santa, but he wouldn't go for it. One thing at a time, I guess.

Mrs. Bedwin greets us with hugs and a cheery smile. She and her assistant Cara relieve us of our suitcases and armfuls of gifts. "Your grandfather is on his way home, so you have a few minutes to get ready." She nods at Cara, who takes Jack up to his room.

"Don't you worry," Mrs. Bedwin says as she escorts me to my room. "Your grandfather will see this young man for the good person he is."

"How can you tell he's a good person?" I ask teasingly.

"He's with you, and anyone you let into your heart can't be anything but a good person."

She leaves me to change into my dinner clothes—a long blue velvet dress I know my grandfather will approve of, with the pearl necklace and earrings he gave me last Christmas. I stare at my reflection, surprised at the confident, sophisticated-looking girl who stares back at me in the mirror. Such a long way from the clueless foster kid I once was. It feels like ages ago that I was wearing clothes a size too small and wondering how to approach my foster parents for money for something as simple as a pair of shorts that fit. Nerves twitch inside of me. If Grandfather tells me he won't accept Jack, what will I do?

I draw my shoulders back. I have Jack now. I don't mind being poor and outcast if I'm with him. And I highly doubt Grandfather would do that to me, anyway.

I turn around, startled to see Jack leaning against the doorframe, watching me.

"You're beautiful," he says, his gaze swallowing me whole. I could live in those eyes. He walks over to me, taking my hand. "If this doesn't work, I want you to know it's completely okay if you leave me to stay with your grandfather."

I raise an eyebrow. "Really?" He's so full of it.

"Hell no." He pulls me to him tightly, lifting me in the air. "You're mine, and I'm yours, and there's nothing Mr. Brownlow can do about it."

"Good." I touch his cheek gently. "Just don't forget it."

He kisses me then, and for a moment I forget all about dinner, all about my grandfather, and frankly about anything other than the fact that Jack is kissing me in my bedroom, and it's all I can do not to lock the door and stay a while. I break away as Cara informs us dinner is ready.

"Let's go," I tell him softly, slipping my fingers through his.

Grandfather is talking to Mrs. Bedwin at the bottom of the staircase as we descend, hand in hand. He looks up at us, his face solemn. He hugs me, his arms somewhat stiff, then looks at Jack.

"Mr. Brownlow," Jack says, extending his hand.

"Jack," Grandfather says, reaching out to shake it. I

know that doesn't mean anything. He's too polite to slap his hand away.

"Thanks for inviting me to spend Christmas here," Jack says.

Grandfather nods once, and he may as well have said, *It wasn't my idea.*

"Well, let's head to the table," Mrs. Bedwin starts. "We've prepared a lovely welcome home dinner—chateaubriand with roasted root vegetables and grilled asparagus."

She continues on about the meal as we walk to the dining room, but all I can focus on is the sharp tension between Jack and Grandfather. This is going to be a long night.

Over dinner, Grandfather asks me about school, finals, and everything someone would ask when trying to avoid awkwardness.

"So you're enrolled at Princeton as well?" Grandfather finally asks Jack.

"Yes, sir."

"He has a 4.0 GPA," I add, but Grandfather keeps his focus on Jack.

"And what are you doing for income these days?" he asks.

I clench my teeth, praying Jack doesn't get offended or nervous. But Jack merely smiles and says, "I do work for hire in computer technology. Helping companies find weaknesses in their systems to prevent them from getting hacked."

Grandfather raises an eyebrow in surprise. He always figured Jack was involved in something shady, but probably in his eyes it was running drugs or guns or something. Or maybe he figured out a while ago what Jack was really up to but wanted to test him.

"So you know a lot about hacking, am I right?" Grandfather asks. His eyes flick to me to check my reaction, but I keep my face expressionless.

"Yes," Jack says. He says nothing else. I glance at Grandfather, whose lips twitch slightly. I have to admire the way he ferrets out information and how quickly he puts two and two together.

"Are you still in business for yourself?" Grandfather asks him.

Jack raises his chin slightly. "No, sir. I am not."

Grandfather nods shortly. "Good. Ah, Mrs. Bedwin," he says as she walks through the door. "This was excellent. Please extend my compliments to Betty Ann."

"Yes, sir," she says, winking at me. I wink back.

The rest of dinner is much more relaxed. Grandfather speaks mostly to me, but he does include Jack in a few of his questions. Most of the conversation revolves around friends and activities at Princeton, campus life, that kind of thing.

"Emerson's coming over later," I tell Grandfather over plates of apple pie. "She finally got her parents to take her with them on one of their trips, so they're leaving early in the morning."

He nods. "Good. It's about time they recognized that the best part of their life was right in front of them."

"I know."

"For me, too," he says. He looks at Jack. "It's no secret how strongly I've disapproved of my granddaughter being with you." He sighs. "However, I will accept that you are together because it's important to Olivia. You seem like you're getting your life on track, and I approve of that. But if you hurt her at all, consider my acceptance of you strongly rescinded."

It's a threat, though a mild one. But I don't care. He'll accept Jack as long as he's with me, which is forever as far as I'm concerned. And one day, I know he'll grow to actually like and appreciate him. As Mrs. Bedwin said, Jack is a good person. He deserves no less.

"That'll never happen," Jack says. "That I can guarantee."

"Good." Grandfather sighs, his gaze softening as it moves from Jack to me. "Merry Christmas, sweetheart," he says, his hand patting the top of mine.

To his surprise, I throw my arms around him and hug him tight. "Merry Christmas, Grandfather."

I catch Jack's eyes, bright with love for me and happiness he never thought he deserved. Jack and Liv— two lost souls who found—and saved—each other. Our pasts may have shaped us, but they don't own us.

Not anymore.

DON'T MISS THESE FANTASTIC READS FROM VIVI BARNES

OLIVIA TWISTED

Olivia and Z's story begins in this tale full of romance, intrigue, action, and of course computer hacking.

PAPER OR PLASTIC

Lexi doesn't think her summer can get any worse than having to work at SmartMart. Until she meets Noah…and things start looking up.

ACKNOWLEDGMENTS

WARNING: If exclamation points bother you, you should probably turn away now. It's impossible to hide my enthusiasm for everyone who's contributed to this book. I love you all!

To Jack, AJ, and Elaine—thank you for putting up with me and my weirdness when I'm writing (and, um, when I'm not)! I'm grateful to have you in my life.

To Stacy Abrams and Tara Whitaker, you are the most amazing editors. I've said it before, but I'm a better writer because of you. I love you—circling YES!

To the entire Entangled team, especially Nancy Cantor, Maddie Pelletier, Melissa Montavani, Heather Riccio, and Christine Chhun—I'm so grateful for your work in bringing this story to life!

To Pam Howell and Bob Diforio, thank you for your support and for navigating me through the weird world of contracts and, you know, that paperwork stuff that makes me LOL!

To everyone who helped shape this book—Peggy "Chai Latte" Jackson, Marlana Antifit, Dennis Cooper, Jennye Kamin, Tori Kelley, Stephanie Spier, Jen Woods, Whitney

Smith, my mommy Patricia Pondant Harris, and Patricia "Strawberry" Taylor—thank you for your critiques, support, and shared laughs! And to Eva Griffin, Tracey Smith, and Peggy Jackson—I'm following my dreams because of you!

(Hey, can't say I didn't warn you!!!!)

To my fellow YA Chicks—Christina Farley and Amy Christine Parker, author visits are so much more fun when we're together! Here's to many more road trips, secret projects (Lynne Matson, I'm never falling asleep again!), and men in the mirror (um, scratch that last one)!

To all the teachers, librarians, bloggers, and media specialists—thank you for your love of books and continual support of authors! And to my fellow YA authors—you know who you are—I'm ever grateful not to feel alone in this world.

Thanks as always to my work team for understanding my never-ending distractions (that's my excuse, and I'm sticking to it!). I'm looking at you, Dina Kuhlman!

Finally, to my darling husband who puts up with me on a daily basis, you're the toast to my jam. Thank you for letting me bounce ideas off you and for suggesting new ways to torture my characters. I love you forever!

Olivia Decoded Reading Group Guide

1. Emerson mentions that her boyfriend's friend dumped a girl by texting her. Is this a common phenomenon in the digital age? Is it right? How should people end relationships?

2. Liv has a hard time making friends at Dalton, except Emerson. Grandfather is encouraging her to develop new friendships. How do people in high school go about making new friends? What has worked for you? How do you act around new kids?

3. Emerson encourages Liv to reveal her secrets to her. How does Emerson demonstrate her friendship to Liv and vice versa? Do you keep secrets from your friends?

4. The novel gives us a glimpse into the underground world of hackers. What did you already know about hacking? What did you learn about their lives and behaviors?

5. When thinking about their abusive lives, Jack states that the members of the house are "all screwed up in one way or another." Is this an excuse for their hacking? Is Jack a modern-day Robin Hood?

6. Jack recalls that Nancy allowed them to hack banks but not to change their report card grades. Do you see a difference?

7. Liv's mother was a drug addict who died of an overdose, resulting in Liv being assigned to the foster care system. How did Liv's childhood affect her new life and her self-esteem?

8. Emerson's parents are never around, too caught up in their business to spend time with her. Is this common for children of wealth?

9. Liv is haunted by the possibility that she takes after her father. Do you agree with nature or nurture as the most important influence on our personalities?

10. We learn that Liv has spent time in therapy, arranged by her grandfather. Liv does not feel it has helped her. What are your thoughts/experiences with therapy?

11. Jack as Z is a "bad boy." Liv admits to being attracted to his dangerous side. Are you more attracted to people you perceive as edgy? Can someone be both dangerous and good?

12. Nancy suggests Liv could help persuade Jack to quit hacking. Liv claims that Jack has to come around on his own terms. Can we influence people we love to stop destructive behavior? Do "interventions" work?

13. Liv deceives her grandfather numerous times in order to be with Jack. Is her relationship with Jack more important than her grandfather's? Do you agree with her justifications?

14. Were you surprised by Jack's decision not to confront his father when he visited the hospital? What other scenarios could you imagine happening in the situation?

15. What did you think about Jen's secret affair with the teacher?

16. When did you suspect that Maggie and Derrick were the stalkers? What caused Maggie to turn against Jack? Was it realistic?

17. Are there people like Derrick out there in the foster care system? Is the foster care system broken? How can it be improved?

GRAB THE ENTANGLED TEEN RELEASES READERS ARE TALKING ABOUT!

LOVE ME NEVER
BY SARA WOLF

Seventeen-year-old Isis Blake has just moved to the glamorous town of Buttcrack-of-Nowhere, Ohio. And she's hoping like hell that no one learns that a) she used to be fat; and b) she used to have a heart. Naturally, she opts for social suicide instead...by punching the cold and untouchably handsome "Ice Prince"—a.k.a. Jack Hunter—right in the face. Now the school hallways are an epic battleground as Isis and the Ice Prince engage in a vicious game of social warfare. But sometimes to know your enemy is to love him...

THE REPLACEMENT CRUSH
BY LISA BROWN ROBERTS

After book blogger Vivian Galdi's longtime crush pretends their secret summer kissing sessions never happened, Vivian creates a list of safe crushes, determined to protect her heart.

But nerd-hit Dallas, the sweet new guy in town, sends the missions-An Vivian's zing meter-into chaos. While designing software for the bookstore where she works, Dallas wages a counter-mission.

Operation Replacement Crush is in full effect. And Dallas is determined to take her heart off the shelf.

CHASING TRUTH
BY JULIE CROSS

At Holden Prep, the rich and powerful rule the school—and they'll do just about anything to keep their dirty little secrets hidden.

When former con artist Eleanor Ames's homecoming date commits suicide, she's positive there's something more going on. The more questions she asks, though, the more she crosses paths with Miles Beckett. He's sexy, mysterious, arrogant... and he's asking all the same questions.

Eleanor might not trust him—she doesn't even like him—but they can't keep their hands off of each other. Fighting the infuriating attraction is almost as hard as ignoring the fact that Miles isn't telling her the truth...and that there's a good chance he thinks she's the killer.

NEXIS
BY A.L. DAVROE

A Natural Born amongst genetically-altered Aristocrats, all Ella ever wanted was to be like everyone else. Augmented and *perfect*. Then...the crash. Devastated by her father's death and struggling with her new physical limitations, Ella is terrified to learn she is not just alone, but little more than a prisoner. Her only escape is to lose herself in Nexis, the hugely popular virtual reality game her father created. In Nexis she meets Guster, who offers Ella guidance, friendship... and something more. But Nexis isn't quite the game everyone thinks it is. And it's been waiting for Ella...